BOOK 2:

LUCK

REBORN
THE BOOK SERIES

Reborn the Book Series: Luck by Torrie Q. Jones

Published by Reborn the Book Series, LLC

Published in the United States of America

www.rebornthebookseries.com

Cover Design & Layout by KLS Designz & Print:
www. klsdesignz.com

Editor: Fluky Fiction

ISBN: 978-1-7370421-3-6

First Edition

DEDICATION

Looks like I did it again. I dedicate this book to the continued support I receive on a daily basis about this amazing story! My creative director Kia, girl! You know how to make a girl's dream come true. I thank you from the bottom of my heart for being a part of this journey. My kids, I hope I continue to make ya'll proud. It's Mommy's time. Keep up the great things you have planned. You got this and I got you!

To my closest and dearest family and friends, thank you. For all the wonderful memories we've shared and continue to make. Man listen, ya'll know I got a dope ass story to tell, so let's make some more history so I can keep turning them into best-selling stories! ☺

RIP Queen, Qua, Val & Mal

LUCK

BOOK 2: LUCK

PROLOGUE

Michiko Tanaka is my name, and I'm the Goddess of Luck. For the past few months, I've been living in NYC with my bestest friend Taki and her boyfriend, the Sun God, Adam. I'm originally from Iya Valley, Shikoku, outside of Tokyo, Japan. I escaped from an attack on my home where my family was murdered. I ran to my friend Taki in the US with some strange angel guy named Dillon. I know bringing my issues to her was selfish but at the same time, her boyfriend is a god too. So, I figured she could help me.

Being a god is no fun. Having to train, learn and meditate all day can be exhausting. At least that was my regular schedule, until that fateful day.

While sitting in one of my strategy sessions, a shake of the building, a loud boom and all of the smoke confused Bisha and I. There was an instant rush of soldier-like individuals that surrounded us. Bisha immediately engaged with the intruders as I was defending myself like I was taught by my Shinigami. I know, weird. We will get to that later.

Swing kick to the right, upper left punch to the gut, hard right punch to the face, I repeated in my head as I "kicked arse," as the Americans would say, I think. Leaving bloody bodies in my wake as I swung. A warm sensation continued to flow throughout my body as I sustained my fighting. I was starting to sweat and feel fatigued as I looked around for Bisha. Sweating and panting, I continued to swing.

An eerie feeling came over me as I began to feel light-headed. I attempted to assess my surroundings when suddenly my vision became blurry and showed scenes and heard noises that was unfamiliar to me. "Get her. I will have that power yet!" I overheard from an unknown voice. Immediately snapping out of those weird thoughts, I kicked one of the intruders that attacked far away from me. Using my small size to duck from another combatant that tried to grab me from behind, I stretched out my left foot to trip him and landed a blow to his solar plexus.

"Ouch!" I said as I heard the crush of bones from the trespasser's chest. I looked around for Bisha and saw nothing but smoke and debris as the noises that sounded like fireworks continued to go off. Detecting someone getting closer as I stayed low in the smoke to search for Bisha or someone familiar, I began to cough from inhaling too much smoke. I scurried to stay low and make my way to somewhere safe. I heard fighting from all sides as the warm cookie sensation traveled throughout my body making me feel like a warm toasted almond. My body began to sweat as I panted for air making the hot flashes more intense.

"Where is she? If you lost her, I promise your spine will be my toothpick tonight," I overheard. My vision began to blur once more as I started to see through the same stranger's eyes again. I began to look around at the unfamiliar faces I saw. Abruptly breaking out of those creepy thoughts, I felt a hand grab my shoulder, and I snatched it as they backed away out of my grasp.

The stranger crouched in front of me and placed his hand over my mouth, whispering, "Shhhh. I am a friend. Where is your father?" Anger burned in his eyes.

Frightened, I whispered back, "I don't know." It was an honest answer. I was unsure of what was going on with my family at the moment.

The stranger stared at Michi with the anger still in his eyes, "Don't get scared now. Stay focused and stay low. We will get through this. I have to find your father," The well-dressed stranger said, sighing as he assessed the area.

"I was studying with Bisha, what the heckles is going on?" I spoke in English, as I noticed the stranger probably was not from Japan due to his terracotta skin color and thick curly hair, slicked back in a long ponytail

He immediately responded in Japanese, "I know your language, so speak freely. I have a lot of questions for your father. Why would the EGU be after you all?" A puzzled look was on his face.

"EGU, who are they? I don't know who you're talking about," I replied just as confused. I spoke again before he could continue. "Wait, who are you? I have never seen you around here before. Believe me, I remember everyone."

The stranger replied, "My name is Dillon, and I will be the only reason you survive this. It is obvious your family was targeted by the Elite Guard Unit. They are a demon army faction that works with the Royal Fallen. Which you probably don't know whom I'm talking about." He sighed and rolled his eyes with frustration.

"First of all, I do know who the Royal Fallen are. My question is why would my family be targeted by them and why aren't the angels here to help?" I remembered that my family did a lot of work for angels and their high connections in Otherside. They were the link to Otherside for a lot of the Otherside creatures in Earth Realm. The Tanaka Clan assisted with the collection and exchanging of Earth and Otherside information with Angels, Demons and Otherside creatures. I figured with all of those connections. How could someone allow the Elite Guard Unit to attack. This had to have had a backing from a powerful crest.

Dillon glanced around the room, "Oh, well. Since you are well versed in our predicament, we will cut this conversation short and get out of here. Once you and your family are safe, we will have a nice discussion." The angel grabbed my hand as he began to lead me towards an area that was covered in destroyed furniture, wall panels, and stone debris, most likely the remnant of my family's artwork.

I recognized the picture that we were crouching directly under. "We are in the family room." I whispered to this Dillon. "My father usually conducted his meetings in the study, which is across the hall," I added, still crouched down and continuing to hold on to the back of Dillon's sleeve.

"Okay. We will check in there and then get you and your family out of here. I heard they are looking for the oldest female child, so I am going to guess it is you." He turned to stare at me. "Again, the Tanaka family is well protected in Otherside, so who would attack them like this?" Dillon said, aggravated as he continued to lead me across the hall.

"Why are you so all-knowing and interested in what's going on here? Like I said earlier, I have never seen you in my compound before. I know every person that has walked through this gate." I slightly raised my voice as I spoke.

Dillon sighed. "Your smart mouth and high-pitched voice will be your death. For now, shut up and listen to me so you can survive!" he spoke through his teeth, a vein coming out of his forehead.

Insulted and aggravated at the being in front of me, I shot back, "I will not tolerate your insolence. You have no right to speak to me in that manner." The warm feeling in my body began to turn hot. My skin tightened, my eyes began to hurt, and I breathed deeply as I calmed myself before responding to this Dillon stranger. "Dillon or whomever you are, you will know who I am!" I was beginning to pant. The sweat poured off me. Immediately, I was interrupted by a loud screech.

Dillon and I rushed towards the scream coming from the study area. I spied on a figure standing next to a pile of individuals lying on the ground. I witnessed the kneeled figure that was my mother and she was screaming at the laid-out bodies in front of her. As she cried, a man with long locs stabbed her in the back, turning the scream to a gurgled screech.

The penetrating cry and sight of my parents stopped everything around me. A fire burned in the pit of my stomach, my skin tightened, and my eyes began to strain and the colors around me started to shift to a tinted gold hue

I immediately ran to my fallen parents, ignoring Dillon and shocking the stranger that used his sword to make my mother scream. I stared at the vile being, my pace slowing the closer I got to my parents, and a loud scream escaped me as I watched the blood flow from their bodies.

The counterfeit soldier in front of me turn to a red goldish silhouette and I felt an airy power around me. I rushed towards the soldier and instantly grabbed him by his hair, pulling out each loc one by one as I felt all the pain that my parents felt before they left this realm. I started to enjoy the torturous expressions on the screaming man's face while I continued to pull at his hair. Amused by the blaring soldier's tears as I threw one of the locs that I had ripped off, I turned to see a group walking towards me.

Four guards led a woman that I did not recognize, but her energy felt so familiar. Unsure of who all these people were and what was going on, I looked around for Dillon and noticed he was standing next to me. The woman spoke to me, but I could not hear her over the screaming man as I continued to pull the hairs out.

Dillon, still immaculately dressed, instantly knocked the man out of my hands and sent him flying across the room towards the group of guards. "Young lady. We will have a discussion of your version of torture later." He continued to stare at the individuals in front of us.

"Why are you here?" is all I could decipher before I yelled again. How could we be having a conversation so casually as my parents lay there dead? The only thing in my mind was my mother's previous shriek as she was killed, replaying again and again. I began to scream louder as my skin began to glow and my eyes started to hurt again. The beings around me started to form into swirling colors and my mind began to show visions of shelves of books, angels, demons and places I did not recognize. My skin began to tighten again as I continued to yell, hurling over in agonizing pain

Images of people I didn't know, unfamiliar foreign places, and glimpses of M started to flow through my head. I started to sweat profusely and took my sweater off. The feeling I got was amazing. "O-M-G!!! I'm about to fuck this shit up!"

Michi walked towards her locker, speaking out in Japanese, "You know, Taki, I would have thought you were born doing this. Your skills are top notch, girlie!"

Taki immediately responded in English, "Girl, I am trying to teach you to be comfortable around here. Let's practice your English all the time for now. You never know when you may need it."

Michi ignored Taki and responded in Japanese, "Look, I've been formally trained to speak English all of my life. So, I don't need to practice. You're just mad your Japanese is getting rusty from being around Sunny too much."

"Sunny?" Taki said still speaking in English, confused at the mention of Michi's nickname for her boyfriend. "Whatever, chick! My language is just fine. You just mad that boy in the dojo hasn't paid you any mind," she teased.

Sticking up her middle finger, Michi turned to Taki and yelled in English, "SHUT UP! I am not interested in that boy!" stomping her feet as she turned to start changing her clothes.

M interrupted the two ladies' bickering, "Stop the nonsense talking and get those bags outside and clean the rest of the dojo so we can get out of here." Then, she walked away.

Taki and Michi stared at each other as they laughed at the disruption. Michi said, "Okay, I'll take out the bags and you start the cleaning."

"Cool," Taki answered, walking away toward the training area.

****

Still in the male locker room, Niko packed his bags--lost in his thoughts. *"Why do I get so nervous around her?"* he wondered as he remembered the match with the girl named Michi.

The thought of losing to her still upset him. Snatching the bag off the bench, Niko gathered the rest of his things and headed towards the exit. "Oh, shoot!" he yelped, accidentally bumping into something.

Michi, annoyed at having to clean up after the students, started to walk towards the door to take the bags out, bumping into the boy from her match earlier. "Hey, watch yourself," she said as the boy walked directly into her.

Niko armpits and hands began to sweat as he looked down at her. "I'm sorry. I wasn't paying attention." He noticed the trash bags in her hands. "Can I take those for you?" he asked, being a gentleman.

Michi, relieved at not having to carry the trash anymore, exclaimed, "Yes! Thank you," then shoved the bags in his hands. "You are doing a great deed for the Tanaka Clan." She bowed in front of him.

Niko was surprised by the bow but understood the custom, and returned the bow as he held both bags. "No need, Ms. Tanaka. I'm glad to help. Now lead the way to where these go."

"Please follow me. Again, thank you," Michi said in her sweet voice. Remembering their match earlier as he followed her, she added, "Just so you know, you're not bad. I've been training since I could walk and your moves are very predictable." They stopped a few feet away from the dumpster.

Niko instantly threw the bags into the big dumpster. "Look, I'm good on the fighting tips. You did your thing, I can admit that," he said as he stared at the beauty in front of him. "So, what brings you to New York? I can tell you're new here," he said.

"Well, I'm here visiting my friend Taki, the tall girl with the big afro!" Michi said excitedly. "I really like it here. Just as busy as the city of Tokyo but with more Americans," she giggled. "Are you from America?" She inquired.

Niko smiled at the squeaky tone of her voice. "No, funny, I'm from Japan as well. I was born on an army base just outside of Tokyo. I'm what they consider an army brat. My family and I moved a lot until I decided to come back to New York to be with my mom's family."

Reaching out his hand, he added, "By the way, my name is Niko."

"Hello, Niko. My name is Michiko Tanaka," she responded, ignoring his handshake and bowing.

Following tradition, Niko bowed. "Nice to meet you, Ms. Tanaka," His face became flushed as his heart rate increased.

"You can call me Michi. We don't have to be so formal," she said with a gleam in her eyes. Michi immediately felt "other" energy getting closer. She plotted to get Niko out of the fray. "Well, it was nice meeting you, Niko. I appreciate your assistance today and look forward to our next meeting." As she turned around, a demon dropped in front of her and then another one behind her, separating her from Niko.

Niko stood frozen, not recognizing the beings in front of him. "What the hell?!" he yelled in confusion as he ran towards the opposite direction.

Michi, glad the human ran away, kicked the first demon in front of her far away as she ducked low and swung her leg out to sweep the other one off its feet. She punched it in its scaly throat just as she rolled back, missing a swing from a sword.

The new player on board was dressed in black leather pants and vest. Michi immediately recognized he was from the EGU that had attacked her home. Instantly, anger burned from the pit of her stomach, and Michi felt the pain in her eyes again as her power flowed through her veins. Rushing towards the guard, she reached him and—using the force from her speed—grabbed him by the neck using her knees. She snapped his neck as the next guard attacked.

Rolling away from the next guard that attacked, crouched low, Michi continued to feel the presence of other EGU soldiers and the growing numbers that they exuberated causing an anomaly in the alley that created a vacuum of energy. Quickly, she ran towards the new guard and knocked him off his feet as she heard a motor noise.

Niko knocked over another guard that had driven his motorcycle onto the scene. He yelled towards Michi, "Let's go!" while reaching out his hand.

Michi realized she was about to be surrounded by an EGU army. Confusion as to why they were attacking her now filled her, as well as whether this human could be involved. Going with her gut, she yelled towards Niko, "Get out of here! You don't have anything to do with this!"

"You need help! I don't know what the hell is going on, but we gotta go! Now, Let's go!" Niko responded forcefully.

Nervous about getting on this stranger's bike and how she would find Taki and M, as all of her valuables were left inside of the dojo, Michi said, "Fine," as she hopped on the back of Niko's bike, kicking an EGU soldier as they sped off.

ON THE RUN

Niko continued to drive down the busy street to get away from whatever he had seen back in the alley by the dojo. Worried he was hallucinating, he slowed down to pull over by an underpass. Stopping and turning off the bike, he slightly turned to Michi. "Ms. Tanaka, don't get me wrong, I'm not crazy. But I don't believe those things were human that attacked you." He shook and rubbed his head now that he had taken off his helmet.

"Nope, you're not crazy. Those things were demons. I'm sorry. They are not after you," Michi said with her head slightly down. "I do not wish to you bring you any harm. I will depart from you. Thank you for your assistance." Getting off the bike, she bowed while she searched the area. Unfortunately, Michi did not go out without Taki or M.

Noticing she did not know her way around, Niko asked, "Do you have a phone? I can wait with you until your people come get you." He was unsure if he wanted to get involved in whatever this young woman had going on.

"I'm okay. I have a special way of communicating with my friends, so I will get to them in no time. Don't worry about me. I will be fine." Just as she finished her sentence, another scaled demon launched himself at Michi, scratching her shoulder.

Michi yelled in Japanese, "Piece of shit! Ouch!" as she felt her power. "You will pay for this!" she yelled towards the creature as she slowly walked to it and grabbed its head, snatching it clean off. Splattering the demon's blood all over and the head and body immediately turning to dust.

Niko, in shock, choked on the dust in the air, snatching Michi's arm to bring her back close to the bike to get on. "Let's go—it looks like they found you again," he said, pulling her onto his bike. As he pulled out, he handed Michi his helmet. "Put this on! This will get bumpy!" he shouted as he revved the bike to gain speed.

"What the fuck?!" Michi yelled in Japanese while she placed the helmet on her head and began to see a rip in the realm revealing a wave of scaly demons coming through from Otherside. Behind her just as Niko was pulling off, she turned her head and couldn't believe the upsurge of demons that were coming through to NYC. She thought, *this has to be someone very powerful and connected to be able to pull this off. I have to find M!* Michi gripped his waist tighter, leaning her head into his shoulder blades.

****

"What do you mean you can't find her?!" M yelled at the angel in front of her. She shouted, "You have less than two hours to give me something, or there will be hellfire to pay!" Then she dismissed the individual in front of her.

Taki interrupted the conversation, "M, don't you think that is a bit harsh. Don't take it out on other people. Maybe she really did get away with the guy from earlier," she said, hoping Michi was somewhere safe and sound.

M, furious at the current predicament, shot back, "There is no excuse, there was obviously a hole in the barriers. How could that many get through? My question is who did it and why did they bring them here?" She was curious on how so many EGU soldiers and scaly demons got through her barriers since she usually produces the most powerful protection barriers due to her experience in the Hell.

Taki thought for a moment before answering. "Do you think it's the same people that are after her?" she said, fidgeting with her fingers.

"They will pray to whatever deity it is they worship that they better not be. I am already gathering information about the Tanaka Clan Raid. Whomever is involved will pay dearly," M said with such malice that Taki felt a chill go down her spine.

They were interrupted by an angel recruit that was usually assigned bodyguard duties. "There were witnesses who reported a speeding motorcycle with a young girl on the back. We will start there. I will notify Commanders Dillon, Mikael and X right away." After finishing, he turned around to leave.

"Wait, before you go, tell X that we don't need the angels help. I will deal with this on my own," M said, then turned to Taki. "Let's go." Grabbing Taki, they disappeared to start her hunt for Michi.

LET'S FIND OUT

Niko, heading towards his house, figured whoever was chasing Michi would never connect him to her. Thoughts raced through his head. *Dog, why are you going above and beyond? Drop her off at the police station. Nah, I can't do that. I know how it was being in a new country with no friends, no help. Damn! What the fuck!*

Niko pulled over into a garage area as he pulled Michi off the bike. "Look, you should be fine here for a few hours. We have to figure out how to get you back to your people. You said demons?" Niko said in one breath, wiping his hands and pacing quickly in front of Michi as she leaned on his bike. "I really don't get what you're saying about demons, but I will take it for what it is." Niko stared at Michi, wondering how she was so calm about the situation. His heart continued to race as she leaned on the bike looking at her nails.

Michi responded, "They only show themselves when it is dire to their cause or when they are on the hunt. In this case, they are on the hunt, and you are not the prey. So, thank you for the assistance, but I will be on my way." She bowed then looked around. "Now, where are you, Sunny?" She tried to sense for Adam's energy signature as she walked away from the garage that Niko had parked in.

"Sunny? Where are you going?" Niko asked, confused, and chased after her. "Do you even know where you are going?"

Michi turned to look at Niko. "No, I don't. Sunny is my friend Taki's boyfriend. Haven't you been listening?!" She rolled her eyes while walking away. "We just started practicing this actually, so this may take a while. I will just walk until I get something." She stopped and closed her eyes to meditate, attempting to contact Adam.

Niko was confused at her behavior and statements. "Um, so you're just going to walk until you find them?" he asked, grabbing her hand to pull at her to come back with him. "Look, come back to my house so we can figure this out. I don't want to leave you out here. Come on," he suggested, tugging at her arm.

"Niko, correct?" Michi said, standing her ground. "I truly appreciate whatever help you have offered thus far, but I will be fine on my own."

Niko felt an intense pull to Michi with a sense of familiarity that always plagued him when he was in her presence. "Michi, look, I got you. Don't leave. We will get you back to your family ASAP. My cousin knows a lot of people here and has a car, so I can take you back to the dojo safely. If that doesn't work, we can figure something out. Just don't leave, okay?" he pleaded.

Michi stood aggravated at the situation and began to assess her next moves, "Okay! I could use some water and a cell phone. Have your people get me some new clothes as well. I can't be outside without my heels on." She looked down at herself then glared at Niko.

"Look, princess, my connections are not that lit. But I can get you some water and you can use a cell phone. You know your people's number by heart?" He motioned Michi to walk with him, "Come on!" excitedly as he led her back to his place.

Michi, unsure of the man in front of her, she suddenly recognized Niko was of "other" by the swirling colors of his aura. Her lessons with Ebisu assisted Michi in acknowledging different kinds of beings and creatures of Otherside by deciphering the color scheme of their aura. Questioning her resolve, Michi doubted his help. "Niko, I do not believe you fully understand what is going on here. As you all will say, the shit has hit the sack. So—" She started, but was interrupted by Niko.

"You mean the shit has hit the fan? What don't I understand? Those things looked creepy as hell! What type of circus act are they?" he said wondering about the snakeskin humanoid looking creatures that chased Michi.

Michi laughed. "You know, I want to go to the circus one day! I want to see the clowns!" she said, clapping her hands in joy. "That will be so fun!" She stopped clapping and took a deep breath. "Okay, okay. Let me stay on task. Anyway, those things chasing me are not part of a circus and are very real. I advise you to leave me be!" She stared at Niko as she spoke to see if her powers reacted to him like Adam's reacted to Taki. Michi always pondered if Adam and Taki's situation was just a thing with them two or something bigger.

She recalled M speaking about an anchor and wondered if she had one. Someone to keep her anchored to this realm, as sometimes Michi wished she could escape to her own space at times. The past few months has been emotionally draining for Michi. Her control of her powers has been erratic as her emotions have been getting the best of her. M and Taki assists her during these difficult times but Michi doesn't like to burden them and sometimes wishes she could escape alone.

Michi noticed things about Adam and Taki that most wouldn't catch. Such as the growth of Adam's power as he described to her. He explained that having his anchor helps him understand the emotional responsibility of this powers.

She snapped out of her thoughts. "Well, that was interesting," Michi said as she realized Niko was just staring at her. "Is there something wrong?"

"No, I was just looking at you. You're beautiful, Michiko Tanaka," Niko said with an intense look, mesmerized by the glow of her skin.

Michi, slightly shocked by Niko's expression of her looks. "Well thank you, Mr.… you didn't tell me your whole name," she said with a smile. Michi stared at the young man in front of her and got lost in a thought that wasn't hers.

Changing her tone, she continued, "So it is you, what is it you want from me? Am I not doing everything you ask?" Michi whispered.

"Um, you're being weird and your eyes are a freaky gold color. How about we get to a phone and call your people. It's in my bag on my bike," Niko responded, nervously walking away from Michi, wanting to get away from the weird situation.

Michi, still in a trance, said, "I don't think you know what I am capable of." She cocked her head to the side as she walked seductively towards Niko.

Niko stepped towards his bike to grab his phone. "Um, look Michi, I don't know what changed your mood, but I need you to relax and call your people so you can get the fuck outta here. I think they are probably worried about you by now," he said as he continued to step away from Michi, but the pull to her increased as he wanted to protect her.

"Um, what? What did you say?" Michi said, snapping out of her trance, eyes still gold and heavily blinking. "I have to find Lady M and Taki. I can't stay outside the barriers this long." She added, "Why can't I feel you Sunny?!" Michi stomped her feet. "I need to change my clothes," she snapped, leaving an airy chill around them.

Niko was intrigued by Michi in the couple of hours he's been around her. "Okay. Here's the phone. I will be right back!" he said, walking away towards a door.

Michi held the phone unsure of who to call since she hadn't used phones since the attack on her compound. She looked around the small garage at the various items sprawled out and the little sports car parked in the corner. Sensing some form of power in the air, she immediately thought it would be Adam or M, but to her dismay her powers were not cooperating with her to pinpoint the source. In frustration, Michi screamed, causing the wall to her left to crumble.

****

"I doubt very much she is still in Japan. It can't be a coincidence that there is a god here in this country as well," Benzaiten said to Bishamonten. "I wouldn't be surprised if our little angel is out here spreading love and positivity!" she said, excitedly clapping her hands.

Bishamonten rolled her eyes at her colleague. "Benzi, I don't see how you are excited about all of this. We have been here in the US searching for Michi for two weeks now. Happens that she might be with that angel. Before her little episode at the compound, I saw her standing next to one."

Benzi started to walk a little faster. "Well, an angel. What was princess doing with an angel? How did one get in the compound?" Benzi asked.

"From what I recall right before the attack, I remember a guard saying a commander angel had come to speak with the clan leader. So, maybe that's who it is. My plan is to see if we can find her friend here to see if she's heard from her. It took us a long time to get here. Three months have gone by, anything could have happened to Michi," Bishamonten said as she stopped walking to concentrate on the energy in the air. "I sense a lot of demon activity here. It will be hard to try to find Michi or her friend."

Benzi stopped her fast-paced walk. "Look, Michi is fine. What I am worried about is how the EGU keeps getting tabs on her. We need more info! I think going back to Otherside will help us get more info as to who is behind this and why!" She halted to stare at a mannequin in the window of a shop they were walking by. "I think I like this outfit. Come, Bisha! Let's shop," she said, skipping excitedly towards the store entrance.

"If you were human, I would swear you have a mental disorder. I see where Michi gets her issues with concentrating from!" Bisha said, rolling her eyes as she followed Benzi.

The two Shinigami had been in the New York area for about a week searching for clues on how to find Michi's friend Taki and possibly Michi as well. Unfortunately, the last known address and job for Taki was a dead end. They were able to settle in a place in downtown Manhattan as they gathered more information about the EGU raid at the Tanaka Compound. The information they had received so far is what led them to NYC and to search for Taki, as she may be the only person that knows of Michi's whereabouts. Both Benzi and Bisha knew that if the EGU had the information, then they would come for Taki as well.

FAMILY INTRODUCTIONS

Michi was waiting for Niko to return as she stared at the giant hole in the wall of the garage. Nervous of how he would behave, she sat on the bike to act like nothing was wrong. *Act like the hole is not there,* she thought, messing with her nails.

"WHAT THE HELL?!" Niko shouted from across the garage. "What happened? Girl! What did you do?" he said in panic. "My cousin is going to kill me!" he panted as he looked around at the hole in the wall. He shared the home with his cousin, and he knew there would be hell to pay.

Michi swiftly jumped off the bike, talking a mile a minute in a mix of Japanese and English, "Look, when I get really mad and upset, I tend to have these episodes that make me do things I don't mean to do. I mean, what do you expect? I'm the Goddess of Luck. I have no control of how these powers work yet. Hence Goddess in training. I thought I mentioned this already?" She continued twitching her fingers while darting her eyes back and forth between the hole and Niko.

"Goddess of what? Wait, you really did this?" Niko said, walking towards Michi to see what the deal was with the woman he stood in front of. "Who are you?" Niko asked, staring down at Michi.

Michi rolled her eyes and sucked her teeth. "I really think you are hard of hearing. I told you. I am the Goddess of Luck, Michiko Tanaka of the Tanaka Clan. If I have to keep repeating myself, I am going to stop speaking to you." She added, "Now, where's my water? I'm thirsty," as she mumbled extra insults in Japanese.

"Look little princess, don't go blasting another hole in my garage wall! I will get you some water and then we are getting you back to your family ASAP. Enough of this weirdo shit for me." Niko continued to mutter to himself, "Goddess of Luck, what the fuck? Demons?! Niko, how the hell did you get yourself caught up in some crazy shit like this?"

Michi interrupted his under-breath rant. "Um, are you talking to yourself? You're the one that is weird. You don't have to be rude. You know. I can hear you!" she shouted across the room.

"Look, I just want you to find your family and be safe. No need to be dramatic—you're the one punching big ass holes in walls. I can only imagine what you do to your boyfriends. Especially since I know you can fight." He added in Japanese, "The men over there probably think you're crazy as hell!" He turned to walk away, amused with himself.

Michi, frustrated at his teasing, yelled in Japanese, stopping Niko in his tracks, "Don't make your head be like that wall."

Niko turned to face her, "Whoa, whoa… I was joking. No need to get all serious! Come on." Niko put his hands up nervously as he watched her eye color flicker from gold to brown back to gold.

Staring back at Niko, Michi asked, "Who are your parents?" She recognized the swirling colors of his aura that confirmed Niko was mixed with demon blood.

"I don't know what you mean. I told you already," he responded, confused as to why she was questioning him about his parents.

Michi searched Niko's features. Recognizing the swirling colors that surrounded him, she continued, "One of your parents is a demon. Do you know which one?" She began to sense another's presence approaching them.

"Yo! Cousin!" Jason yelled from the garage door as it slowly began to open, interrupting the conversation.

Niko, nervous as to what his cousin Jason was doing home early, exclaimed, "Jay! What's up? Meet me in the front. Don't come in here." in hopes of keeping his cousin from seeing Michi and the big hole on the opposite side of the wall.

The garage door was already all the way open. "Man, too late. I am not walking all the way around. What you trying to hide anyway?" Jason teased, strutting in and looking around. His eyes instantly found Michi. "I can see why you didn't want me in here. Well, hello beautiful," he said, walking directly to Michi and grabbing her hand to introduce himself.

"I'm Michi Tanaka." Immediately, she snatched her hand away and bowed to Jason.

Jason, familiar with customs, returned the bow. "My name is Jason Hida. Nice to meet you. Is there anything I can help you with?" he asked, wanting to know more about the woman in front of him while ignoring the giant hole on the opposite side of the wall.

Niko, uncomfortable with his cousin's flirting tactics with Michi, said with a scowl, "Excuse me, Jay, she's good. I am helping her at the moment. What are you doing here? Shouldn't you be at work?"

"Calm down. I'm checking in since Grandfather asked me to see if you were okay today," Jason said, ignoring Niko's hostility while his eyes squinted and Jason licked his lips.

Niko rushed to his cousin's face, blocking Jason's view of Michi. "I keep telling y'all I'm good. I don't need him to keep trying to babysit me. Come on now," he said, clearly annoyed. "We already spoke about this."

Ignoring Niko due to the concentrated power he felt coming from Michi, Jason suddenly remembered the meeting about some new targets the royals were looking for in the area and recognized the name. Jason felt as if he hit the jackpot. Sitting in on a small get together with his father and grandfather at one of the family meetings yesterday, Jason was shown a picture of three Japanese women and was told to contact the clan immediately if they ever ran across them. Fortunately for Jason, one of the women from those pictures was standing right in front of him.

Unbeknownst to Jason, Michi recognized his "Other" characteristics and the change of his aura as she felt the shift of his demeanor after she introduced herself. Michi remembered something Taki told her the other day: *"Stop telling strangers your real name. This is New York City. You never know who people may know around here."* Uncomfortable with the sensation, Michi spoke to Niko, "Hey, Niko. I will take that ride back to the dojo now. Taki and M are waiting for me there."

Niko was weirded out by the tingling sensation running down his spine and was surprised she would be ready to go back there so fast after what happened a couple hours ago. "Okay. Do you think you should go back this quickly?" he asked, confused at her sudden reason to leave.

"I don't think they would have left. Believe me, it would have taken more than the number of soldiers and creatures they sent to get rid of M or Taki. You've watched the way they train," Michi added, looking towards Jason to see his reaction.

Jason immediately smiled and threw on the charm. "Nah, come on, Michiko, right? I don't want you to leave. Come hang with us. I doubt your folks would mind," he said, sliding his way towards her and wrapping his arm around her shoulder.

Niko moved to stepped in-between the two, pushing his cousin away from Michi and himself. "Bro, chill. What you doing? Don't be touching her like that." He stared down his cousin as he sensed warmth emanating from his body causing sweat droplets to form on his forehead.

"Aye, relax cowboy. I see you trying to stake your claim already. I was just inviting her in so she can chill. You know, hang out. Maybe have some fun," Jason said winking at Michi.

Niko immediately swung his left fist, punching Jason in the face. "I told you to stop being so disrespectful," He muttered as he stepped back in front of Michi, not completely understanding why he was overly protective of her.

"Well, look at this. This is what it took?" Jason sneered as he shook his head, trying to shake off the punch he took. "Wow. Well, it looks like we are family after all. I'll be right back."

Niko, confused at his cousin's sudden departure, turned to Michi. "I'm sorry you had to see that. My family and I are going through some things right now. Come on, let's get you to your people."

"Niko, I don't know who you are connected to, but your so-called family is bad news. I am not going anywhere with you!" Michi angrily stated. "I am leaving. Thank you for all of your help today. I hope you survive whatever it is your family is involved in," she added as she turned to leave the garage area from the still raised garage door.

Niko followed Michi, confused at her statements. "I don't know what you're talking about. How do you know my family?" Since she was new to the area, he wondered what she knew about his family.

"I don't know your family. But you are getting on my nerves by not listening. I told you who I am. What makes you think I don't know how to determine if someone is a demon or not?" Michi ranted as she continued her tirade in Japanese.

Niko, feeling an incredible pull to her, rushed towards her. "Hey, hey," he grabbed her hand, pulling her towards himself, "it's okay. I promise that with me you are okay. I will not let anything happen to you, okay?" Niko spoke to her with sincerity. "Let me see where my cousin went and then we can start our search."

"Wait. No. I don't think Lady M or Taki would have left yet. I have a bad feeling about your cousin," Michi quickly replied. She started to speed walk through the open garage door with Niko on her heels.

He grabbed her hand to stop her. "Okay. Okay. I got you. I will make sure you get to the dojo. You have nothing to worry about. Just let me grab my bag and let Jason know I am leaving. He is not like that. Especially towards women. Only thing you gotta worry about is him bugging you for a date," Niko said to Michi. "Please, give me five minutes of your time. Please," he pleaded, as there was slight pain in his chest from him thinking about her leaving him.

"Okay. Fine, hurry up! I am starting to get hot. And it's not a good thing for me to get hot. This is the start of my episodes," Michi said, nervously wiping her forehead and using her hands to fan herself with the rise of her body temperature and the tightening of her skin.

Niko turned to walk away. "I'll be right back. Stay right there. Don't move." He walked into the house from the garage to look for Jason.

Niko stopped suddenly as he heard his cousin's voice. "I'm telling you, it's her. I know what I'm talking about. Also, looks like the little welp has some power. Took for him to find some other type of pussy for us to find out," Jason said into his phone.

"Find out what?" Niko said as he walked in on Jason's conversation.

Startled by Niko's sudden appearance, Jason said nervously, "Aye, cuz. What's up?" as he pressed END on the phone. "Where's the sexy girl? Let's get this party started." He looked around searching for Michi.

"Nah, she good. Who were you talking to? You know Michi?" Niko slowly moved toward Jason.

Jason started to back up, not sure of the swirling colors and power he felt coming from Niko. Jason, a demon halfling himself, never saw or felt power come from Niko prior to this. "Well, this is new. Aye, cousin. Chill. Don't you feel different? That's the question you should be asking. Also, didn't you wonder why all of a sudden grandfather was interested in your health and wellbeing?" he replied, backing himself into a wall of the hallway they were standing in.

Niko did not care about what his cousin was saying. For some reason, his only concern was Michi. "I don't give a damn why you and that old man care about me all of a sudden. Ya'll didn't give a damn about me when my mom died or when I was left alone when my dad was working. Like I said, how do you know Michi and who the hell were you just talking to?" he said, now face-to-face with Jason.

Mirrored this way, the two young men could have been mistaken for brothers. They both stood at about five feet and ten inches tall. Jason and Niko both had a lighter caramel skin tone and dark curly hair. Jason related to Niko by his Japanese father, Jason had a Spanish mother that died young, leaving Jason to be raised with his father.

Being that Niko's mother was Jason's father's younger sister, the cousins grew up close before Niko's mother's death. Their relationship was weird as Jason always had a superiority complex towards Niko. A relationship that became toxic after Niko's return to the family, years after Niko's mother's death Jason would purposely undermine his cousin with unwarranted comments, financial dependence and exclusion from other family members in their age group.

Jason worried about the unfamiliar power the felt coming from his so-called "human" cousin. "Look, Niko. Don't go acting funny now, you know what it is. It's nothing for you to worry about. Since Grandad found out you're really one of us, you have nothing to worry about. Sheesh, I was getting worried for a minute. Thought I was gonna have to kill my favorite little cousin." He chuckled, attempting to walk away from Niko.

"Where do you think you're going? I asked you a few questions, and you didn't answer one of them. Now you're speaking jibberish. Kill me? Kill me?" Niko repeated. Growing angrier and unable to control himself, he swung at Jason again. "Stop playing with me!"

Jason, amused at the newfound power Niko tapped into, stopped Niko's punch. "You know, I really didn't know you had it in you. Wow. My father is going to eat his words. We thought you were a dud. Don't worry, they will be here soon to explain everything to you! So crazy you found the girl. Our clan is going to be the shit now!" he said excitedly. "Now stop trying to hit me. I let you get that one off in the garage since the girl was there. Don't think I will let you do it twice. Especially now that I know I can't kill you," he added.

"Fuck you!" Niko replied, wondering what he felt coming from his cousin and what he sensed growing within himself.

Jason, confused as to where Michi was, asked, "Where's your girlfriend? She's our meal ticket. Grandad will explain when he gets here. Don't let her leave."

Niko stared at Jason like he was crazy. "Our meal ticket? What the hell are you talking about? What did you do?" he blurted out, realizing Jason had called their grandfather.

"Look, all I can tell you is this: your life is about to change. You're not who you think you are. Our family has been around for thousands of years and are starting to get some ground in ruling this area of the region of Earth and Otherside. I think you, my guy, just gave us a bigger jump on taking over," Jason replied eagerly.

Niko was perplexed. "Otherside? Earth? You talking like we're an alien or something. Again, how does Michi fit into all of this?"

Jason slapped his cousin's shoulder. "Bro! Like I said, wait until they get here! Man, I can't wait until you find out everything so I can really talk to you. I will say this, Niko, you are about to be the man! My dad really misses his sister and believed nothing of her was left here on Earth, and I am glad to tell him he still has a piece of her." He reached to give Niko a hug. "Now go get the little cutie so we can make sure they collect her."

"Collect me? Niko, what is he talking about?" Michi interrupted in Japanese.

Niko, surprised by Michi's abrupt entrance, said tensely, "Oh, damn. Michi. I'm sorry. I got tied up talking to my cousin here."

"I can tell you are lying to me," Michi replied in English. She turned to Jason. "Who are you and what demon are you?" Michi snapped at him, eyes turning gold.

Jason's eyes widened with shock. "Oh, this just keeps getting more interesting. I can't answer those questions for you, but you will find out soon enough. Especially since you will be the one answering the questions," he snickered, feeling the others approaching.

"I can tell you are used to dealing with low-levels and demons. I can sense them too, dummy!" Michi said, instantly knocking Jason off of his feet with a quick low kick to his right foot. She landed a punch to his face, instantly knocking him out, then stood up to face Niko. "I was waiting for you and I walk in on you plotting to kidnap me!?" Michi shouted at him, attempting to throw a punch.

Niko dodged her hit and grabbed her hand. "We are not at the dojo—don't do that! Kidnapping? I don't know what you're talking about. I'm just as confused as you are. In my opinion he was speaking in riddles. You walked in on me about to kick his ass for talking crazy. He didn't get—"

"I have to go!" Michi interrupted as an EGU soldier walked in on them.

"Stop! Don't move!" the soldier yelled.

"You!!! I hate you!!!!" Michi shrieked. Her skin tightened, turning a tanned gold color as she continued to scream. She grabbed the intruder by the throat and raised him above her head. "I am going to destroy every last one of you." She threw him through the wall next to her, revealing two more EGU soldiers.

"What the hell are you doing in my house!?" Niko yelled at the one closer to him, grabbing the soldier by the hand and twisting their arm as he threw a left hook. He swept them to the floor, landing a hard chop to the throat. He looked up to watch Michi decimate her opponent by swiftly climbing the tall combatant's leg and grabbing him by the head and arm, causing the man to fall like timber.

Niko reached out to Michi to help her stand. "Come on! We don't have time to argue!"

Michi ignored his outreached hand after knocking out the EGU soldier. "I don't need your help. It's because of you they know where I am!" she yelled while shoving Niko away from her.

"Come on! I have nothing to do with that. Now my cousin, maybe, but I've never seen these people before!" Niko, hot on her heels, shouted as he grabbed her hand to turn her to him. "I want to help you. Also, I want to find out what the hell my idiot cousin was talking about," Niko pleaded.

Michi pulled away from him. "You are dealing with things you don't understand. If your family hasn't told you anything, you are in luck. Shit is about to get reality, as you Americans say."

"It's, shit is about to get real." Niko chuckled. "Michi, I will help you get back to your family. Can you help me figure out who my family is?" he added shyly, looking down at his knocked-out cousin.

Michi, appalled at his question, replied in Japanese, "I'm being chased by demons and you are asking *me* for help?" She walked away from him, talking to herself out loud trying to feel for Adam. "Sunny, where are you?!" Just then, a stronger presence stepped in front of her as she made it just outside the garage.

"Well, hello, Ms. Tanaka." He bowed. "My name is Touma Hida. Let's have a chat. You are completely surrounded. I doubt very much you can escape. We heard about your episode at the compound, so believe me, we are prepared. I just want to talk," he added at the end in an attempt to ease her.

Michi's golden eyes revealed the auras of about fifty soldiers surrounding the house between Otherside and Earth realm. She knew exactly who she was dealing with since she knew it was the EGU that attacked her home in Japan.

"I noticed. I doubt that's enough to take me. I guess you know who I am then?" she questioned, wondering how he was connected to the EGU. "I know for a fact you are not EGU. How do you know me?" she added to insult him.

Touma Hida was not impressed with her tactics. "I am not the idiot my son is. I will say, you are correct. I am not EGU, I am something bigger than that. I am the head of the leading demon clan in this area. EGU had no choice but to come to us for help and direction for this region." He swayed side to side. "You see, Ms. Tanaka, I don't want the royals or EGU here in my space. SO, I rather they collect their belongings and be on their way. Please, don't make this difficult," Touma cunningly said.

"Uncle Touma? What are you doing here?" Niko rushed over. "The house is being attacked. Help me help my friend here."

Touma, tired of the charade he had to show his nephew all of these years, sighed. "Niko, it is about time you learn a few things tonight. First, it looks like you are not all human as we originally thought. Second, you came across something that may help in our cause. Now grab the girl and let's go."

"Uncle Touma... I'm not human—what does that mean? Grab her? Our cause? Uncle, you sound crazy right now," Niko reacted, becoming even more puzzled.

"Boy, do not test my patience today," Touma responded. "Grab the girl and I'll explain everything to you. I'll even tell you about your mother," he added with a smile, knowing that topic was delicate for Niko.

Niko contemplated his uncle's words. "Hey, you will tell me about my mom?" He put his head down, moving closer to Michi. Niko rubbed her hand with his finger. "Uncle T, you know that's real low to use my mom. Of course, I want to learn all about her. That's why I moved with you guys! You barely talk about her."

"That was my baby sister. I loved her, but she chose her fate," Touma retorted with malice as he stared at Michi. "You, my lady, are more than they told me. Who are you?" Touma said, adding, "I was wondering why the EGU came all the way here for a mere girl."

Michi realized the EGU hadn't told him why they wanted her. "I don't know why those creeps are after me. I just know I will destroy them for murdering my family," she said. Michi realized Niko was stalling, as he was still clinging to her hand.

"You know, Uncle, I always knew you were into some shit. Why didn't you tell me?" Niko interrupted. "I can't believe this. What are you? What am I?".

Touma, now inpatient, shouted, "You are a demon, boy! My sister unfortunately fell in love with a human and had you. Like I said earlier, she chose her fate. As for me, you will learn more about your family after we deal with the guests that we have in our area. Wait here." He walked away like he was waiting for something.

"We can get away. My cousin's car is in the front. I have the keys and my emergency bag is right by the exit where we can run," Niko whispered to Michi. "I am not letting my uncle take you to anybody!"

That strange sensation overcame Michi again, and she began to see through the eyes of someone else: *We are almost there. Stall for another ten minutes. I will make sure your deal with the royal family goes through. Thank you.* The call ended, the speaker looking out the window.

"Michi, Michi!" Niko shouted. "You, okay? Come on!" he exclaimed, shaking her.

Michi immediately snapped out of those other thoughts. "I'm sorry, that happens sometimes. FYI, they have about fifty soldiers surrounding this place. Some I can see, some I can't. I'm not sure how we can get out of this," she whispered back to Niko.

"Watch this—follow me," he eagerly replied with a smile. Niko grabbed Michi's hand and walked to his left. There were no EGU soldiers on the side of the garage he led her to. He snatched a bag from under the luxury car parked there and then began to run towards the exit. Hearing a yell in the distance, Niko turned to make sure Michi was on his heels. "GET IN!" he exclaimed, having already unlocked his cousin's car. Not seeing his uncle, Niko got in the driver's seat.

Michi was annoyed by Niko's lack of decency. "So, I really had to open my door myself? You are so rude," she complained, slamming the door.

"Are you serious?" Niko replied as he started the car and peeled off. "Sorry, princess. This is not a date. This is an escape. I don't even know where I'm going," he said, glancing over at Michi as he drove.

Michi looked out the window as Niko drove. "I hope the rest of your family is not as crazy. That was not a pleasant introduction."

"You talking like you're going to marry me one day. With you being the Goddess of Luck and all, I hope I don't become the dessert when I meet yours," Niko said to lighten the mood.

A sudden sadness fell upon Michi as she thought of her family, "I don't have family anymore. My family was murdered by those EGU ass whoops! I promise I will kill them all!" Her eyes and skin started to turn gold again.

"I am so sorry!" Niko responded, removing one hand from the wheel to grab hers while he continued to drive. He lifted her left hand to his lips to kiss. "I am so so sorry. I wish I could take all that pain away. Also, it's ass wipes." He chuckled. He added, "Can you think of any landmarks that you may recognize that's in the area you live in??" He wanted to lift the somber mood.

Michi noticed what he was doing, and responded in Japanese, "I have no clue. The way M and Sunny travel, we don't drive. Taki and I walk around when we are at the dojo. I think we should go there."

"Don't you think that's the first place my family and this EGU will look for you?" Niko grew suspicious of the reasons why his family and the EGU were after Michi. He thought, *is what she's saying is true? She's a god and some wierdos are after her?*

A familiar energy signature revealed itself to Michi, "Sunny, is that you?" she spoke to the sensation. "O-M-G. Sunny, it is you!" She began to think harder so she could reach Adam.

"What are you doing?" Niko sensed that Michi was doing something important, so he held her hand tight and glanced over at her, feeling a tingling sensation throughout his body.

Michi answered him casually, "I'm looking for Sunny, that's how I will find Taki! There he goes. Come on. Be careful. I just learned how to use this power. Sunny taught me. M said I wasn't ready, so she wouldn't teach me. I can't believe—"

"Hey, hey!" Niko interrupted her rant. "What are you saying?"

Michi, excited that she could get back to Taki, said, "Hold on. It will be weird at first." Using her powers, she pinpointed exactly where Adam was.

TWO GODS

"Sunny! I found you!!" Michi exclaimed, just as she popped in on Adam with Niko still holding her hand.

Adam, startled by Michi and company's abrupt appearance, finished wiping himself, "What the FUCK MICHI?!" he shouted as he was getting off the toilet seat. "Why the hell are you in my bathroom?" he said, fixing his clothes. He then started to stalk toward Niko. "And who is this?" he asked, immediately recognizing Niko was a half demon.

"Don't go boom!" Michi replied to Adam, jumping in front of Niko as she noticed Adam's eyes were on fire. "He helped me get away. They are after me again. Where is Taki?"

Adam was mad at Michi for involving a stranger. "She and Mel disappeared looking for you. Last we heard, they left the angel guards and went looking for you on their own. I've been trying to call Kisha since. That still doesn't explain why you brought a newbie with you," he said, still sizing Niko up.

Niko, slightly intimidated by the large man with the burning eyes, said, "Look. I don't know what's going on. I just wanted to make sure she got back to her family." He gestured his hand out to Adam. "My name is Niko Black. I know Michi and Taki from the dojo."

Adam was not impressed, and ignored the offer of a handshake. "I don't care where you know them from. I want to know why you are around and what your plans for them are?"

Michi, not happy with the way Adam was questioning Niko, stepped in. "Look Sunny! He is my friend. Stop being mean. He just went against his family for me!" she yelled as her eyes turned gold.

"Hey, Mich, cut it out. Calm down. I won't hurt the kid. But you know he can't be in the mix," Adam responded, as he was noticing the clash of him and Michi's power with the faint crackle in the air and slight wind beginning to move about the apartment.

Michi started to calm herself. "Okay. Kay. Sorry, Sunny." Looking back at Niko, she began making introductions. "Niko, this is Sun—I mean, Adam. He is Taki's boyfriend I told you about. He is going to help me find Lady M and Taki."

"First thing's first. Stop calling me Sunny in front of people, Michi! Second, we will take the rest of this conversation outside my bathroom.," Adam said, washing his hands. He gestured for Michi and Niko to get out of the bathroom to give him some privacy.

Michi looked around the penthouse. "Sunny! This is nice. I see why you want Taki to move in with you." She sat on his couch as Niko followed her lead.

"We are not talking about Kisha and me. Let's get back to the people chasing you. I already texted Uncle Mike." Adam stood over them.

Michi bounced in her seat and clapped with joy. "Whooo! I get to see the angels finally! Lady M always got her panties in a crunch so much that I haven't seen Dillon in a couple weeks and I haven't seen Mikael or X since my first day here. I heard he is so cool!" she said, grabbing Niko's leg with her eyes shining bright gold.

"Angels? Did you just say angels?" Niko replied. "Michi, what are you talking about?" he said, confused, but he felt the same warmth that flows throughout his body when she touches him as she rested her hand on his knee.

Michi scowled as she removed her hand and stood up, "You are so annoying. I've been telling you stuff all day! You don't listen and it's starting to really annoy the hell out of me." She began to just rant in Japanese with her eyes turning gold again.

"Mich, calm yourself down little girl!" Adam reached to touch her.

Niko promptly stood up to disrupt Adam touching Michi. "Hey, you don't have to touch her.", he said, grabbing Michi's hand. Niko felt the tingling sensation again, and he was still unsure of why he all of a sudden was so overprotective of her.

"So, Michi, you found yours already?" Adam said to both individuals in front of him.

Michi switched back to her regular self. "Found my what?" she said, sitting back down on the couch and gesturing for Niko to join her.

"I'm okay with standing up. All of this is getting a bit too weird for me," Niko said, wiping sweat from his forehead. "Is anyone else hot?" He began to fan himself.

Adam laughed at the two clueless lovebirds. "Look, Niko, right? Sounds like Michi here already told you what the deal is, right? You're going to have to roll with us for a while until we get with Mikael and M. So, it's all good. Sit tight. You're good here."

"Let me be honest. I don't know what the hell is going on. She speaks with a mix of Japanese and English. Most of the time I can figure out what she is saying, but sometimes I can't. I know she keeps going on about the goddess of luck and that EGU agents are after her."

Michi interrupted the two men, "I am sitting right here. Now you are admitting that you don't understand me. Making me have to repeat myself is going to irritate me." She checked her nails, adding, "I haven't worn heels in about 5 hours, this is getting bothersome."

"You know, you're really reminding me of M right now," Adam responded. "Let me try to get in touch with them ASAP," he added, walking away and pulling out his cellphone.

Niko was nervous, as he wanted Michi to know he was trying his best to be supportive. "Look, Michi, I will try my best to understand what is going on. I'm sorry my family is helping the EGU. Please, just let me help you, let—" He was interrupted by Adam.

"What you mean your family is helping the EGU?" Adam asked.

Niko instantly began to sweat as his eyes believed him to feel as if he was looking at the sun. "Look man, I didn't know my family was into this stuff. I had no idea they were after Michi." He shook his head, trying to forget the memory of his uncle talking to him about his mother.

"Who are you? What do you want with Michi?" Adam spoke forcefully while towering over Niko and staring down at him.

Niko slightly trembled, replying instantly, "My name is Niko Black like I said before. I know Michi and Taki from the dojo. I found a dojo that I like and my cousins told me it was a respected training facility. I want to bone her—I mean, damn she's hot. For some reason I feel like I have to protect her," he spat out, covering his mouth. Why had he just revealed all of that information?

"Oh shit. Well at least we know he is as corny as he looks." Adam laughed, looking Niko up and down. "What else don't you want us to know about you and Michi?" he added.

Niko covered his mouth just as he began to speak. As he finished, he removed his hand from his mouth. "Why am I answering you like this?"

"Because I am willing you to answer me. I got powers too. Not just Michi. Just make sure you stay on our side. Keep your family away from Michi. I do not need Kisha getting on me," Adam answered. Adam sent a text message to Taki as he continued talking to Michi and Niko. "Look, we are about to head somewhere to meet my people. It may not be a good idea to stay here right now. My place is not as protected as our usual spots. M's place is the best. So, come. Mich, we are about to be out. Grab ya boyfriend and pay attention to my energy signature. Might as well make this a lesson," he said, grabbing Michi's shoulder.

****

Taki paced back and forth as she watched M speak into the phone. What she heard of the conversation made her nervous.

"Look, I don't care who has to die! I want to know who sanctioned the EGU raid on my place of business!" M screamed into the phone. "Whomever this lieutenant is, he will learn his place!" She clicked END.

Taki looked at M. "Lady M, who was that? Have you felt Michi? I don't have enough power left from Adam to do an energy search."

"For a second, I did, and then she disappeared. I regret not teaching her my power now," M answered. "I know Adam has been teaching her to travel without me behind my back, so hopefully she will find him. I don't want those angels involved. They will make this situation more complicated," she sneered.

Taki did not understand M's current frustration with the angels, as she thought they made peace months ago. "Well, shouldn't we let them help us? You know, teamwork makes the dream work!" she shouted enthusiastically pumpng her fist in the air.

"Stop it with your dramatics. I do not want them involved and that's that!" M stomped away. "I'm going to change. Get in touch with that boyfriend of yours and see if he has heard from Michi. I am telling you now, the war is starting. This will not be easy. I will not need you two being so rebellious right now," she added.

Taki faked appalled by clutching her imaginary pearls with raised eyebrows. "Oh, what in the heavens do you mean, Your Highness?" She bowed. "Look, I think I proved I can handle myself. Also, I know how serious this is, but you know I am not moving without Adam with me. So, the angels will be around. I'm telling you, M, they can help us. Now, stop being a meanie."

THE ANGELS

"Now, what do I owe this pleasure?" Dillon spoke into his cellphone. "Really, well thank you for that information." What he heard on the other end slightly frustrated him. He ended the call and then sent a text to X, *Meet me at the castle. I'll be there soon.*

He yelled back to Mikael while he looked around his office area looking for something, "Look, we will not have any assistance with the extra EGU agents in the area. The Eastern region is immersed in battle with a strong family army and can't lend us any assistance at this time."

Mikael stood in the entranceway of Dillon's office, "I knew that already. I don't understand why you keep thinking we have to win this by the book. We obviously have more assistance in the two gods on our side than the army we command," Mikael said, just as frustrated at the lack of resources to assist them in the war that continued to rage on unbeknownst to regular humans.

Dillon, prideful in his reasonings for not siding with the gods, responded, "We have reborn gods that are being trained by the former queen of the brutalist part of Hell. You expect me to trust that!"

"I expect you to trust the Ultimate High, as this has to be happening for a reason. You are acting as if there is some type of conspiracy behind these gods returning!" Mikael shouted back to Dillon.

Fully understanding what Mikael was insinuating, Dillon huffed. "Of course, there is a conspiracy behind these gods returning. We have not received any updated orders, nor have we been in contact with headquarters in almost an eon! How do we not know this is not the demons somehow manipulating the energies they are trying to control?" Dillon said, glaring at Mikael with a slight force of energy in his tone.

"Look. I can understand why you feel this way, Dillon, but we have to have faith that the Ultimate High sent the gods back to help us. I practically raised one of them and regardless of what you say. You know Melchorde is not on the other side. I will not get into the past, but don't act like she is not family because of you," Mikael sneered back. "Also, your power does not scare me and never has. My energy is on par with yours now so please, stop with the threats."

Dillon walked to face the angel, "Stop testing my patience. Regardless of how much you think you are on par with me, you should rethink that. I will forever be the commander of you all. Don't forget it." With that, he walked out of the office leaving Mikael behind.

Frustrated that he hadn't spoken one word to Melchorde since the day the Goddess of Luck brought him to her home. The shock of seeing M stirred a mix of anger and sadness, evoking long-buried memories. Snapping out of his memories, Dillon left for his meeting with X to see what X learned from the psychic demigod Lucia.

****

"Well, look at you beautiful. I see you're still teasing me. Got any good information for me today?" X called out to Lucy as he walked into her shop.

Lucy, knowing she had to continue to assist the angels, replied, "Only that the EGU is here and that they have a lot of info on you all. I do not know how, but they do." Adding, "And I like looking good for you, my handsome knight in shining armor," and winking at him.

"Well, I like looking at you. But I see those assholes are still at it. Okay. Well, I'll make sure everyone stays on high alert." As he finished speaking, his phone rang.

"Yea. What? HOW IN THE FUCK did that happen?" X shouted into the phone. "What do you mean they disappeared and they don't want our help? Yo, you're not giving me any good news. I am hanging up." He pressed END.

He sighed heavily and rubbed his chin. "Well pretty lady, you are right. The EGU attacked Mel's dojo and Michi is missing," X said, unsure of what was going on.

Lucia was sure that Michi was safe. "Well, she's fine. She has to go through this." She recognized that all of this was connected to the bigger picture. "Look, handsome. I have clients coming soon. Ya'll don't need me right now. But soon, you will. Stay safe and keep in touch. I gotta go prep. Later!" she said, disappearing into the back of her shop.

X chuckled at her sudden disappearance and turned to leave as he felt a familiar presence outside the door. "Well, if it isn't Chain Face. You've been MIA lately."

34

"I've been playing tag with demons and angels lately. They still can't believe I exist," he said chuckling and clenching onto the blanket that laid on his boney shoulders.

X was in awe of the power that pulsated from the individual in front of him. "Well, I can see why. We don't know what you are ourselves," he replied, curious as to if Chain Face would reveal his true nature and identity.

"Don't be slick. I am not that dumb. In due time, you will learn of me and my kind. Also, at this time, you should lay low. The angels should not involve themselves in demon family issues. Leave it be. It will all work out. Just be supportive of Taki with her pretty self. Oh my god Adam is so lucky, and so are all of you! She has touched you all and it will shine through when necessary. That's all I am to reveal at this time. Gotta go!" he said, immediately disappearing.

Popping back in front of a startled X, Chain Face continued, "She is coming for you. Just watch. You will know, but you must first get to know yourself. She will need your other side to be her guidance. DO NOT FAIL HER, Xeno!" Then he disappeared again, leaving no trace of his appearance.

"What the heavens?" X stood shocked by the eerie feeling left by Chain Face's words. "Who is she? Know myself? Other side? This guy really needs a mental institution for supernaturals," he chuckled, picking up his phone to see a text from Dillon and responding, *I am on my way.*

ANCHOR, WHAT?

Mikael was slightly startled by the sudden appearance of Adam, Michi and Niko. "Well, isn't this going to be interesting. What do I owe this pleasure? I thought you were missing?" he said, looking towards Michi. He added, "And why is this half-demon with you?"

"Am I the only one that didn't know I was a half-demon?" Niko responded to Mikael's question.

Michi, irritated at Niko's lack of seriousness around the angel, responded, "Look, I know you're new to our world, but calm down and let us do the Q&A. Sit tight." She pointed him towards a seat that was near them to his dimay.

"Hi Mikael! I haven't seen you in a while. I was hoping you could shine some light on the events that are happening and get me in touch with Lady M and Taki," Michi said, bowing in front of him, then ranting in Japanese to Niko.

"She is as hyper as you stated, Adam." Mikael chuckled at Michi. "Well, hello, Ms. Tanaka. I have heard great things about you." He returned the bow. "I do wish we would have had more time getting acquainted. Far as Melchorde and Ms. Mashiro, they are no longer in contact with us. They have gone out on their own to find you. We heard about the attack on Melchorde's dojo. They left shortly after. I take it the queen doesn't want our help with this. At least that is what she told the guards," he said, thinking of why the EGU would suddenly attack. It's been months since Michi had been with Melchorde and Taki.

Adam immediately sensed Mikael's assessment. "FYI, this dude family is involved, so maybe he can tell us something," he said, staring Niko down.

"Stop being rude, Sunny! You already forced him to tell you who he is. He doesn't know about the EGU besides what I told him," Michi interrupted the angel and Sun God talking.

Raising his hand like he was in class, Niko said, "You actually haven't told me anything. It's been in bits and pieces. I've been feeling really strange since I've been around you. I think, I think—" Niko passed out immediately.

Michi rushed to his side and attempted to use her power to heal him. Her eyes and skin immediately turned gold, and she began a chant in Japanese.

"Michi, what in the universe?!" Adam said. "I've never seen you at full power like this?"

She stood up and looked at Adam and Mikael. "I've never tapped into my full power like this? O-M-G! Sunny! You're literally on fire! I see fire when I look at you! Mikael, you are the pure energy of the Ultimate High." She walked towards Mikael to stare. "I know I must not go too deep, but I just want to touch it!" she said as she reached out to Mikael.

"Little one, stay focused! I see you have an attention issue." Mikael swatted away at Michi's reached out hand, immediately cutting his energy signature off and snapping Michi out of her trance. "I see gods are not immune to the pull of the light," he said. "Well, back to business. Adam, please call Takisha immediately." Mikael was nervous at the god in front of him as he knew she had the power of Luck. He never understood those gods' powers. He just remembered one of the Shichifukujin was playful, very mischievous, devious and hard to keep under wraps. She reminded him of her. He knew a few of them survived the Days of Hunt due to their cunning ways.

Mikael pulled out his phone to send a text, "While he tries to reach Ms. Mashiro, I will try to reach Dillon. I know he will want to know you are safe."

"How is my Dillon? I miss him. He is so cool. I am so grateful to him and how he kept me safe. Lady M is a meanie and doesn't let me see my Dillon. Look, Niko. Niko, wait until you meet my godfather, Dillon. I can't wait—" she stopped her rant as she remembered he was still passed out on the floor.

Adam laughed at her lack of attention. "Godfather? That's interesting. Michi, this is exactly what M was talking about in class. Your mind is everywhere but here. Do you know what you did to the dude? Remember you are at full god strength. Your skin and eyes are still gold, Michi," he said, reminding her of their circumstances.

"Oh yea! He's fine. He's new to all of this and his brain didn't take it too well. I just healed his brain and told him everything that is going on," Michi said, shrugging her shoulders.

Mikael asked, confused, "What do you mean told him everything?"

"I showed him everything that I've been trying to tell him all day. I inputted the images from my thoughts into his mind. When he wakes up, he will know what is going on so I don't have to keep repeating myself. It is so annoying and irritates the heckles out of me," Michi ranted then continued in a mix of Japanese and English.

Mikael realized she had a serious attention span issue. "Ms. Tanaka, please stay focused. That is a power that hasn't been around in a long time. Implanting someone's thoughts into another being is next level god powers."

"Uncle Mike, her powers *are* next level. She does that all the time. When she and Kisha want to talk without me knowing she does that. She even knows how to block me from reading when she is doing it. Funny thing, I think she taught Kisha how to do it. Since Kish siphons my powers, she can do it too."

Mikael was slightly surprised at what he heard. "Are you telling me your girlfriend can siphon the powers of another god? Now that is interesting. I thought as an anchor, you are only able to siphon from the god that you anchored to?" he spoke inquisitively.

"I don't know. I didn't know it either until this one slipped up and told me one day. I've been attempting to learn that before I met her, so I find it kind of cool," Adam said with a smirk.

Mikael shook his head. "You really thought to do that? Why?" Mikael asked, wondering what Adam was thinking.

"Honestly, if this so-called war gets as nasty as M and you are saying it's going to get, we're going to need every advantage we can get. Me being able to relay messages to you all without the enemy knowing or even when we're far apart would be excellent, so you're damn right I thought of that," Adam replied to Mikael.

Mikael was intrigued by the seriousness Adam was taking towards his participation in the war. "Well, I am glad you even think to assist us. Now back to Ms. Tanaka here. I am sorry for all that you've been through. I really hope we can help you against the EGU. The good thing is you found your anchor. Assuming you two gods are at full strength due to your anchors being around, we may have a chance against them. We also need to figure out which crest the EGU are working for. Maybe that can help us get a leg up on them. Once we convene with Melchorde and Ms. Mashiro, we should be able to collaborate on a resolution to this matter."

"Dillon said you always spoke like you're in a business meeting. I really appreciate your concern. Don't worry; you've all been touched by me, so nothing is going to happen. We just have to make sure she doesn't get what she wants," Michi said in a trance.

Mikael, confused, went to grab her, but he was interrupted by Adam. "Stop! Don't touch her—she's officially in her God state. M and I learned to let her speak like last time and she will return. None of us figured that part of her power out yet. Her books don't even mention it," Adam said, not meaning to add the last part.

"I will make sure we all survive. It will be brutal, but we all will make it! Now I must rest." Michi giggled as she passed out next to Niko.

Adam said, "Told you," He shrugged, looking at Mikael. "You know we never finished telling her about the anchor thing."

"How could we? The girl's mind runs ten miles a minute. I am surprised she keeps up with us all, concentrating on so many things at once," Mikael said staring at the petite girl with power radiating from her that was on par with Adam's.

Adam glared down at Michi and Niko. "Look Uncle Mike, I know you don't fully trust her. But she is on our side. She is very spontaneous and reckless, but she really is for us. M is working on helping her control her power. Please don't worry and don't involve more of the angels. We have to keep this under wraps. The EGU is working with some powerful demons, and we can't afford to let ya'll lose more soldiers right now." Adam turned to look at Mikael. "Don't get too involved. For some reason, I feel like we're going to have to trust M and Michi on this one," he added.

"You may be right. To be honest, we don't have the extra resources to help, so I am relying on the two gods I have on my side to assist with these issues." Mikael replied confidently.

Adam was glad he and his godfather were on the same page. "Well, good. It's funny, Michi called Dillon her godfather. I wonder why?" he asked.

"I think she bonded with him during their travels together in reaching Taki. In the short time they spent together, he kept her safe and guided her to safety. She appreciates that," Mikael responded. "Interesting, I would have never thought Dillon would get close to anyone. Let alone a young human girl. Well, at least *thought* to be human at the time."

Adam immediately replied, "Nah, remember, Michi always knew who she was. Knowing her, that's the first thing she told him. That she was who she was."

Mikael nodded, fascinated by Dillion's relationship with Michi. "Well, that's even more interesting, as Commander Dillon was one of the leading factors in the Days of Hunts. Because of him we decimate—I mean… Never mind." He stopped in his tracks.

"Don't get all quiet now. You know, out of all I have learned, I have not gained any knowledge of this Days of Hunts you speak of randomly. I even noticed the grim look on M's face when she mentions it. I think we have time to discuss it." Adam glared at Mikael.

Leaning on a pole, Mikael sneered back, "Look, that is not a topic that anyone who was around during that time likes to discuss. I thought with you being a god now you would be privy to that type of information, as I do not care to speak of it unless necessary."

"It's okay. We don't have to now, but believe me, we will all discuss it! I want M and you around for that conversation. Even bring in Dillon," Adam replied. "Now, to get in touch with Kish. She hasn't responded to any of my messages. So, it's time to show her how much of a creepy boyfriend I can be," he said as he began to pinpoint her energy signature.

Closing his eyes in concentration, Adam added, "Melchorde is trying to hide her and Kish's energy when they travel, but I never told her I can always find Kisha regardless of what she does. Be right back." He left Mikael alone with the passed-out Goddess of Luck and her anchor.

MICHI FOUND

"Didn't I tell you I will stalk you to the ends of Earth, girl," Adam whispered in Taki's ear as he popped in on her while she watched M decimate a squad of EGU soldiers in a dimly lit parking lot M she was on a phone call.

Taki yelped at his sudden appearance, "WHAT THE HELL?! Adam, why and how are you here? I know for a fact M don't want ya'll to know where we are."

"Mr. Moore came even though he knew I was cloaking our location. Interesting," M said, irritated that he knew where they were.

"Look, I wouldn't normally do this, but I know where Michi is. That's the only reason I came," Adam immediately replied as he watched the darkness pour away from M.

Taki was relieved that Adam was not being a creep. "You know you should have led with that, because we seriously were gonna have a conversation later at home," she said, folding her arms.

"I love the way you just said *at home*," Adam grabbed Taki's hand and planted soft kisses while a fiery blaze danced in his eyes.

"Don't make this about our residences. Where is Michi?" Taki giggled, happy that he knew to find her once Michi found him.

"Where is she, Sun God?" M immediately interrupted the love birds.

Adam towered over the two women. "She is at one of Mikael's safe houses in Queens. Before we go, I want to tell you both what's going on. She is not alone."

"What do you mean she's not alone?" both women shouted at the same time making Adam jump back.

Taki shifted her gaze to M. "Sorry," then turned to Adam. "Spill!" she said knowing Michi probably didn't want Adam to speak with them before they saw her.

M wondered how she found Adam. "So, I see you teaching her behind my back helped our cause. I truly didn't think she was ready due to her lack of concentration."

"I was shocked she took to it so well. She definitely has a lot of work to do. But back to what I was saying, because you're going to want to hear this." He paused, then continued. "She found her anchor. Some dude named Niko Black. I willed him to tell me who he is. He's a half-demon that has family that is involved with the EGU squad that's searching for Michi. He never knew he was a half-demon. Haven't got to the part of what kind of half demon, as he and Michi are passed out at the moment." He looked directly at M. "She went into a trance saying it will be brutal but we all will survive. This time she was in full god-state while she was fully conscious before the trance."

M was surprised at what she heard. "Well, it looks like she is fully syncing with her powers as well. Not as dramatic and intense as your rebirth." She glared at Adam.

"Remember, she was trained to be a god all her life. I didn't know any of this existed before I became a god," Adam snapped back.

Taki instantly knew where this was going. "M, you are such a troublemaker, and Adam, why do you respond to her? You know you can't win against the Queen of Shade."

"Now, can we go get my best friend? Oh yea? Adam, how do you know that this Niko Black is her anchor?" Taki added.

Adam stood next to Taki and wrapped his arm around her shoulders. "He siphons from her like you do me. I noticed immediately. We'll discuss how they found me later. Let's go. I know that little busy bee is up already." He paused. "Oh yea, she planted what is going on in his head, so he already is up to speed with everything."

"SHE DID WHAT?" M screeched with enough force that caused the pavement to crack next to them and the car alarms to sound off. "Let's go now! I will have her head!"

****

X walked towards the pacing Dillon. "What's got your panties in a bunch?" he snickered, and added, "Like that one? I stole that one from Taki."

"Your obsession with these humans is annoying," Dillon retorted.

X, not impressed with Dillon's somber attitude, scoffed, "Not my fault you walk around as salty as humans and don't enjoy your time doing anything. What do you want anyway?"

"I want to know what that psychic girlfriend of yours found out for us?" Dillon said.

X responded, "Nothing really, just that the EGU is on to us. It wasn't her who I got good info from." He paused, then added, "I ran into Chain Face. He told me to make sure we sit this one out. He said not to get involved in demon family affairs."

"What does that mean? What demon family?" Dillon asked. "Well, I know you heard about the attack on the dojo by now. I also wanted you to assist me in finding Ms. Tanaka."

X was shocked at Dillon's request. "Wait, did you just ask me to help you find Michi?" he chuckled.

"Don't make me repeat my myself. You are already walking on thin ice with me, Xeno." Dillion slowly paced toward the curious X. "Do not question my motives. I am looking to make sure the last of the Tanaka Clan is safe. Unfortunately, she happens to be a god. We haven't received any orders to destroy Adam. I take it headquarters will be learning of Ms. Tanaka soon." Turning his back to X, he continued, "Until otherwise, we will make sure the EGU is not successful in destroying the Tanaka Clan. Now, come. Let's start with Mikael."

X understood what Dillon meant. "I am calling him now. Do you really think—"

He was disrupted as Mikael spoke into his phone, "Aye! I'm checking in with you about Michi. Heard from Mel or Taki?" He listened to Mikael's response.

"What is he blabbering about now? Why are you not repeating what he is saying?" Dillon anxiously said to X.

X waved his hand at Dillon, placing his finger over is lips. "Shhhh," he ordered as he continued to listen to Mikael.

Dillon raised his eyebrow staring slightly up a X. "DO NOT—"

"Look, Mike was getting to the good part. Let's head to the spot in Queens. Short story. Michi is passed out with some dude that is probably her anchor, and somehow, she found her way to Adam and Adam took her to Mikael."

Dillon furrowed his brow. "Anchor? How and who?"

"I am just as confused. Oh yea, he's a half-demon," X said, unleashing his wings to fly towards the safehouse.

CLOSE ENCOUNTERS

"Well, isn't this a surprise. What do I owe the pleasure of this phone call?" Jade spoke into her device. "I have no clue on where my former student is. I heard she got involved with some of the angel scum over there and haven't had contact since." She paused, listening. "Well, I advise you to tread lightly. I got word from my side that she is now under the care of the former Queen."

Jade listened again. "Heed my words: this will not be taken lightly. If your plan doesn't work. I promise you my family will not back you. Goodbye."

She ended the call knowing that she would eventually have to go to her father about the events with Taki, Michi and Melchorde and how they were connected. This would reveal that she always knew about Taki and Michi. Unsure of how to move forward, Jade placed a call.

"I'm glad you answered, sister. FYI, that Lieutenant Zerrick is coming for you. For some reason, he's after your ransom and he has a good amount of info on Michi." Jade stopped and listened to Melchorde's response. "Father will not be pleased with your take on this. Nor would he like that we hid Michi from him. I will not be brought down for you!"

She ended the call. Jade knew she had to choose a side eventually but was unsure of which was right. "Be careful, baby girl. Only choose the winning team," she said, staring out her office window.

****

"Benzi, did you feel that? I know that was Michi," Bisha immediately interrupted the spur of the moment shopping spree that she and Benzi were on.

"I felt my princess. I wonder what she was doing? Come on. Let's go!" Benzi flayed her arms, throwing the clothes she was holding onto the ground. "We don't have time for Earthly Travel. See you soon!" she said waving and disappearing right in front of Bisha.

"How do I tolerate two of you?" Bisha heaved a sigh as she followed Benzi's energy signature to the spike they felt from Michi.

"Oops. Looks like princess has already left this area." Benzi sighed, scanning her environment.

Irritated, Bisha said, "Yes. But we are now surrounded by EGU soldiers. Benzi, that is why we should investigate first."

"Well, we can just leave or we can beat one of them to a bloody pulp until we get the info we need. Either way, I'm down," Benzi replied with a gleam in her eye.

The ladies' conversation was interrupted. "Well. This is a surprise I did not intend to get today," the familiar seductive voice called from behind. "It seems my plan didn't work to rid the rest of you back at the compound. I still can't believe you would trust a human girl is our leader! Fukurokuji would be so disappointed in the choices you've made. I will correct this, and I will become the Shichifukujin," Daikoku said.

The shocked Benzi and Bisha stood with their backs touching in a defensive stance. Bisha unleashed some of her own power and ran directly to Daikoku landing her first hit on the arms crossed Shinigami. Benzi raised her hands to the sky and twirled in a circle as a faint gold light surrounded her as she disappeared and reappeared in front of each of the soldiers, cutting off their heads, annihilating them one by one.

"You will pay for what you did to clan leader!" Bisha screamed, landing strong punches on her crossed arms as Daikoku continued to block the barrage of hits.

"You will not stop me! I know how to find the child. You think you are the only ones linked to her?" Daikoku said, changing the pace of the fight by using her right arm to block Bisha's punch and landing a strong uppercut to Bisha's chin and knocking her away. "You're supposed to be the warrior. I told you. I am best to lead you. Follow me, Bisha. I promise what I can offer is more than you can imagine. I have lived gloriously with the power I've accumulated."

Bisha tightened her fists creating them to glow. She suddenly launched herself at Daikoku swinging a volley of punches "You will not touch her. I promise you, Koku, you will join Fukurokuji very soon," she said while adding more power to her punches.

Daikoku reacted to the punches with heavy puffs, attempting to block them but feeling the might of the Warrior Shinigami, Bishamonten.

"Bisha, come! I found her again! Koku, you will pay dearly for what you did to princess. But for right now, we will go," Benzi said placing her hand on Bisha's shoulder, following the trail of Michi's energy signature.

"I WANT THEIR HEADS!!" Daikoku screamed at the remaining EGU. "How did you let them get away!" she turned to the approaching Touma Hida, "You did not attempt to stop them at all, half-breed. I told you that I would be the reason your deal with the royals goes through."

"I do not interrupt cat fights. But you will learn your place in this area, Shinigami. I do not answer to you. This is a favor for a friend. You, my dear, are NOT my friend. As for those two, you clearly underestimated your hand. I will get with Zerrick and find out what the EGU is really doing in my area.", Touma sneered, walking away.

****

"Hey guys! You found me. I am so happy that you found me!" Michi exclaimed at Adam, Melchorde, and Taki at they returned.

"Thank the Ultimate High. Ms. Tanaka's vocabulary is very extensive and vibrant," Mikael said, rubbing his forehead.

Adam laughed at Mikael, "I know what you mean."

Taki interrupted the men talking, "Don't be talking about my friend." She nudged Adam in his side and pulled Michi into a hug. "Girl! I missed you and you only been gone for a few hours. Where the hell you been and who is this man with you?" Taki pointed to the still passed out Niko.

Michi shook her head shyly. "Well, how about I just show you. My day has been off the hiz-anes," she said, attempting to impersonate the rapper Snoop Doggy Dog. "You know! I want to go to LA so I can meet Snoop Dogg." She paused. "Sunny, teach me how to get to LA," she said, leaving Taki and walking towards Adam.

"Ms. Tanaka, focus. Stay focused," M said. "We want to know what happened to you."

"Oh yea. It's too much to tell. Let me show you," Michi said, her eyes instantly turning gold. "Let me show you the way as the way was shown to me. Like I said before, your paths have been blessed by me."

Her eyes closed, skin turned solid gold, and raised her hands to her head with sighing. "See, Taki, didn't I have a cool day?" Michi shouted excitedly towards Taki, continuing to implant her day's activities in the heads of everyone around her.

Taki yelled, "Michi!! Michi! Stop! Stop!" as if she was fighting off some type of power. "You're out of control, girlie!" she yelled at the goddess.

Michi looked down and noticed she was slightly floating in the air with sizzling power. The people around her were all in defensive positions, as Michi had released too much power trying to incorporate her day into everyone's head.

"Oops. Sorry, I've never tried to implant memories into more than one person's head at a time. My bad, guys!" She looked around at the angel, sun god, her trainer, and her best friend. "Calm down. I'm okay. I got this under control," Michi added, slowly soothing herself to relax the others around her.

M was impressed with Michi's use of power. "Seems as if you had an eventful day," she said, remembering bits and pieces of Taki and Michi's conversation of her.

"Ms. Tanaka, that was amazing. But please, don't ever do that again," Mikael interrupted, waving his finger to show Michi the cause of her actions.

Michi's raised eyes and mouth wide open, she began to laugh as she accessed broken furniture and windows on the opposite side of the room. "Oops. I'm sorry."

The living room they were in was completely destroyed. The couches and chairs that previously occupied the area was turned to ash and the large windows that was directly behind Michi were shattered. Nothing was left besides the gods and angel with Adam holding the still passed out Niko.

"Well, at least we know who the players are. Who is Touma Hida? Looks like nerd boy here really doesn't know what he is," Adam said, interrupting the awkward silence.

X started, "Yo! Michi, how many times do we have to tell you—" He stopped in his tracks as he stared around at the scene of destruction and then the nervous Michi standing next to Mikael.

Dillon followed X through the loosely hinged door. "Well, looks like we missed some exciting activities. Explain, Ms. Tanaka."

"Godfather! I missed you." Michi, eyes still gold, rushed towards Dillon. "Where have you been! The EGU came for me again." She continued her explanation to Dillon in a mix of Japanese and English with her arms wrapped around his waist.

Dillon held the small goddess, remembering his worry for her while holding her chin. "It's okay. It's okay. They won't get you. You're safe now. I am glad you found your way back. Are you okay? Did they hurt you?" He stared into her gold eyes.

"I'm okay! I just showed everyone what my day was like and got a little carried away with my power. I was really excited. I would show you and Xeno here, but I don't think I can right now," Michi responded to the angel in front of her.

Everyone's facial expression froze in shock at the exchange happening in front of them. The angels were flabbergasted at the Dillon's fatherlike actions and tenderness towards Michi. Adam and Taki were surprised that Dillon was being nice to anyone. M, however, stood with a stoic expression to not reveal her true feelings.

X cleared his throat. "Anyone want to give us the short version? I see this is a lot to explain." He stood scratching his curly afro.

"Michi was kidnapped, found out the dude she liked at the dojo is her anchor and is related to a family that is connected to the EGU that killed her parents and is chasing her. She found me and now we're all here trying to figure out the next move," Adam answered.

Taki nudged Adam at his lack of other details. "There is a lot more going on here, A."

"Hey, I gave the cliff notes version. That's all he needs right now. I don't know about ya'll, but I feel a very powerful presence about to pop up on us right about now!" Adam's eyes flared into dancing flames while his fist was a blazed and raised into a fighting stance.

****

Benzi burst in running towards Michi, shouting, "Princess! I am so glad I found you! O-M-G! Are you okay? What did those vile EGU agents do to you? Where's Taki? Is she okay?" She continued a barrage of questions as she hugged Michi.

"Young lady! Where have you been?" Bisha immediately followed in questioning Michi as well.

Michi, excited about her Shinigami finding her jumped up and shouted, "Benzi!!! Bisha!!!! I thought you were dead with Papa!! Mama is gone and so is little brother. I really thought you all were gone. I saw Ebisu die too. I saw all them die, Benzi!" The air around her began to crackle while she laid in Benzi's arms.

"I know, princess, I know," Benzi soothed as she held Michi tight, rubbing her hair.

Bisha checked their surroundings and recognized Taki and Melchorde. "Hello, Ms. Brown and Ms. Mashiro. Thank you for protecting Michi."

"You know that is my purpose. Tell me, how did you find her?" Melchorde replied. "I know you all have a link to each other. During Ms. Tanaka's time here, her powers have been very erratic and unreliable."

Bisha, not liking the way Melchorde spoke of Michi, said, "She is a child that witnessed her entire clan slain. OF COURSE, her power is inconsistent right now. We always told you all Michi's powers work off her emotions. If she can't control her emotions, she can't control her power. She is a human with the power of all of the Shichifukujin. This has never happened before."

"Are you insinuating that Ms. Tanaka cannot handle the power of the Shichifukujin? Sounds as if your take on this is on par with Daikoku. Don't think I am not abreast to the activities that were going on. Senior Tanaka made sure to keep me in the know about the issues that were coming up." She placed her hand on her hip and leaned to the side, "He let me know that he wasn't happy with the way things with Daikoku were being handled."

Bisha, immediately understanding M's implication, responded, "Are you trying to say that we agree with what Daikoku is trying to do? We would never harm Michi. As her Shinigami, it is our job to protect her. Guide her to understand the extent of her power and her purpose. We all have a job, Melchorde. We do it."

Benzi interjected, "Don't say we! The queen is talking to you." She pointed at Bisha, "I told you, she's my Michi-ban!" The pale Shinigami with a long dark bone straight high ponytail and dressed in a silver all sequin jumpsuit with silver stiletto pumps that still made her shorter than everyone in the room besides Michi said.

Bisha moved towered over the former demon queen. She stood almost as tall as Taki but not quite. Bisha dressed her in traditional fighting gear that consisted of black ninja like jumpsuit covered by a short gold and black kimono. She kept her jet-black curly hair in a tight high bun. Her gold kimono sparkled against her skin as she spoke, "What is *your* job exactly?"

The angels, sun god, the goddess and Taki stood off to the side as they witnessed the intense exchange between the Shinigami and the former Queen of the Golden River Realm as the two went back and forth in English and Japanese.

X interrupted, "Bisha, as in, the Bishamonten. Yo! You are one of the best sword fighters in all of Otherside. I always wanted to meet you. I'm X" He reached out to shake her hand.

Bisha, ignoring X, continued, "We do not have time for formalities or petty conversation. For one, I do not agree with Daikoku. If the Ultimate High rebirthed my leader into the body of an extremely hyper human, I will do my best to continue my service as I always did. "Now," she continued, "we ran into the EGU and Daikoku at a house not too far from here. It seems we just missed Michi from that area."

She was interrupted by the now woke Niko. "Sounds like you were at my house. Who is Daikoku?" he questioned.

"Niko!! Finally! You should be all caught up, as I made sure you were able to hear and feel everything that was going on." She sucked her teeth with irritation "This would have been annoying trying to explain." Michi rolled her eyes.

Standing next to Adam, Niko rubbed his head. "I know. I have a massive migraine trying to process it all. Can we have a discussion later on about how I do not like your way of communication?" Niko retorted. "It makes my head hurt. Oh yea. What's this thing about how I'm your anchor?"

"Yes, I noticed you said that, boy," Benzi spoke at Niko and then turned to Adam. "How did you assess that this half-demon is in fact her anchor?" she questioned him.

Mikael stepped out from behind M. "Benzaiten, it's been a long time."

"I thought that was you back there. I recognize that handsome Dillon from anywhere." Benzi gleamed while clapping her hands. "It's been at least a thousand years. Still playing human savior I see. How are you involved in all of this?" she asked, surprised that Dillon and Mikael were involved, as they were high level angels.

"Sun—I mean, Adam here," Mikael pointed towards Adam, "is my godson. I helped raise him and he happens to be Ms. Mashiro's boyfriend."

Benzi clapped with joy as she walked towards Taki. "Taki! My girl! How I have missed you!" She grabbed Taki's hand and immediately started speaking in Japanese, attempting to catch up.

"Benzi! Stay focused! We now need to figure out what we are going to do next," Bisha sternly spoke towards Benzi.

M was not surprised, as she remembered the lack of concentration from both Benzi and Michi. "Look. What information have either of you gathered before you got here? Michi has been here with us for the last three months."

"Melchorde, please don't start this again. We are all trying to work together here." Taki was interrupted by a loud thud that broke through the window, revealing a large swarm of bug-like creatures that started to form a cloud around Michi.

An abrupt scream leapt from Michi's throat, as she was petrified of bugs. Niko instantly shot across the room to grab hold of Michi while the others attempted to rid the area of the bug-like creatures. "I got you!" Niko said, holding her so she couldn't see or feel the bugs.

"Adam, take Taki to safety. I believe the EGU—" Mikael said just as EGU soldiers started to pile in from the broken window.

Adam grabbed the first two by their throats as they attempted to run past him to grab at Michi and Niko, and using his fire, he set the two demon soldiers on fire and watched the two instantly turn to ash. He then set his sights on the soldiers coming through the window.

Mikael, Dillon and X covered each other's backs continuing to decimate the soldiers that made it past Adam. Mikael said, "I am happy I told the workers and the other angels to leave. Can I suggest we start buying houses in Long Island? Living in the city is starting to become troublesome."

"I know. Anybody have a barrier up?" Dillon replied, using his foot to break the leg of the soldier in front of him then using his left hand to knock the soldier away. "I actually liked this suit. Someone is going to pray to their deity that they do not meet me!" he added, looking down at the red colored goo from the dead bugs that were left behind on his suit.

Benzi and Bisha were fighting the soldiers near them, and Bisha yelled, "Benzi, protect Michi!"

"I don't need protection! Get these bugs away from me!" Michi yelped as she tucked her head under Niko.

Niko attempted to protect Michi from the bugs. "I got you. Don't move," he said, holding Michi as his body started to feel warm again.

"Move, move! I feel really hot. I don't want to hurt you," Michi said, pushing Niko back. Feeling herself begin to sweat and her temperature rise, she warned, "Don't touch me! I might hurt you," as her skin and eyes began to turn solid gold. Her voice became trance-like as she raised up out of Niko's grasp. "How dare you! You all will know the power of the Shikifukujin!" she shouted, releasing a power that rocked the building.

"Michiko! Michiko!" M began to yell. "Stop! Don't do it!" she begged, remembering the story of the aftermath of Michi's last outburst at the compound.

Niko glanced over and saw M's expression and grabbed Michi's hand, feeling the heat continue to rise and then immediately sensing something within himself grow. The power of protection, strength, and a sense of animalistic instincts grew within his body. Niko shouted to the sky, feeling the change in his back and muscles, the red film over his eyes, the instant sensation of warmth and ethereal power.

What is this feeling? Niko asked himself as an EGU soldier reached out to grab Michi. "DO NOT TOUCH HER!" he roared, snatching the arm off of the soldier, and began to devour the rest of the soldiers that continued to pour into the already ruined area.

Michi watched as Niko's body got bulkier, his movements became faster, and it looked as if horns were protruding his head. She couldn't tell with how fast he was moving as she attempted to access her surroundings.

Watching M fight a gang of EGU soldiers, the angels were fighting their own group of soldiers while Adam and Taki held their own against this army that kept pouring through the broken window. Feeling that familiar sensation again, Michi stood up and watched as two modelesque individuals began to walk towards her.

Michi's golden eyes showed her a male being with an aura that showed a diverse mix of colors and a female figure that aura shined bright gold surrounded by green.

DAIKOKU, HAVE WE MET?

"So, you all are here, which makes this even better. I told you, Bisha, you should have joined me earlier today. Now you will join Fukurokuji, Ebisu and the rest of us that were too weak to survive!" Daikoku yelled out at the volley of fights in front of her. "Come Zerrick, let's decimate the rest of these weaklings so I can gain the power of the Shichifukujin and begin our plans for Otherside."

Unbothered by the chaos that was going on around him, Lieutenant Zerrick responded, "Are you sure this time? I am tired of searching universally for this power that you continue to seek. I just want the Golden River Realm's former queen. She will be my prize! That will start my takeover of Otherside."

This lieutenant stood about six feet, five inches tall, was extremely bulky with slightly tanned olive skin. His hair was dark brown and spiked. He watched his environment with his brightly colored red eyes. Early on in his training, he was teased for being too pretty to be a warrior. Resembling the likes of human celebrities, Zerrick fit in perfectly on Earth. As Daikoku would constantly remind him, she was his only equal, as she was more than beautiful. Daikoku herself was pure beauty, she stood about five feet, eight inches tall with jet black hair tied back in a high bone-straight ponytail that reached the bottom of her waist. Her skin was a tanned golden color, similar to Michi's when she was at full power. She was dressed in a black jumpsuit with a short gold kimono with red and black dragons all across it. Daikoku glared at Michi with hatred.

Her walk, aura, looks, and voice all screamed seduction and power. Daikoku was the Shinigami that had the power of the Shichifukujin that controlled power over business, trade and wealth. She had a knack for controlling operations, soldiers and accumulating wealth.

"You are not the true Shichifukujin, I am!" Daikoku immediately swung to attack Michi, who was hunched over from the bugs surrounding her and Niko fighting EGU soldiers in front of her.

Michi instantly felt the attack coming from Daikoku, ducking down and landing a swift kick to Daikoku's leg to push her back. "Why do I feel like I know you?" she said towards her opponent. Skin and eyes still gold, Michi began to have visions of the person in front of her. Images of actions with this person along with basic info.

"Daikoku is your name. You are my Shinigami. You do not attack your master!" she yelled, standing up and releasing some of her power in an attempt to make Daikoku submit. Michi slowly began to walk towards Daikoku as the air around her sizzled. "You are MY SHINIGAMI! I AM YOUR MASTER! HOW DARE YOU?!" she bellowed, pointing her index finger towards Daikoku, ignoring the few remaining bugs

"What is this?!" Daikoku sensed the need to stand down and bow to Michi. She began fighting her body's commands. "You are not my MASTER! YOU ARE TOO WEAK, HUMAN!" she yelled back while continuing to fight her body, which suddenly released, causing Daikoku to slightly fall onto Zerrick.

"Continue attacking the little one!" Daikoku shouted out.

Lieutenant Zerrick yelled towards his soldiers and bugs. "No problem. I noticed too. She is petrified of the smaller creatures. I hate these things, but it's so much easier to get to humans this way," he responded, looking down at the still weak Daikoku.

"You will not touch her!" Niko turned to see the fight behind him getting more intense. Michi stood in front of two people he didn't recognize as she attempted to fight the bugs that surrounded her. "I got you!" Niko spun around and yelled a wretched shriek, causing the rest of the bugs to explode. "I will kill you all!" He launched himself at Zerrick.

Michi immediately followed, attacking Daikoku with her left fist. "I am your master! YOU WILL LEARN YOUR PLACE!" she screamed, landing her first punch on the Shinigami. She followed through with a bombardment of hits that landed on Daikoku, causing some damage.

"Michi! Stop!" Bisha yelled out. She stopped her fight with an incoming EGU agent and ran to stop Michi.

Niko immediately sensed Bisha's intent to grab Michi. "DO NOT TOUCH HER!" He grabbed Bisha's reached out arm, preventing her from getting to Michi. He began to violently attack her with his right hand with a hail of punches that landed on her arms as she attempted to block them. The force of his open palms allowed his claws to leave bloody marks on the back of Bisha's forearms as she continued to prevent his blows.

Zerrick had already begun to try to fight with M, as he felt the half-breed was beneath him. Misleading Niko while he moved to attack his target, Zerrick attempted to try to attack M as Mikael and

Dillon immediately disrupted their fights with the EGU soldiers to attack the lieutenant. M watched as the angels protected her from the EGU leader.

Michi still continued her attack on Daikoku, while Daikoku attempted to block as many hits as she could. "You will know your place! This is not how you conduct yourself as my Shinigami!"

Niko knocked into Daikoku while he continued his attack on Bisha. Bisha, not understanding how this human-demon half breed could be getting the best of her, tapped into her powers and turned the attack in her favor, landing powerful punches on Niko's rib cage and dodging his hits.

"STOP IT, BISHA!" Michi shrieked as she noticed the fight between a transformed Niko and Bisha. "Stop you two!" she shouted, blasting Daikoku and Zerrick with a gold-colored light and crumbling them both to the floor.

Michi grabbed Niko from behind, feeling the intense power he radiated. "Calm down. Calm down. I'm okay." She used her power to try to calm him. "I'm here. Don't worry." Michi rubbed the scaly skin and claws of the now fully transformed Niko.

"GRRRRRR!" Niko responded and stopped in his tracks, feeling the heated sensation on this back. *What am I, why do I feel this way? Why does SHE make me feel this way?* Niko's thoughts ran through his head. When he noticed his now clawed hands, he stared down, suddenly realizing his transformation. Immediately, he was shocked by a sudden pain in his stomach. "Why?" He looked up at a dazed Daikoku with her topaz-colored eyes piercing through his soul, her knife thrusted straight through his gut.

Michi could feel the cold metal run through Niko as she felt his pain through her touch. She let out a loud screech that caused the room to shake, windows shattered and the building walls to started to crack.

Adam snatched Taki and Mikael, disappearing from the soon-to-be annihilated area. M had grabbed Dillon and X, leaving Michi and Niko with Zerrick and Daikoku and the two other Shinigami fighting the EGU soldiers that continued the attack on the building.

"HOW DARE YOU!" Michi growled as she stood over the bleeding Niko. "YOU ARE MY SHINIGAMI AND YOU WILL NO LONGER DISRESPECT THIS CLAN!" She continued her tirade towards Daikoku as Michi's power continued to grow, glaring at her enemy as her skin tightened and glistened in solid gold. Eyes of pure gold burned while her hair whipped past her as if wind was blowing around her.

Daikoku, immediately feeling the surge of Michi's power, wanted to submit. Defying her body's needs and fighting off the effects of Michi's previous energy blast, she stood up much taller than the Goddess of Luck. "I will be the Shichifukujin! I will take what is mine!" She leapt to attack Michi.

"You really think you can take my power!" Michi shrieked, causing the building to shake and tearing away at what was left of the apartment. Michi reached her hand out towards Daikoku and began a chant in Japanese.

Daikoku suddenly stopped in her tracks, unable to move as she scowled at the god in front of her. She understood the chant and that this could be her own demise. How could this child god know the chant to take the power of her Shinigami?

"Michi! NO! YOU DON'T KNOW WHAT YOU'RE DOING!" Benzi shouted from behind Michi. Grabbing Michi's arm, she pleaded, "Stop! Please! Princess!"

Michi responded in a trance-like tone, "YOU ALL WILL LEARN I AM YOUR LEADER NOW! Fukurokuji will not allow you to continue to defy me! Ebisu has also agreed that I am the new leader! Hotei and Jurojin also said it's me! Daikoku, Hotei told me what you did!" Her screaming got louder as the building rocked and the others around them were trying to escape the devastating power Michi was exuberating.

The EGU soldiers continued to scatter while a few of them grabbed the passed-out lieutenant to leave the area. Benzi and Bisha were behind Michi as she continued her chant.

"Michiko! Please. Don't do this! I don't want this for you! You will kill her! Ebisu wouldn't want you to do this!" Benzi shouted.

Bisha looked down at the passed-out Niko and noticed his wounds were healing. "Mich, Michi! Look! Look! He is okay. You healed him. You healed him! Stop this now!"

Just as it seemed as if Michi would destroy the building, two soldiers came and snatched Daikoku away and escaped as the power surrounding Michi began to fade.

"YOU LET HER GO! WHY, BISHA?!" Michi screamed at the two Shinigami as Niko still lay passed out. "She killed them, she killed them all! You don't get it! Mama, Papa, my little brother! All because of her, and you stopped me!" Her yell turned to a screech as the building continued to crumble beneath them. Michi glowed as her power continued to peak. "YOU WILL PAY! You all will pay" she growled as her eyes pierced through Bisha. She bent over to touch Niko and disappeared in a flash, leaving the half-crumbled building with Benzi and Bisha standing within it, lost at the recent events.

GONE AGAIN

Taki continued her piercing yell as Adam continued to drag her away from the crumbling building. "Let me go! I can't leave her! A! Let me go now!" she pleaded while attempting to touch his bare skin so she could siphon some of his powers. Unfortunately, he knew immediately what she would think to do and held her from behind.

"Come on, baby girl. You know Michi is fine. Calm down. Please," Adam whispered in her ear in an attempt to calm her down. "I can feel her, she is—" He stopped mid-sentence.

Taki heard a loud boom come from the building behind them. Immediately snatching herself free from Adam since he was too distracted, she rushed towards the building, but Dillon and M stopped her in her tracks.

"We just came from there. She is gone," Dillon said with a sad sigh.

M stared away from the group ignoring Dillon as she observed humans beginning to crowd the area. Dillon glared towards M's direction.

M interrupted the awkward silence, "She has disappeared again. I felt a spike in her power a couple minutes ago, and then it was gone. No one is left in the building. We made sure to evacuate the humans and it looks like we are going to have to make something up. This is going to bring a lot of human attention."

"I don't give a damn about any of that! Where is Michi?!" Taki yelled out again, unsure of why she had an uneasy feeling about Michi, Niko and whoever those other people were.

Taki jerked back, "Oh shit!" Startled by the two Shinigami appearing right next to her.

"Come, we must find Michi!" Benzi grabbed Taki's arm and turned around to leave but was unable to do so.

"Where do you think you're going?" Adam's eyes shined with flames as he raised his energy level to overpower Benzi's and her attempt at departing to find Michi.

Benzi cocked her head to the side, confused. "He stops me from leaving?" She realized he was able to disrupt her energy transfer and trapped Benzi with the group.

"Yes, he is the Sun God and she is his anchor. One thing he is good for is making sure my charge here is safe," M spoke towards

Benzi. Attempting to get the bug debris out of her long ponytail, she continued to speak, "Adam, can you sense Michi at all?"

Adam's chocolate brown eyes turned to dancing red flames as he stood stoic. "No. She's gone. No. That little twerp is blocking me. She never knew how to do that!"

"We are not dealing with the Michiko we know anymore. She's obviously awakened her full powers. We have to find her," M said remembering the anger she felt right before the building began to crumble.

Bisha was pacing back and forth as she kept repeating to herself, "I had to stop her. I had to. I couldn't let her do that," shaking her head as she paced.

"You had to stop her from what?" M said with a raised brow.

Benzi skipped in between the circle of the group, "Queen Melchorde, please. You have to understand, we had to stop her. She knew how to take her Shinigami's power."

"And, how would that have been a problem if Michiko took Daikoku's power?" M glared at Benzi.

Bisha stood up for herself, "Look. Michi taking Koku's power would have killed her. She's not ready for something like that. Michi can't handle killing another person. We don't know what that would have done to her or her power."

"What we do know is you stopped her from eliminating whatever threat Daikoku is to her and this realm," M sneered.

Bisha stomped towards M scowling as Benzi held her back. "I do not regret not letting Michi kill Daikoku. She is not ready! That is for us to handle! You will not make me feel guilty for not allowing this child god to kill her Shinigami! We already don't know the extent of Michi's power. We have never had all of the Shichifukujin powers in one entity before!"

"You can continue your walk over here and see why I am still called the Queen of Hell." M glared at Bisha. "Benzaiten, you will still perform your duty as the Goddess of Luck's Shinigami and protect and serve her. You better get your counterpart on board or there will be serious consequences. My only concern is Michiko Tanaka is safe and back with her friend."

Taki stared in shock at the intense conversation between M and the Shinigami. "I don't know what the hell y'all are talking about right now, but where is Michi!" her voice cracked.

"Look. This is a serious discussion, but humans are starting to gather. I don't think this is a good idea for us to cause more of a scene." Adam nodded toward the crowds of people staring at them and the demolished building. "I know the police are not far—" He was cut off just as someone walked up to them.

A low voice said, "You guys are always causing trouble. You wonder why the demons run this town." Then, it started singing the hit song "Run this Town" by Rihanna.

"Chain Face!" Adam exclaimed. "What's up with you? Where you been?", He went to shake his hand.

"Aht aht, no grabbing. We are BFFs and all, but no touching, Sunny!!" Chain Face jumped back. He looked directly at Dillon. "Look, I will take care of this. You all have a serious problem. FIND HER! She will ruin EVERYTHING!" he shouted. "Go! Now, the boys in blue are almost here and you all look suspicious." He shooed them away from the area.

Taki grabbed Adam's hand and stared at him. "You will help me find her, A! Ya'll will not do this without me!"

"I got you, baby girl. Let's get out of here first. M, where we going? I am taking them with us," Adam said.

Bisha responded, "Taking us where? We are not your prisoners!"

"Technically, you are my prisoner. You will not leave my sight until we find Michi and she decides what to do with you and Daikoku. Benzi," M continued sarcastically, "do you disagree with my stance on this situation?"

Benzi did not want to side with M but understood her predicament. "No, Your Highness, our services are yours to use as you see fit until we find our master." She put her head down.

"Thank you, your services will be appreciated." Turning towards the group, M continued, "We will convene at the Castle of Angels. We will need all the help we can get. The EGU will be recouping and prepping for their next attack. So, let's prepare," she then immediately disappeared with Dillon and Mikael.

Bisha said to Benzi, "You are really going to trust her? Come on, I wasn't wrong."

"I know what you were trying to do, but we know Koku; she is going to kill Michi. I wonder if maybe you should have let Michi end it all." Benzi squinted her eyes and shifted to her left side while stroking her long ponytail. "Come, we must obey for now. We need them to find Michi." She shrugged her shoulders.

Adam looked over at the other ladies and grabbed Taki to follow M's energy signature to wherever they were headed.

MICHIKO THE GODDESS OF LUCK

"WHO THE HECKLES DO THEY THINK THEY ARE? I HAD HER! I HAD HER!" Michi screamed aggressively, pacing back and forth. "AHHHHHHHHHHHHHHHHHHHHHHH!" she screeched at the memory of Bisha stopping her.

Looking around at the debris surrounding her, she fell to her knees with tears in her eyes. Michi felt her skin tighten; her eyes hurt until all she could see were colors with sparkles of gold. Looking down at herself, she saw the hard gold texture of what used to be her skin. Speaking in Japanese, she exclaimed, "Wow, I really am solid gold. I like this," while staring down at her skin.

Snapping out of her inner thoughts, she shook her head. "I will destroy them all! Bisha will learn her place!" and used her power to stalk her prey. "There you go!" She teleported herself a few feet away and, with light steps, slowly crept through the passageway. Michi rapidly used a small blade to stab her opponent from behind, causing him to fall. Catching him on his way down to cause no noise, she said to herself, "Good, last one."

She opened a door, ignoring a yell from the other side of the room. "Who are you!?" the voice yelled towards Michi.

"I am the Goddess of Luck. I can be your lucky charm or a wicked curse. You better tell me about Lieutenant Zerrick and his little bitch Daikoku, and also the Hida Clan. I already know you work for them, so don't even start with the 'I don't know them.'" She suddenly appeared next to her target and stabbed his left hand with her small hidden blade as she grabbed his hair.

With his head pulled back, he gasped out, "Who are you!? I can't tell you anything and you know this! I am a mere human. You killed all my special guards—where are my human guards!?" He yelped with pain and watched the blood drip from his hand.

"It's disgusting how you are involving humans in Otherside's affairs. They are safe. But like I said. I want to know where I can find them, and how do I find the EGU Headquarters?" Michi released the man and skipped away from the desk to sit in front of the victim.

The man feared for his life as witnessed a young girl made out of solid gold and exuded a feeling that made the hairs all over his body stand. He watched the stranger sitting in front of him and stammered,

"I really don't have any idea what you mean by headquarters. I am a human. I've never even been to Otherside."

"Thank you for that information." His statement confirmed EGU Headquarters was in Otherside and not Hell. "Also, what are they doing here? A lieutenant and his flooky shouldn't be able to come to Earth Realm without some high-level influence. And who are these human half-breeds, the Hida Clan?" She got up from the chair and began to prance around the room. "Remember, my knife is still in your hand, so please don't lie and don't become unlucky along with your bloodline for the next thousand years." She smiled as she continued prancing.

The human man was sweating profusely, frightened, and in excruciating pain. "Look, all I know is the chick, and its flunky not flooky, isn't well received by the EGU, but for some reason their lieutenant is helping her find something. He is using the Hida Clan to navigate Earth Realm. Also, she paid and did favors for some high-level demons in Otherside to get a pass to Earth Realm. She is definitely on borrowed time, but I guess if she finds what she is looking for, who can stop her?" He sighed, "Can you let me go now? I told you good information. Please. I have a wife and kid."

"You aren't worried about them when you are doing deals for demons?" Then, Michi added in Japanese, "You are lucky I am in a great mood. I will not curse your bloodline." She turned to walk away, but looked at the man once more. "I will be back to visit," she told him before disappearing in front of him.

****

Michi was back at her makeshift home for the time being. "Niko! Niko! Where are you?" she shouted while searching for him.

"Michi, where did you go this time? I woke up looking for you." Niko walked towards her from a dark area of the room.

Michi was excited that he was feeling better from the fight with Daikoku and Lieutenant Zerrick. "I went to get more information for our trip. I am close to finding a way into Otherside."

"Are you sure you want to do this? Why not call that big guy Adam and your friend? I know they can help us," Niko responded.

Michi's eyes began turning gold. "I will not involve them in this. I will defeat my Shinigami on my own!"

"Mich, come on. You know they're looking for you. Even your other Shinigami are probably worried about you." Niko rubbed the back of his neck and started to move towards her but stopped short about five feet. "It's been about two weeks now. I've surprised they haven't found us yet."

Michi ran close to him, knocking on his head, while speaking in Japanese, "Come on, silly. Of course, they can't. One, I'm blocking them from finding us, and two, why would they come to this place? It's in ruins." She put her head down in sadness.

"What's wrong?" Niko grabbed Michi's chin to lift her head to him. "Why the sad face?"

"It's in ruins because I did this. I ruined my home," she said grimly.

Niko grabbed her into a hug. "Michi, it's okay. You did what you had to do to protect yourself. You got out safely."

"No!" She immediately pushed him away. "Everyone else died. My dad, my mom and my little brother. Even Ebisu died." She stood in front of Niko, holding her head high. "I am going to do this on my own. I thought you would help since you're my anchor. But you can go back to your family if you want."

Niko walked back into her personal space. "I told you I will stay with you regardless. I just think we could use some help." Niko looked down at her. "Stop telling me I can go back to my family. We know that's not an option. But since I am helping you find your people. I figured you could help me find mine." He smiled. "I told you I still don't understand this anchor thing. I mean. I feel it. You do something to me. But I want to know more," Niko said, still looking at Michi.

Michi pranced away. "I know. I am still trying to figure out how to get to my books. I've only been able to get there myself once without Sunny. Once I learn how to get back there, we will be able to get more answers."

Niko yelled towards the prancing Michi, "What books? What are you talking about?"

"Come on, keep up. The place I told you that keeps all the books of the Gods and their roles and blah, bah, blah. I remember Ebisu's teachings used to tell me about this place. You humans…

Well, technically you're not human, you are a half-breed. So, I don't know if this statement will apply to you. But, —"

Niko interrupted her rant, "Michi, come on. Stay focused for me. I am really trying to keep up with all of this."

Niko attempted to wrap his head around the things that he had learned, including the story of the EGU agents and how they worked for the Royal Fallen Family Crests. To Niko's understanding, the Royal Fallen were the elite fallen angels that started the hierarchy of the fallen, demons, and other creatures of myth. All the things that he read in books and saw on TV were real.

"Michi, start over please. What place are you talking about?" Niko continued their conversation.

Michi stopped prancing and looked at Niko. "Oh yea, that's right. The Akashic Records. There's so much information there. I saw a few about me—O-M-G. It is so much."

"What do you mean it's so much?" Niko asked, confused.

Michi cocked her head to the side. "Don't you remember? I told you they don't have a clue how I was created. There's never been a God like me before. The Shinigami that are left behind are the ones that formed the former Shichifukujin. I am THE Shichifukujin. I have the power of them all," Michi said, smiling.

"Wow. So, you are one of a kind?" Niko said to her, feeling her power flow through him as he held her hand.

Michi giggled, "I am. Are you trying to flirt with me? I think we should start training for the day and then go get some food. I want some sushi."

"I think I want to stand right here just a little bit longer." Niko brought Michi closer to him and leaned down to kiss her.

Niko felt the power coming from Michi as it flowed into him. He stopped himself from going further as it scared him how her power made him feel. "Okay. Let's go."

"What's wrong? You okay, Niko?" she responded in Japanese. She felt him pull away as she got closer.

Niko instantly perked himself up some. "Yea. I'm ready to train. If I stay here with you, little cutie, we won't get anything done." He let her hand go and started walking towards the training area.

"Okay. I'm about to kick your arse again," Michi replied, sensing he was lying. She hoped her power didn't scare him since she confirmed he is her anchor by the way he siphoned her powers when he touched her. She skipped to walk next to him and he grabbed her hand, causing her to blush.

Niko stopped his walk and squeezed her hand. "First, it's ass. And…" He paused, then turned to her. "Look, all of this is new. Powers, gods, demons and fallen angels. Just be patient with me."

"I will, Niko Charles Black. But for now, I am your sensei and none of your anchor stuff matters. We need to properly prepare for where and what we are getting ready to do. Now let's fight!" Michi said, swinging her left leg towards Niko.

DAIKOKU

"YOU ARE NOT MY MASTER!" Daikoku leapt up from her sleep surrounded by EGU guards and servants.

Lieutenant Zerrick stepped from the shadows. "You are finally awake. I thought we would lose you. We have too much to accomplish for you to perish now. Come. We have planning to do." He walked away from the bed and out the room.

"Where are we?" Daikoku groggily replied, rubbing her head, unsure of how she ended up in bed, and attempted to get up. One of the servants came to assist. "MOVE! I don't need your help!" She held onto the bed post trying her best to stand on her own. Daikoku's body felt like an iron weight was sitting on her head and feet. She looked down at her hands dressed in only her black jumpsuit. "That bitch almost absorbed me," she whispered. "I will kill her!" she said, raising her voice.

Lieutenant Zerrick yelled from the hall, "How long do I have to wait for you to be by my side? My patience is weighing thin on what our next moves will be."

"My apologies, Lieutenant. I'm coming." She stood up with all her strength and walked towards the door. "We will defeat them. Now that I know the last two are with her, we can get rid of them all," Daikoku said, now bowing in front of the lieutenant.

"I'm glad we share the same sentiments. This chase has been rather exhausting. I am ready to make my move," The lieutenant responded, walking around her. "Now, get yourself together. We will be departing to Otherside soon. I have to report in."

Daikoku panicked, as she wasn't ready to leave Earth yet. She knew she needed at least one more Shinigami power before she returned to the kingdom she came from. "Are you sure? Is there a rush?" She turned, still bowed to Zerrick.

"No. But we will leave this place and regroup before our friends find out our real reason for being here. That debacle a couple weeks ago does not sit well with the family. It brought too much human attention." The lieutenant stopped walking. "Me doing all of the thinking is making me rethink your position. Don't go losing your edge now." He walked away, never looking back at Daikoku.

Still bowed to hide the anger that showed on her face, she slowly breathed out, "I will kill you all."

She launched herself up, still in the hallway, ignoring the pain that flowed through her body. She yelled to the servant, "Find me a nice outfit and get Jade from the Golden River Realm for me. I need to speak to her at once!"

Daikoku walked back to the bedroom and stared at herself in the mirror as she contemplated her next course of action.

****

Bisha gazed out the window still considering if she was wrong about letting Michi defeat Daikoku. "I hate this for her," she spoke out loud and turned to face Benzi.

"I do too. My little cherry pop hasn't had a mani/pedi in almost a month and we haven't been shopping in forever. This group is boring!" Benzi interrupted Bisha's quiet time as she stood and stuck her tongue out at one of the angel guards that were always watching her and Bisha.

They were holed up in a room at the Castle of Angels. For the past few weeks, Bisha, Benzi, the angels and the Sun God have been looking for Michi. "She can be anywhere on the planet or Otherside," Benzi said.

"I know. That's not what I am worried about," Bisha said, ignoring Benzi's other comments. "Koku will kill Michi for what she tried to do. This will not end well, Benzi. Now that we know it was her that led our leader and the others to their deaths," she added.

Benzi furrowed her brows and gazed out the same window. "I am really pissed about that. For her to have stooped so low to have been working with the Royal Fallen and the angels at that time. She's been betraying us for a long time. I always suspected it was her that led the angels to Fuki. Hote (Hot-tee), I didn't know she did that to him."

"What did she do to him?" Bisha turned to Benzi. "I don't know what you are talking about.

A tear fell from Benzi's left eye. "I saw it. I saw what she did to him when Michi was absorbing her."

"You saw it? Absorbed? Is that how that goes?" Bisha sighed.

Wiping the tear, Benzi responded, "Yes. Somehow, the witch Koku figured out back then that we are able to absorb each other's essence to become The Shichifukujin. We didn't know that. How did she figure that out?" She put her hand on the glass window and it immediately shattered, causing Bisha to jump back and alarming the angel guard.

"Benzi, calm down. I am just as pissed as you are. Do not cause issues with these angels. We still don't know the extent of that Sun God's power. He is extremely powerful and will be a problem if we have to fight them," Bisha said, turning to apologize to the angel guard. "Don't worry, she won't hurt you.

The angel guard stood in shock at the mess made from all the broken glass and immediately left the room, closing the door behind him.

"Bisha! I'm sorry, I can't help it. I am so angry I cannot contain myself. You wouldn't believe what I saw. Koku has done some evil and disgusting things. Michi saw all of that. It's like she was absorbing her being. I am worried that could have had a negative effect on Michi. I never knew we could do that. It's like we aren't individuals at all. We are really one." Benzi placed her hands on her head.

Bisha worried for her friend. "Look, Benzi, it's okay. We have always known our purpose. Once the others died, we lost our way, but having Michiko and the Tanaka clan has helped redefine our purpose. DO NOT lose sight of that now!"

They were interrupted by the door opening. "Come on now, we have you as guests and this is what you do? I know we need to redecorate and shit, but damn," X playfully said as he entered, followed by M.

"Well, do you care to explain? Bishamonten?" M, the petite woman, said while stepping from behind X.

Angry that she was to blame, Bisha spat, "Always looking for the bad in people, former Queen of Hell."

"I am the former Queen of the Golden River Realm. If you wish to use my title as an insult, I suggest you get it right." M smirked with a raised eyebrow.

Benzi instantly broke the cold chill in the room. "Your Highness, my apologies. I am the one that did this. My emotions got the best of me. Please let me know what I can do to help fix it."

"It's okay. We've been meaning to upgrade this place. To be honest, we are about to leave anyway. M thinks we need to make a move soon. M, explain the plan. I will get the others together and let them know our plan and get prepared," X added and walked out.

"Aww, white eyes is so damn handsome." Benzi clapped her hands. "Your Highness, how are you around all of these fine ass men? It would be hard for me to concentrate."

Sarcastically, Bisha interrupted Benzi, "You never concentrate anyway." She turned towards M. "Former Queen of Golden River Realm, what did he mean we are leaving? What is going on?"

"Ms. Brown to you is fine," M responded and turned to Benzi. "These feathered bird brains are perverts, so do not think I would ever look at them in that manner. We—" M scowled.

Benzi immediately interjected, "Weren't you and the other one—"

"SHUT YOUR MOUTH!" M bellowed. She smoothed out the mauve colored pant suit she had on. "We will depart in the next hour. We have information that Michiko and a half demon have been raiding EGU hideouts around the globe. Unfortunately, we do not know where they are, but we have intel on where they are going next. So be ready to go, as we will not be returning to this place for a while." After finishing her sentence, she left the room.

Benzi, still shocked at M's reaction to her, said, "Well, I can tell somebody hasn't had their back blown out in a long time." She held her hand on her chest, acting appalled.

"I can see exactly where Michi gets her ditziness from." Bisha shook her head. "DO you ever take anything serious? Did you hear what she said! That means Michi is looking for Koku! Koku will kill her if Michi finds her!", Bisha anxiously added.

Benzi shook her head innocently as she held her chest with sincerity, "First of all, I am paying attention. That's how I know M hasn't had any dick in a really long time. And I know the situation we are in. Honestly, I knew Michi would be looking for Koku. I am not surprised. Bisha, we are dealing with all of our powers. She is angry. We have to find her."

OTHERSIDE, WE GO

"Michi, baby. Don't you think that's a bit much? He won't tell us anything if you make it to where he can't talk. Come on. Let him speak." Niko pleaded with Michi as the couple has been raiding EGU hideouts together for about two weeks now. Their trust and bond together have grown rapidly as they navigate their anchor relationship and traveling in Otherside.

Michi was still angry at the large demon and his teasing of her being a pipsqueak before she punched him and he fell to the floor. "He will not make light of my size. As he can see, I am more powerful than him." She looked down at the demon. "Don't like getting beat by a girl?" she uttered, hovering over the demon.

"You will pay! I promise you will not last here," the demon responded in ragged breaths.

Michi was not intimidated by his remarks. "Yea, yea big guy. You're like the tenth being that has told me that since we got here. Guess what? I'm still here. As you can tell, I am not human, demon!" she shouted as her skin and eyes turned solid gold.

"Babe, stop toying with the demon and let's ask some questions. We need to leave. I feel more of them coming," Niko interrupted her conversation. "Now, tell us where the EGU headquarters are!" He kicked the demon in the face.

Michi had learned in the past few weeks that her powers were still growing. She had attempted to reach the Askashic records more times than she could count but to no avail. So far, she had figured out a few of her powers, and one of them was reading an individual's intentions and thoughts if their mind wasn't strong. She knew this demon was buying time. "See, you are not as smart as you think. I am not some mere human causing trouble. I am the Shichifukujin and I will destroy this EGU thingy ya'll got going on here!" she declared as her eyes burned bright gold and her hair whipped around her face with the energy around her continuing to rise.

"Baby, come on. Come on. I always tell you: don't get that pissed! We don't want anyone to know who you are. We still don't know where we are and how this place works," Niko interjected, grabbing her hand. He felt the energy flow into his body as his protection for her grew. "Come." He grabbed Michi's other hand, facing her towards him. "Calm yourself. You got this." He leaned down and whispered in her ear. "I promise when we get back to our spot, I will make you some good food and do some spicy things to get you in the mood," he teased while his foot was pressed against the fallen demon's throat.

Michi's eyes turned back to their regular brown color. "Ohh, you are really trying to distract me now. I wasn't going to kill it. I was just scaring it a little bit."

The demon choked out as Niko pressed his foot harder, "You both will perish. The lieutenant that you are after is one of the most brutal and hateful ones of our kind. I promise your disrespect will not be taken lightly." Then pushed Niko's foot off of his throat as the demon jumped up and leapt towards the couple.

Michi lifted her middle finger and then using her powers she caused the demon to turn to ash.

"Michi, did we not speak about that before we got here? No turning the last one into ash. We needed him to navigate Otherside. We don't know anything about here." Niko patiently reached down and kissed Michi on her forehead. He smiled at her.

Michi placed her head on his chest, feeling Niko's calmness and appreciated his accepting attitude when she messed up. Her voice grew with excitement, "You know, it feels as if I am connected to you when we share moments like this. I'm surprised you haven't run off yet." She paused. "I know you are not comfortable with all of this."

"Yea, but I am comfortable with you, so don't worry. I need you to calm down so you won't get us into some shit we can't handle. We're in Otherside now. Rules may be different. Regardless, I got you. Now, come on. Let's get back to the spot," he assured her.

Michi and Niko had been able to infiltrate Otherside and immediately started attacking EGU strongholds. Michi had learned a lot about the power she wields. Being able to find the EGU strongholds with the information she collected the past few weeks from humans she had interrogated throughout Otherside. She had mastered her way of not traveling as a human. Those secret lessons with Adam proved to be helpful.

Regardless of being raised by her Shinigami, experiencing the power was different. Her first attempt at getting them both to Otherside was an experience, as she learned she can crossover anytime like how she witnessed with Adam and M. Her issue was figuring out how to get Niko over. They discovered that he was able to crossover to Otherside with her when he was in his full demon state. That's what the couple called it since he didn't take on full demon appearance and powers. Based on this discovery, as long as he had a bit of Michi's power flowing through him, he didn't have to always be in the full demon state while they were in Otherside.

"Come on, Mich. The others are here," Niko pleaded with her as he felt a swarm EGU soldiers approaching.

Michi continued to search for survivors from her latest attack. "I mean come on. *Somebody* is still awake. I feel and hear them." She paused and quickly turned around. "There you are! Found you," she exclaimed as she located a smaller demon hiding under a table near the corner.

"No, no! Please don't hurt me. I am not EGU. I was here on business," the small, horned demon pleaded with Michi. "Please. I won't tell anybody and I will go about my business." He attempted to walk away.

Now in his full demon state, Niko stood right behind the demon. "Mich, let's go. They are here," he said as an EGU soldier rushed through a collapsing door to attack Niko. Niko dodged the attack, knocking the soldier out.

"Okay. Little guy, answer a couple of questions," Michi said, grabbing the demon by his collar. Michi produced an energy barrier around the area they stood in so no more EGU units could attack them. "We're good now. Talk." She pulled a chair from the debris for the demon to sit down.

The smaller demon watched as the EGU soldiers continuously banged on the invisible barrier with infinite attempts to break it. The soldiers looked like mimes attempting to entertain the masses. "Look, little girl. You're not that much bigger than me. Let me go. I don't want nothing to do with you humans and half breeds."

"As you can see, tiny horned dude, I am not human. Don't be prejudice against half breeds. It's not his fault. Shit, he didn't even know until like a month ago he was half demon. And we don't even know what kind. I mean, his horns look similar to yours but—"

Niko interrupted her rant, "Baby, come on, stay focused. I don't think it's a good idea to taunt them. Look. They're coming at us full force and I think more are coming." He watched the growing mass of soldiers banging on the invisible barrier.

"Okay. Okay. My boyfriend here. Oops. I just said boyfriend." She paused and looked over at Niko. "I'm sorry. I don't think I should be calling you that. Is it okay if I call you that?" She frowned then smiled at him.

Niko sighed and smirked. "Michi, baby, we have to go. You can call me whatever you want right now. We will discuss our relationship status when we are not surrounded by demon soldiers trying to kill us."

The little horned demon stared at the strange being in front of him, "I want no parts of you two. This girl is a dingbat and you just let her be. Get me the hellfire away from you two!" he said, attempting to get up from the chair that Michi had placed him in.

"Come, you will be our guide," Michi said, grabbing his shoulder and Niko's hand. "Back to our hideout." She disappeared, and the surrounding soldiers descended on the now empty space.

****

The demon immediately began choking as they all arrived back to the underground level of the former Tanaka Clan's headquarters. Michi, unsure of why he was choking, crossed them back over to Otherside. "You've never been to Earth before?" she asked, confused by why he was choking as if he couldn't breathe.

"No, dumbass! I am a demon! I do not belong on Earth Realm. I'm lucky I am able to work peacefully in Otherside!" he panted. "FYI, I don't breathe! My energy is not accustomed to Earth Realm, so my body is unable to stay there."

Niko stood in front of the demon. "Watch your tone talking to her!" he snatched the demon by the throat. "Don't end up like your friends in Otherside."

"Be nice, Niko. He's scared. He's a demon, so they probably lack manners," Michi interrupted, placing her hand on the demon's shoulder. "He's going to play nice since he knows that he can't escape." Then, she sent them back to Earth while she created an invisible energy barrier around the demon's body. "Now you should be good to be here. Don't worry. After you answer my questions, we're packing up and leaving this joint. I have an idea of where we should go next."

The demon eyes widened at his ability to be outside of Otherside or Hell. stared down at himself and then looked around. "Broad, what the hell did you to me? I feel a tingling sensation throughout my body. Feels like a light cloth is wrapped around me." He began to run his hands over himself.

"It sort of is. I wrapped an energy barrier around you so you can be here. Now, first, I'm Michi and this is Niko," Michi replied, pointing to Niko. She continued, "So stop with the name calling, shrimp!" She whipped her hair back. "I am a god and I am going to destroy the EGU. Tell me all that you know about them."

The demon shivered at the energy that poured off her but still didn't believe her. "Um. Well. I would believe ya, toots, if gods weren't all but destroyed." He chuckled nervously. "By their own kind too. Not too many can still talk about the Days of Hunts. Happened secretly during the last Angel/Fallen War."

"Yea, yea. I've been trained on that damn story since I could talk. I really am the Shichifukujin. For some reason, I was reborn into this realm with the embodiment of all seven Shinigami of the Shichifukujin, and the EGU attacked and murdered my family. Now I want them all dead!" Michi said to the demon.

The demon jumped up and walked up to Michi to stand in front of her. "The embodiment of all seven?" He stared into her eyes. "Shit. I see why you're batshit crazy. All seven of those idiots would make me crazy too!" the demon added, stepping back. "My name is Putzin by the way. Damn girl. I can tell you ain't lying. There is no way you filleted that whole stronghold by yourself on top of being able to have little poor me in Earth Realm unless you are one of them. Like I told you. I'm lucky to be out of Hell."

"Well then tell us what you were doing at the EGU stronghold?" Niko grabbed Michi to sit at their makeshift table they had created. They formed a small living area within the debris of her former home. Unfortunately, the Tanaka Clan did not make an underground safehouse.

The demon still stared at Michi. "You are one weirdo." He hopped on the chair next to Niko. "Duh, sell information. That's how I got my pass to be here. I mean, I've been here so long that I don't get bothered. Otherside is way better than the H-E-double hockey sticks."

Michi laughed, "Hey Putzin! How do you know that joke? You said you've never been to Earth before."

"Look, dingbat! Just because I can't go to Earth Realm doesn't mean I am not in the know! We got those electronics ya'll got and watch the stupid shit on those idiot boxes too." Putzin stood up to look around. "I'm hungry." He twisted his head side to side.

Michi eyes turned gold. "You little munchkin. Sit! Answer some more questions and I might let you get a snack. Unless you want me to start being your unlucky charm." Michi grinned, her bright gold eyes twinkling mischievously.

Startled by Michi's reaction, Putzin started talking. "Well to let you know how Otherside works, it's a parallel realm to Earth, so technically if you have the right power, it's nothing to transfer between the two. To my understanding, nonhuman creations such as myself will never attain that power. Even the most powerful demons that I know of need special access to come over here. So, you causing the ruckus that you did will definitely bring notice to Otherside and possibly the other place."

"I don't care about that. Tell me about the EGU and where their stronghold is. I want to find someone," Michi responded.

Putzin looked at Niko sitting next to Michi. "You and goldy here better take notes. Lieutenant Zerrick has been around for a long time and has earned his title as the Punisher in his ranks. He pulverizes anything in his way. What that demon said earlier is true. And whomever is helping him is just as powerful. I advise you to leave them alone. Besides them, you will have the others to think about. The EGU works directly under the Royal Fallen, and believe me, you don't want that smoke!" He stopped talking to Michi and pointed to Niko. "Put her on a leash or something."

Michi immediately went to hit the small demon, but Niko stopped her. "Babe, stop. Like you told me. Be nice. He is not wrong either." Niko planted a kiss on Michi's cheek. He sat down, placing her on his lap for her to face the demon across from them. "Whomever is helping him is some bitch named Koku trying to kill Michi here. They are the ones that attacked Michi's family."

"They attacked humans? In the open?" Putzin said. "Look, I want no part of this. I've heard some rumors about the lieutenant recently. I want to continue minding my business and exist. I am not ready to return!" he exclaimed, jumping on the table and wiping himself off. "Get this barrier off me and return me to Otherside."

Michi stood up. "No! You will sit and tell me all that you know and do for the EGU and tell me where the GOT DAMN STRONGHOLD IS!" she shouted with a force in her voice that it caused Niko to stand.

"I procure and sell information for them. I've been working for two Royal Crests for the past thousand years. This faction of the EGU has been around the longest and works with some powerful beings, toots. I don't know where their stronghold is. I am just a low-runner and don't get caught up in the politics of this place." He paused. "Wait, why the hell did I tell you that?" he looked around.

Michi smile and grabbed the little demon by his left horn. "I willed you to! Now, where is another stronghold that belongs to them? We need a place to lay low anyway. We can't keep coming back here. They will find what is left of this place eventually."

"I think we should stay here until we can figure out where the next place Koku and Zerrick will be. If we ambush them, you can defeat her like you almost did before and this will be all over." Niko said to Michi, gleaming.

Putzin slapped his hand against Michi's for her to release his horn. He scurried away. "Do you really think the lieutenant is going to be fine with what you two have been doing? I bet you Otherside in the Eastern Region is buzzing about some batshit crazy human fucking with the EGU. You don't know what you've started."

"Eastern Region? What are you talking about?" Niko asked.

Putzin responded harshly, "For you two to be as strong as you both are, you are fucking morons. How the hell are you invading a place and have no clue how to navigate the world? Know anything about the creatures that you are dealing with? I mean, shit. Just let me take you to the lieutenant myself and let him off you both. I can't believe this. I am really in Earth Realm with dumber and dumbest."

Through clenched teeth, Michi said, "For a small fucking point in the universe, you speak as if you don't know I can and will return you to the hellfire you came from. You are really starting to irritate the heckles out of me!" Michi growled and moved to attack the demon again.

Niko grabbed her again. "Babe, come on. He is harsh but he is not wrong. We have been going about this all wrong. We do need to make a better plan."

She whipped around to face Niko with her golden eyes. "The plan was and will always be to go to Otherside, hunt down every EGU stronghold until we find this lieutenant and Koku, and kick their asses." She paused, then brightened. "Aye! I remembered that one. Before I used to say arses but I think that's a British thing. But this time—"

"Babe, stay focused please. You are doing it again," Niko said pointing around them.

Michi looked around and noticed everything around her had turned to solid gold, including the little demon. "Oh shit!" She grabbed the solid gold demon's hand and began a low chant as his body began to loosen from the gold prison that Michi trapped him in. She continued as Putzin's eyes were widened in shock. "Like I said! He is just a lowly lieutenant! There is no way he can defeat me. Koku is my Shinigami and she will learn her place!" Michi raged.

The small demon realized he was utterly petrified of the unfocused, ditzy and the most powerful being he has ever run across in his lifetime. His voice cracked, "Michi, you said your name is? Please do not ever do that again." He cleared his throat. "Look, I will help you. Don't ask me why. It's for my own reasons. Okay?" He paused and waited for a reply.

"I could care less about your why. At this point, you try anything funny or weird, I'll just turn you into my favorite golden munchkin statue," Michi said with a huge smile.

Putzin ran behind Niko. "She really fucking scares me."

"Stop playing around. Fine. We don't care about your why. Just tell us what we need to know," Niko grabbed the demon by his right horn and picked him up like a toddler and placed him in front of him.

Putzin stared at Michi as she stood off to the side playing with her hair and looking at her nails. "We must first have a study session on Otherside and how it works. I will get you to a place that the EGU train their recruits. Like Michi said, he is just a lieutenant. But he isn't any lieutenant. He is on his way up in the ranks and he gets to pick who his team is. Where I am going to take you, Zerrick should be there or at least they would where he is."

Michi clapped her hands. "Oh cool! Field trip!"

THE TWINS

"Get your bitch ass up! Are we still locked up? I thought Mother was going to get us out," Dante said to the sleeping Deuce.

Deuce turned over, removing his tangled hair from his face. "Every day you ask the same questions. Of course, we are still locked up. Grandfather is toying with us at this point," he answered his twin, remembering the nightmares he'd been experiencing since being where they were. "I doubt very much they will take what happened lightly. Mother isn't the favorite like a certain someone, so I know we will pay."

"That is why we must take over. This old hierarchy shit and ancient ways is bullshit. I truly believe Grandfather is scared to try to unite us. He doesn't think he's strong enough because he's too worried about his so-called boss!" Dante shook with rage. "We can definitely make all those other Royal Crests our bitches and take over this whole damn universe. We are the strongest of them all!"

Deuce shook his head. "Grandfather doesn't understand what the consequences would be if he attempted to unite all demons and fallen under one kingdom. Of course, the idea is there. Can he really do it, is the question. Will fate allow such a thing? Will HE allow such a thing? Dante, don't be an idiot. Our plan was fun, but failing has shown me a whole new perspective on things." He sat up excitedly. "Brother, Gods have returned. Do you understand what that means? Also, I need to see her again. I am telling you. She is our connection to all of this."

"You're just pussy whipped with no pussy. Leave that human girl be! We have better fish to fry! I no longer want to be sitting here like a caged animal. I want to finish what we started and rule Otherside so we can start the takeover of all of Hell!!" Dante exclaimed just as the door opened.

Seraphin cleared her throat while walking through the door. "So, boys, I see the excitement for life hasn't escaped your hearts yet. I know Father has been making sure you learn your lesson with your indiscretion in Earth Realm," she said to her sons.

"His means of torture are not very fun. He could at least let us fight back or warn us." Dante shivered with his head down.

Deuce chuckled, "You know. If I didn't know any better, I'd say he is trying to break us."

"Unfortunately, he was not happy that we didn't tell him about Melchorde and that damn Trystan! He ruined everything. I told you not to allow him to do that," Seraphin responded.

Dante stood up. "This one was too busy playing weakling that he allowed that lowly demon to get a bit over his head. It's Number Two's fault that he even got in our way! That demon will pay!"

"Calm down, Number One. You don't have any room to speak. It was your job to make sure Deuce was able to keep him in check. It looks like he played both of you. Now he survived. Father hasn't returned him yet. I don't know what he is waiting for! He better not say anything!" Seraphin exclaimed, angry that Trystan survived his role in their plot to take over Otherside and Earth.

Deuce was supposed to lure him in with finding the foreign power that happened to be Adam. Using him was easy since he was connected to the human massacre that was linked to that power a few years prior. It was Seraphin that sent Trystan and his team to kill the beings in that area to claim the foreign power, but the plan was botched due to Adam.

The twins stumbling across their aunt that had been missing for a couple thousand years was a bonus. But the twins keeping that secret from their superiors, and especially their grandfather, had led to their imprisonment within their realm. Seraphin has been trying her hardest to convince her father that it was all Melchorde's fault and that the twins were trying to stop the overzealous Trystan while also trying to gain notoriety by capturing Melchorde. So far, it was to no avail. She'd been patiently waiting to see what her father's next move for her sons would be, but she doubted he would get rid of them, as they were his only biological grandchildren. Unfortunately, she was the only one of his daughters to be betrothed and to successfully carry children.

"Mother, don't worry. The decade I was training with that barbaric moron, he didn't learn a thing about me or our plans. He was just as shocked as we were when Melchorde was first seen. His obsession with her caused my plan to fail."

Deuce added, "About Melchorde, I thought you said you were the only one to reproduce?"

Completely ignoring her youngest son, Seraphin said, "Be prepared at all times. He will be testing your resolve and loyalty to this family. Father is also taking into account that you both are being questioned on your allegiance and ability to be a part of the hierarchy of this realm. You both wasted too much time doing absolutely nothing to gain us ground. I've been telling you both it is time for you to show that you are my sons!" Smoothing her silk clothing, she continued, "Now, you both will do whatever it is you have to do to get out of this hell realm and get back to what I've been raising you for!" And with that, she left the twins to themselves and their punishment.

****

"I will murder those two arrogant pricks!" Trystan growled in pain. Having been chained to the wall since his capture, he had never fully healed from the fight in New York. Being tortured here, his hatred for the twins that was the only thing that kept him thriving. He whispered to himself, "I am going to break his neck and drink his blood."

A door creaked opened as a large figure with some metal tools in his hands stood there in front of the disheveled Trystan. "Well, you're awake. Anything to tell me today? The twins already told us what we needed to know. We just need you to tell us who was the cause of the fire. We can't measure your burns or the power that was welded in those chains. Maybe if you cooperate, we can get those injuries healed."

Trystan continued to ignore the guard that had repeatedly come to ask the same question. Each time, Trystan would remain silent. Endure the torture that was dished out to him. And then start over. He heard everything as he was being transported to his new home. Unfortunately for Trystan, he was in too much pain to pass out. He learned of the twin's identity and learned that the boy that came and rescued Melchorde was a Sun God. At least that's what he heard one of those Angels say before they disappeared, and that the twins were related to Melchorde. He also heard when the Royal EGU arrived on the scene that it was Lord Belial that sent them to clean up the twins' mess.

"I will kill you ALL!" was all Trystan could muster before his torture began again.

THE SEARCH

"Okay. We are officially in the heart of the Western Region in Otherside," X said to Chike. "The others should be arriving soon. There is a place that M and I had information put out that Daikoku and Lieutenant Asshole will be. Hoping a little hot head and naïve petite goddess will come."

Chike understanding X's plan, asked, "Do you really think she will fall for that? I mean, come on. She's a fucking genius. She can't be that slow."

"Have you met Michi?" X whipped around to face Chike. "She's a fucking three-year-old in the body of a twenty-five-year-old with the powers of all the Shichifukujin. I can't imagine what goes on in that brain of hers. You don't even get it. We have to find her ASAP! This is worse than Adam's temper tantrums." He turned to continue to lead Chike to their destination.

Chike chuckled, "Where are we going anyway? I know in this part of Otherside the demons have more control, right?"

"We're headed to one of our safehouses on this side. It's a small house. Not as grand as the castle but good to use." X sighed. "Unfortunately, you are somewhat right about the demons, but as long as we don't start trouble, we should be good. They have more contracts with the creatures in this area. Also, in some places of Otherside, the war between Heaven and Hell is not tolerated."

He stopped as the trees opened up to a garden, turning to Chike. "They have their own hierarchy over here in certain places. Specifically, the southeast part of this land. Why do you think places like the southern US and South America have so many beliefs of things of 'Other'? That area is controlled by Otherside creatures and our involvement is heavily rejected. It's like its neutral ground for the angels and demons."

Chike remembered his teachings. "Yes. I was told specifically there are areas of the world that have closer connections to Otherside and that's how some humans learned of it and its beings."

"Actually, that is not fully true either. From what I understand, some of the humans connected to the light or dark have the ability to get there. Unfortunately, they are considered "other" and if they learn or stumble across the thinnest layer of the realms' connection, then they will have access to Otherside. But I haven't witnessed any officially crossing over. Some have come close while others thought they were here, but it was just some entity messing with them trying to cross. As simple as it sounds, it does require a lot of power to cross both realms. Beings such as myself and other warrior angels have the ability to cross due to our positions. Most beings don't have the power and require contracts or help from others who have the ability to cross."

He walked the plush pathway that led towards the house. "Remember, this area is not as up-to-date as other places of Otherside, so our phones are not useable nor do we have a lot of backup. I have a small team scouting the area making sure we are good to move towards the EGU training camp."

Chike followed closely. "I figured that and made sure our phones were configured with satellite settings. You told me the realms are basically parallel, so I figured the global satellites in Earth Realm should work in the remote places in Otherside." Checking his phone, he continued, "See. One bar at least. No FaceTiming or shit, but we could at least text or call."

"You know, I like you kid! Don't think I forgot, you never told us who you're working for. It's obvious it's an angel, so I won't pry. But whoever it is was smart to bring you to our side. You, Adam and sexy chocolate are the closest to humans being here in Otherside I can think of. I keep telling our other angel generals we need to get with the times." He walked to the door of their new hideout. "The demons are working with the humans and beings of Otherside to gain more followers and power in this war. While us angels are following a tradition that's constantly trampled on and destroyed. You can't even fathom what I've witnessed in the over three millennia since I was born."

Chike was still taking in his surroundings, as X's description of a small house was not accurate. The small house X mentioned was the size of one of the castle towers of the Castle of Angels. "Yo, X, your version of small house and my version of small house are two different things. This is a slightly smaller version of the damn castle. You're old as hell, my g! Over three thousand years old?"

"Shut up! Not too old to kick your ass! This place is hella small! I don't have my own wing!" X rubbed the back of his neck turning to look around the area. "Come on. Let's get ready while we wait for the others."

****

"Where are we meeting handsome white eyes?" Benzi used her hand to fan herself as she zoned out thinking of X. "I can't wait to see him again. He is such wonderful eye candy. Even with the scar."

Adam chuckled at Benzi's question. "Actually, he won't be joining us. He is with the other ladies and Chike. They will be checking somewhere else while we check this location, they sent us. Supposedly, both of these places could be Michi's next target." He checked his phone's text message from X, "Uncle Mike, you all caught up and ready? I know you've been off doing your own thing. You good? Angels need more help?"

"I am well-informed to the situation at hand, Adam," he responded. "I am fine. Angel operations does not need the help of the Sun God Ra at this time. Thank you for your concern." He smiled at Adam teasingly.

Adam had his eyes on Benzi. "I hate when he calls me that. Lucy already told you I am not Ra. I am the Sun God Adam!" His eyes set ablaze as he slammed his hand on a wall.

"Now, Mikael, why would you rouse this young god?" Dillon interrupted the back and forth. "We are almost at our target area. I suggest you all be quiet."

Benzi pranced in front of the group as they walked through a parking lot of an industrial area that led to a warehouse. "This place looking creepy as hell. My princess has no business being in a place like this. Let's hurry up and get this over with so we can find my Michi-ban!"

As the group went to launch their attack, Dillon placed his arm up to stop them. "Wait! Look!". He pointed towards a side entrance of the warehouse. Two dark figures revealed themselves near a back entrance that was in sight of the current group. The figures pushed a smaller figure into the doorway of the warehouse confirming three intruders entering.

Benzi immediately ran towards the entrance without warning to the others, reaching the door just as the main entrance of the warehouse exploded open. "Oh no! Our cover is blown! Let's go! That's probably her!"

Dillon rushed towards the opening of the blast searching for survivors or Michi to question. "Over here! This leads to the base of the camp," he shouted towards the group just as a dozen or so EGU soldiers popped up.

Adam, ignoring Benzi, ran past the soldiers A peculiar sensation stirred within the warehouse's core peeking Adam's curiosity. "I am going to follow her! I know this is Michi!" He rushed towards the energy signature he felt.

Dillon attempted to follow Adam just as an EGU soldier dropped right in his path, blocking him from continuing. Using his swift speed and power, he grabbed the soldier by the face and slammed him down on the ground and used the next soldier to stand in front of him as a boost to hop over the rest of the soldiers that were attempting to descend on the decimated area.

"I will follow Adam—take care of these mongrels!" Dillon yelled to Benzi and Mikael.

Mikael, already engaged with the EGU, shouted, "Do not lose them!"

Benzi joined the fray using her small frame to annihilate the onslaught of enemies that moved towards them. "Is this all y'all do? This would get on my nerves!"

"It is our job to stop the darkness from overshadowing the light," Mikael replied, stomping on the soldier that he dragged down.

Benzi was unimpressed with the righteous talk. "Yea whatever. I am tired of fighting. The few weeks we've been with you angels, that's all you do. Whomever doesn't follow your so-called light, you destroy. Ya'll wonder why Otherside is siding with Hell."

She dodged a swing from a soldier and used her elbow to hit the back of their neck, and then used her left leg to add more force to the fall.

"Ouch," Mikael said watching Benzi. "You know, we do not destroy everything. It is our job to make sure the demons do not take over. "I think that's the last of them. I see you are just as good as usual. Nothing has changed."

Benzi looked towards the handsome caramel skinned man. "Well, I'm glad you finally remembered me, handsome."

"How can I forget the beautiful and vibrant Benzaiten. I heard you and Bishamonten survived the Days of Hunts. I'm sorry to hear what happened to Fukurokuji. I always considered him a friend." Mikael paused then added, "Just know, I always denied pursuing you when it was requested. My colleagues know you two survived, but I guess since you were under the protection of the royal fallen family you work for, that pursuit was not continued."

Benzi clapped her hands. "Good to know, Mikey! You were always my favorite angel to work with and I was sad we had become enemies. Now it looks like we are back on the same side. Since its two gods that have returned, this has to be the work of the Ultimate High. They must have recognized their mistake!"

"My creator doesn't make mistakes. We were required to do what was necessary! You remember those times. The gods were out of control," he scoffed and began to walk away. He paused. "Come, let's find Adam and Dillon."

Benzi skipped after Mikael. "Whatever you need to tell yourself to feel better about it. You know what happened was wrong. Don't worry, I won't hold it against you." She caught up to Mikael then slowed to walk at his pace. "I will warn you. If the decision to purge them again is handed down, there is nowhere in your Heaven, Otherside or Hell you all can hide if a hair on my Michi's head is touched," she said with a grin.

"Honestly, I believe it is my creator that has allowed them to return. For unknown reasons to us angels. At this time, we are allies, Benzaiten, and it would be my honor to continue working with you. Now, let's continue searching for Michi."

Mikael bowed with a gesture for Benzi to walk ahead of him as she skipped passed him with a luminous smile that matched her silver outfit.

"You little demon, where did you get your information from? I can sense the angels and Adam are here." Michi pulled her hand back, threatening to slap the demon.

Putzin cowered as he covered his small body, "I don't know what you're talking about. I was told that there are two places in this area that Zerrick frequently gets information and new men to add to his group,"

Niko interrupted their conversation as a group of EGU soldiers appeared in front of them, stopping their descent down the steps. The first soldier reached to grabbed Putzin as Michi turned two of them into gold statues and kicked them down the steps. Niko snatched the soldier away from Putzin and flipped the soldier over the banister. "We have to leave now. I don't think Zerrick and Koku are here. They would have immediately shown themselves."

"Hmm, you are right, handsome, and the fact that Adam is right behind us means we have to go. I know I can't out run him. I'm trying my best to keep us concealed, but it's getting hard. Something else is here. What is it? I want to see it!" Michi dashed away, using an EGU soldier as a glide to jump down the stairwell with.

"Michi!' Niko yelled down the opening. "Putzin, follow her! I will take care of these idiots!" Niko used the power he had siphoned from Michi and continued to fight the EGU soldiers just as Adam arrived at the top of the landing

"You little motherfucker! Where have y'all been? Kisha has been worried sick about Michi!" he shouted with his eyes dancing like fire flames. He went to approach Niko just as more soldiers began to attack them both.

Michi instantly reappeared next to Niko. "We have to go! You will not believe what I saw!" She gasped as her eyes met Adam's. "Hi Sunny! Bye Sunny! Let's go you two!" She grabbed Niko's hand and Putzin's horn, disappearing from Adam's sight.

"That damn Michi!" Adam growled, punching the EGU soldier that was attacking him. Slowly breathing out small flames, he raised his hand and fired a small flame that lit only the EGU soldiers that were standing in front of him on fire. He watched as they all burned, using his frustration to rid the staircase of the rest of the EGU.

Seeing Adam's work, Dillon rushed to the staircase. "Well, it seems you learned not to cause too much structural damage with your power. Where did she go?"

"I don't know. I can't feel her. She's blocking me still. Little brat. She's gotten stronger. I sensed it. I wonder what she saw. I'll be right back. I feel something weird down there too." Adam teleported away, leaving Dillon on the stairwell.

Bisha pranced her way to where Dillon remained. "What did we miss? I felt my Michi and that Niko guy. What is that weird energy signature?"

Mikael added to Bisha's questions, "Where is Adam?"

Dillon with a heavy sigh as he sensed the incoming EGU soldiers approaching them, "I know you both feel the enemy coming, yet you two are asking such feeble questions. Let's get back above ground and prepare for the fight." He rolled his eyes and answered them, "For your information, Adam is investigating the strange phenomena under us and Michi disappeared before I arrived on the scene."

Adam interrupted, "Let's go. We have to meet with Mel now. I don't know where we are, but downstairs looks like a fucking science horror show. Come on, we have to go!" He grabbed Mikael and Dillon by their shoulders while Benzi held Mikael's hand and they left the now destroyed EGU stronghold.

****

"Lieutenant Zerrick, thank you for joining us. Please have a seat," the youngest of the Cressius Crest, Isis, spoke. She guided the lieutenant to a seat at the table surrounded by other EGU lieutenants that serviced the family. She continued, "I regret pulling you from your current task, but it seems that you and your—" she cleared her throat, "company," she gazed towards Daikoku, "have been causing some serious issues with the EGU. More than a dozen of our strongholds in the northeast region have been attacked in the last two weeks. Care to explain?"

Before Zerrick had a chance to respond, Daikoku spoke up. "Your Majesty, if I may, we are in the midst of acquiring something very peculiar and powerful for the family. And we—" Her voice immediately cracked and she dropped to her knees from the cold and excruciating pain that came from her stomach area. Her insides began to stiffen from the ice that formed inside her.

"No, you may not. Lieutenant Zerrick, please teach your pet the rules of her place. She is for only your pleasure and guidance for our business in Earth Realm," the royal stated. "Back to my question. Lieutenant?" she asked with a raised eyebrow.

Zerrick shifted in his chair as he rubbed his forehead removing the small sweat beads, as he knew that her patience was very thin with "Other" creatures. Even Daikoku, though a powerful Shinigami, in Otherside and Hell, she was almost like demon food. "Your Majesty, I just became aware of the attacks on us as I returned from Earth Realm. Unfortunately, I had more than enough clean up to do from the catastrophe that happened there. Our human authority connections are not happy with all of the demon activity in that area that came with the loss of life and structures." He added, "I have a plan for both the humans and this minor issue with our bases."

The other lieutenants stared at the beautiful woman at the head of the table. "Zerrick, do you have any idea who or what would dare attack my EGU stations?"

A lieutenant added, "I have my soldiers telling me that a goddess is attacking our bases because of you and that bitch!"

Isis interjected on the lieutenant's rant, "No one asked you." She closed her fist tight and used her power of ice to freeze both Daikoku and the interrupting lieutenant's hearts, causing them to squeal. "Oh, I forgot I still had you under my power." She grinned at the kneeling Daikoku as she released her grip. The rude lieutenant continued his squeal as his body turned to ice and then dust. "Now back to you, Zerrick. As you can see, I am not in a good mood."

The lieutenant sat in silence as his nerves shook with rage. "Your Highness, I apologize for the inconvenience and disservice. I will make sure this situation is handled immediately."

She replied, "The reason you are not ice dust like Lieutenant asshole here is because I heard you were doing such a great job in Earth Realm. I heard we couldn't have chosen a better demon for the situation at hand."

He replied, "I am grateful for this opportunity and I am doing my best to keep our interests in the northeastern region of Otherside and Earth Realms my first priority. Daikoku here has done a wonderful job of keeping our financial interests and investments on

Earth in great standings. Regrettably, as mentioned earlier, it is the human authorities that are becoming a little more troublesome. I do have a plan that will negate any issues their involvement may bring."

Isis was unamused at his adding Daikoku to the conversation. "I am not interested in the financial aspect of your position. I am interested in the increase of our presence and contracts with those humans. We will continue to gain footing in that area so we can continue moving forward with our family's plan for this part of Otherside."

She stood. "Enough of Zerrick bashing, this goes for all of you. There has been confirmation that two gods have returned to our realms. At this time, we only can confirm the Shichifukujin has returned." Isis paused and smirked towards Daikoku before continuing, "and the other god we cannot confirm their power. I have my scouts working to find out. I would like to add that the former Queen of the Golden River Realm is working with these new gods."

One of the other lieutenants raised his hand nervously.

Isis nodded with approval.

"One entity as the Shichifukujin, that's unheard of. Also, is former-Queen Melchorde's ransom still up for grabs?"

"I heard her father placed a pause on the ransom as it is only for his family to capture her. I am interested to see what he has in store. If we run across her, it is still within your right as EGU to capture the traitor," Isis answered.

She sat down and began her conclusion, "Now that that is out the way, your new set of orders." She barked out the orders for the other lieutenants, "Zerrick, you will return to the Northeastern Region and continue your work on Otherside. As of now, your activities in Earth Realm are suspended. There is no need for you to return there at this time. Also, we will not need you for this god situation, so make sure your team stays away from our other operations. "We already lured a potential threat to one of our hideouts."

She crossed her legs. "So, start there. Now, if your investigation of the base attacks begins to interfere with the other situation, you are to immediately report to me. Are we clear? My family wants to be involved in all things going on with this issue at hand."

Lieutenant Zerrick, totally understanding his boss's stance, repeated back his orders, "Yes, Your Highness. I will continue my duties with the Northeastern Region operations. I will also look into the attacks against us. If these gods are involved, you would like me to inform you before I make any moves against them."

Isis got up and seductively walked towards Zerrick. She grabbed him by his face and began to kiss him passionately. Daikoku stared with disdain as the other lieutenants just watched. Zerrick's body began to convulse and move as she held his face.

Daikoku watched as his face began to turn to ice from under the kiss. Isis raised her head to stare at Daikoku, the ice slowly fading from Zerrick's face. "I'm glad you understand. All of you are dismissed. I better have better news next time."

Zerrick rushed out of the war room of the EGU Headquarters heading towards the area assigned to him. His veins were seething with hatred. Unfortunately, his general was loyal to the Royal Cressius Crest, leaving Zerrick with no choice but to follow. That was one of the reasons why he decided to team up with Daikoku and help her achieve the Shichifukujin power. With that kind of power, he knew he could at least take over a part of Otherside and start his path toward uniting Otherside against Hell and the Angels. He knew a woman like Daikoku could help him achieve such a goal.

Since the Days of Hunts, the few surviving associates of the gods that did live were not trusted and were often held in contempt in Otherside by angels, demons and Otherside creatures. Daikoku had earned her place as a great business woman and trader in Earth Realm and Otherside. Her cunning and conniving ways helped her gain her notoriety and that's how she got the attention of the Royal Tohr Crest.

For the past few decades, they'd been lending her out to other families, causing her to question her need for them as her own power continued to grow. This led to her being paired with the Cressius Crest and meeting Zerrick. Unfortunately, family members such as Isis liked to remind her that she didn't have as much power as she thought. Daikoku knew if she continued her path towards coming the Shichifukujin, there would be nothing and no one that could stop her.

Daikoku followed the angry lieutenant down the hall to their quarters. She knew he was fuming as she was and stared at him with passion in her eyes. Neither one of them spoke to the other as Zerrick grabbed Daikoku's head and started kissing her passionately down her throat as he began to rip off her kimono and the top of her jumpsuit. He wrapped his large fist around her neatly placed ponytail while his tongue licked down her neck and bare shoulders.

Daikoku wrapped her left leg around his waist as she led him to the chaise under the large window in his office. The both of them rubbed against each other like warring beasts as she began to loosen the tight leather uniformed pants that the lieutenant had on. Using her hand to remove the snapped area of her jumpsuit, she allowed his manhood to penetrate her as they both began to lose themselves in the violent actions, they considered sex.

****

Michi couldn't understand why she didn't send them back to their hideout. She was nervous and felt her anxiety getting the best of her. "I'm sorry y'all. I will get us back. Give me a sec." She darted her head back and forth, searching around for a clue to where they were and what could have gone wrong.

Putzin looked around. "What is this place? Your little tingling thing on me stopped."

Niko stood in front of Michi and watched as her eye color switched from their regular brown to gold and back to brown. Niko knew this was the beginning of her panic attacks. "Baby, it's okay. Breathe." He felt the tremendous power flowing through her.

"I'm okay, handsome. I got it," she said, slowly breathing. "I will not let this power control me," she finished, and Niko started to yell.

Standing in her vicinity, his feet and legs began to turn to gold. Michi yelled, "I'm sorry! I'm sorry! I can't stop it." She squeezed her eyes shut with tears flowing down her face.

He fought through the pain. "Baby, I promise I'm okay. You got this. Come on. Breathe for me." Niko slowly breathed so Michi could mimic his movement.

"Okay." The glowing water flowed down her golden cheeks. "Okay." She copied his slow breaths, and the surrounding energy continued to subside and his feet return to normal.

Putzin watched the couple. "Get a damn room." He walked back towards them. "Where did you send us, toots? Some weird dude won't let me past the gates."

"Gates?" Michi said excitedly, the tears still wet on her cheeks. She rushed past Niko towards the gates Putzin spoke of. "We made it! I did it!"

94

Niko, released from her gold, followed her confused. "What are you talking about?"

Michi started rambling, "I told you I needed to get to my books, and I never knew how to get to my books, and now we are here." She continued excitedly, "Come on! I get to see them again!" She pushed the gates open and the large door opened in front of them, leading them into a large empty space.

Niko and Putzin followed. Putzin yelled into the vacant area, "Hello!" He looked around, "Where's the weirdo robe dude? He was just here at the gates talking about how I wasn't invited. What happened?"

Michi pranced around. "We are here at the Akashic Records. You probably couldn't get in because of me. I'm the reason why we have access to this place." Shocked at them two being so quiet, she spun around to see why.

"Yes, you are correct, Shichifukujin. Goddess of Luck, now that you are fully synced with your powers and anchor, you now have access to your purpose and the information needed for your role," a large, robed man spoke from the left corner.

Niko and Putzin were overwhelmed by the being's presence and passed out behind Michi.

The robed man continued, "No one is to know the true reasons for the rebirths. Access to the first two gods is available. The third and fourth will be revealed soon. Melchorde's role is to continue to guide and protect. Learn your role and place in the cosmos, as you will sit with fire creating anew." He disappeared at the end of his sentence, leaving Michi to read.

She stared behind her as Niko and Putzin was still passed out. She skipped over to the shelves of books and picked one from the bottom self. "The beginning? This is boring?" She sighed heavily and rolled her eyes as she sat crossed-leg next to Niko as he slept.

ALL TOGETHER NOW

M looked over at Bisha while witnessing the Shinigami take a couple blows from the soldiers that were attacking her. Unfortunately, they were led into a trap at the location they were given. Now they were fighting to escape the heavily forested area that consumed them. "Ladies, gain some ground by heading to the treetops. Chike, use one of the large fire blasts to slow them down. X, follow me!" She stopped to allow a large amount of EGU soldiers to surround them.

X stood at her back. M used X's knee to jump on his shoulder to backflip into a spin with her twin swords unsheathed in both hands that allowed her to cut the heads off a handful of soldiers. He watched as she landed on her feet. "You're not gonna be using me as your jungle gym!" he shouted towards her as he pulled his battle axe from his sheath and began slaughtering the dozens more that kept coming for them.

"Shut up and fight! I'm trying to let Taki and Bisha get to safety so we can get the hell out of here., M responded.

X lowered his brows and rubbed his temple, "I mean, we have Bisha and Taki, Sunny's princess. I watched her siphon some of his power before they separated," he panted taking a break from the fight.

M grabbed X's arm and swung him to her left side, causing him to miss being stabbed by a sword. She stomped her right foot and immediately kicked outward towards the soldier while exposing her right shoe knife that used the soldier's chin as a bullseye. "Pay attention. This is a waste of our time. They are keeping us from something!"

A scream split the air. M whipped her head around and saw a large fire light the sky up a few feet ahead of her. "Shit! Takisha!"

"Mel, wait!" X shouted. He began to run after her because he saw the same fire blast. Upon his arrival, following M, he saw a large hole in the ground covered in soot and Bisha in the middle of the smoke.

M stared at the passed out Bisha. "I know you're not dead! Where is Takisha?! I do not feel her presence!"

"I don't know! Someone attacked us as soon as we got to this clearing. I did not recognize the uniform." Bisha gritted her teeth in pain. "Whoever it was, it was a fallen!"

The air around M's ponytail began to rise. "You mean to tell me that Takisha was taken?!" Her reds eyes glowed with anger while the air sizzled around her, "WHAT THE HELL?"

The land around them began to quake as a large presence appeared next to Bisha. The temperature in the area was quickly rising. "WHERE IS SHE!" Adam growled with flames flicking out his mouth. "I can't feel her at all! Where did she go! I left her with you DEMON!" he began to walk towards M.

"Sun God! I'm in no mood for your temper tantrums!" M turned to X. "Find Chicky in this debris and get to the tower where we're all supposed to meet. I will deal with this one here. X, DO NOT let Bishamonten out of your sight."

Adam stood with all the fury in his body starting to take over. "I said WHERE IS SHE!" he roared with a fiery blast coming out of his mouth.

"Ouch!" Bisha jumped from the large fire breathing man. "He could roast us all! I thought Michi was bad."

M's large leather wings quickly expanded with the pulsating blue that leapt in different areas of them. She allowed herself to get closer to Adam as he stared in confusion. "Come boy, you will find Takisha. Calm yourself." The bladed tips of her wings began to melt. "You will pay for this, Adam," she said through gritted teeth, trying to ignore the pain from his burns.

Adam no longer created the large cylinder that used to engulf him, but when his power did get out of control, the water in the area around him would begin to dry and everything in his vicinity would melt.

His eyes glared at M while his teeth showed in a smile as they both became surrounded by a light that caused Adam's presence to fade.

X walked towards where Bisha was still lying. "Chike, did you see any more EGU soldier behind us?"

Chike called from not too far behind him, "No. It looks like the blast scared them off. I caused a few big trees to fall back there, so most of them were trapped anyway. Can you tell me what happened?"

"I really don't know, my guy. What I do know is we better find Taki before we have two on-the-loose gods running around this universe fucking shit up!"

M looked up, panting. "That boy is getting strong. I don't know how many more times I can contain him. He is a fully developed god now. My powers will soon be nothing but a pinch to him.

X said, "Fuck that. We put down more powerful ones than him. Is he okay?"

M answered while she stood up, "Adam is fine. He just needs to cool off so we can figure out what happened to Takisha."

Chike gasped, "Somebody took Kish? What the fuck?"

X added, "Duh. You didn't get that from the way his big ass came in like a hungry dragon looking for food? I can't wait to see that Baby G again. He acts so irrational when it comes to her. We gonna have to get that out of his system. We're in a war!"

M interjected, "All of you are idiots. Takisha is not involved or will ever be involved in that damn war! Grab the Shinigami and let's go before I leave you all."

X picked up the injured Bisha and stood next to M. "Can we travel your way. I am not flying her."

"I don't want you carrying me either!" Bisha squinted her eyes as the angel who held her. She attempted to jump put stopped herself since she felt so weak.

M held onto X's vest and whispered low for only he could hear, "You need to learn that power on your own. You will learn your other side is more valuable than you think." She smirked as they all disappeared to meet back with the other group.

****

"Where am I?" Taki asked the dark stranger. "What do you want!?" she shouted at the man pacing in front of her.

The man ignored her questions and began to search Taki. She had on a pair of black cargo pants and a black hoodie that had her other favorite rapper, Tupac, on the front. He continued to pat her down until he found her phone and snapped it in half.

"Now that I know you aren't being tracked or spied on... who and what are you? You can't be a regular human," the low gritty voice of the stranger spoke for the first time.

Taki glared at the handsome face that was within two inches of hers. This man stood a little shorter than Adam with a dark hazelnut complexion and hair that looked like black ramen noodles that sat just

98

short of his shoulders. "Who the fuck are *you* is the question! You just go around kidnapping random people, asshole?" The stranger chuckled, "Feisty, I like. It's obvious you're not human. You wouldn't be able to breathe here. Also, you don't smell human or Other. What are you?" He moved back in closer to sniff at the air around Taki.

"Ew. Move creep-o!" She shied away as far as she could since the stranger had her pinned against a stone. It seemed like they were not far from the area he took her from. Taki recognized the emblem on his jacket. "How do you know—"

The stranger instantly knocked her out. "Not yet, little lady. Come. Someone wants to meet you," he said before disappearing.

WHAT DO YOU KNOW

Adam sat up from what felt like a blackout. He looked up and saw Michi, Niko and a small being with horns a few feet away from him sitting at a table talking.

"How did I get back here?" he asked, rubbing his head.

Michi pranced over to him and bent over. "Hi Sunny! Glad you're awake. You came here and started at me like Arrrrr!" She mimicked a monster attacking. "Then you passed out. Taki told me you do that sometimes, so we just left you there. I mean come on, I know you can't die from a bump on the head." She paused, "I mean, can you? What happens if we crack our skulls? Can we survive that?" and she continued asking questions in Japanese.

"Michi! Michi! What the hell is going on? What are you doing here?" Adam asked and looked back at Niko and Putzin. "You brought them with you? And who's the demon?" His eyes flared into dancing flames.

Michi stepped back and began speaking in Japanese to Adam, "Don't be mean, Sunny! You know Niko, and Putzin is helping us get around Otherside." She sat down cross-legged in front of Adam. "I am on my way to finding them. Don't try to stop me!" Michi glared at Adam, her eyes turning gold.

"You know I am not scared of you, Michi. Your powers don't work on me. First, I don't want to stop you. Second, you can't do this on your own. M is worried and so is your Shinigami. Talk to them, Michi." Adam tilted back on his arms while still sitting.

Michi and he had trained a little bit for the small time they were around each other. The fact that they were both gods intrigued them and they would sit after training and talk, going back and forth to assist each other with discovering and exploring their powers.

"I know you're not scared. But I don't want ya'll interfering. So, I need you to sit this one out, big guy," Michi responded. "Well, as much as you want me to. I will not. They took Kisha, Mich. We were out searching for you, and some random motherfucker snuck up and snatched her up. At least that's what I got from M." Adam stood up and walked over towards his book collection. "You know, the weird part is every time I randomly pick up a book it picks up where I left off."

Michi got up and pranced over to the shelves of books that had her symbol. "They took Kisha!" she exclaimed and then paused. "I realized that too, Sunny! Looks like we have to read from the beginning."

"Yes, they did, and that's just boring." He stepped from the column of books and walked towards Niko and Putzin. "Yo, Niko!"

Niko, surprised by Adam's friendliness after their last encounter, asked, "You're not mad at me from earlier?"

"Nah. I'll probably fuck you up when we have to practice later," Adam told him with a grin. "Yo, why didn't you try to get in contact with one of us? She can't be out here by herself being crazy. I know she was trained damn near like a ninja goddess and shit, but damn. She wild."

Michi skipped over with a book in her hand. "Shut up, Sunny! Putzin, meet my bestest friend in the whole universe. Taki's boyfriend, Sunny! He is—"

"I told you to stop calling me that! You said it like ten times already!" Adam shouted at Michi, flames dancing in his eyes. "I'm Adam the Sun God!" he said as fire flickered at his feet.

Putzin jumped back. "What the fuck freak show is this? All these humans with powers just poppin' up like popcorn."

"What you know about popcorn, little guy?" Adam said to Putzin, slowly walking towards him.

Putzin ran behind Niko. "Not a damn thing with you looking like that, Sunny—I mean, Adam," he stuttered.

Michi interrupted, "Adam, stop it. You are such a tease."

Adam laughed. "Nah, for real, who is he?" His eyes still danced with fire flames.

"I told them I would help them. My name is Putzin." The small demon walked up to Adam to shake his hand.

Adam extended his large hand to Putzin. "What do you want with Michi?" His voice echoed in the stone room.

"Really nothing, but I figure I could use her to get rid of my bosses," Putzin said, instantly covering his mouth. "What the hellfire!"

Adam stalked closer to the small demon and grabbed him by the horn, lifting him up off his feet and bringing him to his own face. "Oh, really! What else haven't you told Michi?"

"That I'm an information broker for the EGU and I am the one who fed the information to the angels about the two locations for a trap. Michi here was too powerful for the trap." He gasped. "Why the hell am I saying shit I don't want to say!?" he exclaimed.

Adam looked at Michi. "You didn't will him to answer your questions? That's sloppy, Mich! He could have been lying to you the whole time." He threw the demon to the ground. "Get a better handle on that power, and I promise you won't have to worry about people—" He paused. "Well, beings lying to you. Shit even works on the angels."

Michi clapped. "Oh. Let me do it!" She concentrated. "Where are you from?"

Putzin looked at Michi confused. "I told you I'm under the Cressius Crest.

"Ooooh…Ohhh." Michi jumped with joy. "I usually can only do this when I am angry! He told me he was an informant but not the extra stuff."

Adam sat at the head of the large table. "Don't trust anyone from Otherside. Including the Angels. Don't get it twisted. They are about good and all that, but if the plans are not in their agenda, they don't give a fuck. So, in my opinion, they may look like the bad guys here in Otherside. I've haven't been to the clouds yet, so I haven't met many fans of the Angels."

"What do you mean?" Michi fidgeted on a chair at the large table. She shifted her hands to rest on her chin to listen to the Sun God.

"I mean since I've been traveling with the Angels to Otherside with them. I see that they have a lot of enemies over here. There is a lot of shit they don't talk about. The cloud part is I haven't learned how to get to Heaven yet." He felt around the large metal like table with a weird looking symbol that he couldn't quite make out. "If we have access to Otherside and this place, you think we don't have access to Heaven or Hell? Let's be for real, Mich. We are gods."

Michi thought about what Adam was saying. "You're right. I believe we can get there too. I got to Otherside relatively easy. I just had to figure out how to bring Niko with me. Also, I was able to make it for Putzin to stay in Earth Realm. I—"

"You did what?!" Adam slammed his hands on the table and stood up. "How the hell did you do that? What does that even mean?"

Michi jumped up and walked towards Putzin. "I don't know, Sun—I mean A!" She paused and laughed. "See, I remembered your name! That's what X, Chike and Taki call you as a nickname!"

"Michi, stay focused!" Adam said, shaking his head.

"Oh yea. Like I said, I created a barrier so the little demon here could stay on Earth Realm. When I first took him there, he was choking and the atmosphere was taking his energy away. So, Fuki showed me how to create a barrier around his body to protect him from Earth's atmosphere."

Adam pondered what she said. "Fuki? That's right, you get the information from all the Shinigami?"

"No, unfortunately at this time only Fuki, Juro, Hotei and Ebisu talk to me directly. I think that's because they are no longer part of this world. I will always have access to the powers of Benzaiten, Bishamonten and Daikoku even though they still exist because I am the Shichifukujin. But the spirits of the ones that are no longer here I can speak to directly," Michi said, sitting in a chair at the table with the symbol of a golden tree at the top. She continued, "Is this some kind of special table? I didn't see this symbol when I first got here. Why are you at the head?"

Adam looked behind him and saw his chair had a burning symbol at the top. He answered, "I don't know, I remember Lucy saying I was the most powerful of them all. Do you think there will be more of us?"

"This is a pretty big table. I would hate to not have company!" Michi said excitedly. "Then again, why? Like why the Sun God? Why the Shichifukujin? And why the others if there are more? There has to be a reason, and why us?"

Adam stood up. "I don't know, but I do know one thing. We better find Kisha, or the demons and angels will have another problem!"

****

Mikael paced back and forth trying to contact Chike using his cell phone.

Benzi sat looking at her nails. "I'm hungry and need a mani-pedi as soon as possible. What are we doing?"

"Mikael, is the new angel answering? If not, we will regroup until we hear from them. It's obvious this was a trap. They underestimated Michiko and paid the price. I am curious as to why the fire boy ran off like that. Something must have happened to Takisha," Dillon said, standing next to Mikael searching for his phone in his suit.

Mikael attempted to send a text message and pondered on Dillon's words. "You think so?"

"Of course. One minute he was here being his usual sarcastic self and then I felt a flux in his power, and then he disappeared. I can tell he is near Melchorde," Dillon answered while smoothing out his navy-blue pin stripe suit from the fight.

Mikael was shocked that he said her name. "Well. That is good to know. Let's meet them at the rendezvous point and see what we missed."

As Mikael turned to fly away, Melchorde instantly revealed herself next to him. "Melchorde! Where is Adam?"

"The Sun God is fine. He will get back to us once he calms himself." She glanced over at Dillon, getting an uneasy feeling in her stomach. She turned to look only at Mikael and Benzi. "Takisha has been taken. We believe it was a Royal Fallen as Bisha did not recognize the symbol on the uniform or if it was a uniform."

Dillon interjected, "What do you mean you don't know? Now we have two rogue gods running around with unimaginable power!"

"Adam is not rogue at this time," M replied, never looking at Dillon. She inhaled and exhaled deeply while rubbing both her temples. "He will not be a problem. At this time, the EGU have regrouped and will start hunting for anyone responsible. We have to find Michiko as soon as possible so we can find Takisha."

She stood with no shoes on as her heels were lost during the last fight. Her ruffled suit set was torn and dirty as she reached out her hand to Mikael. "Come, I will get us to the safe house faster."

"I will meet you all there," Dillon said, abruptly releasing his wings and disappeared into the sky.

Mikael stood staring at the reddish pink tinted sky, turned to look down at M. "I have a feeling this isn't going to get easier."

"Mikael, nothing is easy. It's how you respond to it that will determine the efforts needed to solve or eliminate the issue," she said.

Benzi pushed up from the wall she was standing next to. "This is so boring. I can't wait to get to a spa! FYI, I feel Michi. For some reason I can feel the need to get to her. But I can't. I'm not sure if you know what I mean."

"No. We have to go! Both places we were led to were traps. I know it! There is no reason why they would have come for Takisha unless they are looking for Michiko too," M said to Benzi.

Mikael contemplated what M said. "Melchorde, we saw Michi. She was here with Niko and another being. How would she have known we would have been at either place?"

"I don't know, Mikael. There is no way they could have been as prepared for us as they were. These are outskirt recruiting centers. There shouldn't be as much activity out here as it is," M replied. "Come on. Let's get with the others and make a plan to find Takisha and Michi before Adam makes our situation worse."

She rose from her forced slumber. Shaking off the eerie feeling from being knocked out, Taki stood and assessed her environment. She was in a small room with just a bed and wooden door. No window, and the air was much heavier than it had been her first time in Otherside. She started checking her pockets and then remembered the dark stranger from earlier had broken her phone.

She glanced at her smartwatch and noticed there was no signal to send a quick text to Chike or Adam. She got up to check the door, but then it slowly began to open. Taki watched as a beautiful fair-skinned woman walked in the room, causing Taki to sit back on the bed. The woman had dark curly hair that stood like a bright red cloud around her head and face that sharpened her almond shaped red eyes that matched her hair. She was dressed in a black leather pant suit that hugged her small curves in the right places but not tightly enough to disrupt her movement if she had to fight.

"So, the beautiful Taki Mashiro, or should I say Takisha Williams. You know, if I didn't know any better, I would think you are one of us. Your aura is freaky! I love it," Seraphin said to Taki, taking a standing position diagonal from Taki to block the door.

Taki immediately sized up her new acquaintance. "Well, you know who I am. So, who do I have the pleasure of meeting today? Why couldn't you just invite me over. Kidnapping is not really nice nor does it say friendly,"

"Consider this a little family reunion. I won't reveal all to you, but I needed to see you for myself. I can't believe those two didn't see it.", Seraphin said gazing at Taki. "Father is going to be so interested in this!" She sneered as an eerie feeling crept up Taki's back.

"I will say this. You don't know what you are involved in, little lady. Well, you are not as little as I thought you would be. You are tall. Where do you get your height from?" Seraphin asked.

Before Taki could respond, Seraphin answered her own question. "Let me guess, your father?" she added with a smirk.

"How do you know me?" Taki asked curiously. She had a little bit of power left over from siphoning Adam earlier and noticed this woman was not an angel. She gave off an aura that reminded Taki of M but not as cold.

The woman giggled and folded her arms. "Who doesn't know the HUMAN charge of the former Queen? You are very popular in these parts. No one ever really knew who or what you were. Glad I do now."

The woman moved to leave and Taki jumped up. "Why did ya'll kidnap me? You can't make me stay here!"

Seraphin turned to respond then stared at Taki for a good two minutes before speaking. "Stop being dramatic. You are not kidnapped." She sighed. "What Father does will determine how long you have to stay here. Get comfortable. FYI, NO one will ever find you. Even with that little watch. Get relaxed for the time being. Take a nap. We will discuss more later." Seraphin walked out, leaving Taki alone.

****

Melchorde led the group through the large door and saw Bisha, Chike, and X sitting down in an area in large wooden chairs with purple and gold cushions. "I have to go. I will return so we can regroup and find Takisha and Michi. When he returns, do not let Adam go off on his own looking for Takisha," she said before instantly disappearing.

Mikael, said, "Chike, for some reason I couldn't reach you. I thought our phones functioned here?"

"Aye! Mikael, sorry my man." He pulled his phone out of his pocket. "My jack is busted. We were getting it in today! I didn't know the EGU had so many soldiers in their ranks. We were ambushed something serious. That's how that mysterious motherfucker got Kish."

Dillon added to Chike's story, "Well, we ran into Ms. Tanaka and that half-demon. They were at the other location for some reason. That's when Adam chased them and led us to an ambush as well, leaving us to fight while Ms. Tanaka got away."

"How did Baby G leave ya'll then?" X interjected.

Mikael answered, "Adam led us away from the building not realizing we were already surrounded by an EGU unit as well. These were not recruits. These were more seasoned soldiers and required more attention than we expected. Especially with Adam disappearing in the middle of the fight."

"You should have seen how he popped up on the scene looking like a fire-breathing demon hunter." X laughed. "He was almost spitting fire while he spoke, he was so angry. This was before Bisha told us what happened. He knew immediately."

Bisha added, "Yea. That was scary. The whole area was melting. But I still want to know who took Taki. That attack was a surprise. One minute she and I were going to the treetops trying to get away from all those EGU soldiers and next thing I know, there's an explosion and Taki was pushing me out the way of a ball of light."

"Kisha pushed you?" Chike asked while he was adding up all the stories. "Sounds like the EGU anticipated both places being attacked. They underestimated Michi while we were led into a trap by whoever fed us the information about how we could catch up with Michi."

Dillon looked at the younger angel. "That about sums it up. This puts us back at square one with finding Michi and then no idea how to find Takisha."

Immediately interrupting the conversation, the squeaky voice of Michi called out to everyone, "Did you all miss me!" Michi, Adam, Niko, and Putzin all arrived, startling Mikael and Chike while X and the two Shinigami felt the shift of them coming.

Benzi and Bisha rushed over to Michi fawning over her as if she was their child while Adam went to chat with Chike, Dillon and Mikael.

The room was booming with chatter from everyone catching up with Michi and trying to understand who Putzin was just as M returned with a grim look on her face.

"All, I ask that you save the reunion and catch up for later. I have returned with some news. Takisha is currently in Hell. It has been confirmed, that is why Adam can no longer sense her. Also, I verified that Daikoku and Lieutenant Zerrick are back here in Otherside. It was his superiors who coordinated the ambushes today which leads me to believe that we are dealing with two different Royal Fallen Crests and multiple EGU factions. We are caught in the middle of a war between these two and Takisha is one of their pawns in all of this."

Adam's eyes danced with flames as his body radiated a mass amount of heat that began to scorch the stone under his feet. He asked, "Then how do we get to Hell to get her, and why would she be caught in their war?"

M with gritted teeth. "I was only able to find out that she was no longer on this side due to a favor that was owed to me." She sighed. "Unfortunately, that is all of the information they would give me. But I do know that the Royal Fallen Crest that employs Lieutenant Zerrick is involved in today's events and possibly Takisha's capture."

"Why would the lieutenant want the other human girl? He just learned of Michi's attack, let alone her friend Taki was in the area," Putzin interjected. "I don't know where you people are getting your info from, but the lieutenant didn't take ya'lls friend."

M, as if just noticing the tiny demon, looked down at it with her brows furrowed. "Why is this creature here? He is one of their minions. He could be the one that led us to the traps."

"He actually is." Adam came to stand in the middle of the floor. "I willed him to tell me who he was and what he didn't tell Michi. He works with the EGU and wants to use Michi to get rid of his bosses, as he put it."

Mikael walked towards Putzin from where he was standing next to Dillon and Adam. "So, who is your boss and why do you want them gone?"

"My boss is Isis and she is a sadistic bitch that makes my life a living hell," Putzin answered Mikael while covering his mouth. "Why the hellfire do I keep doing that?"

Adam responded, "I'm not the only one that can make you willfully to answer truthfully." He looked towards M. "So, what do we do now? You know I am not going to wait for ya'll to find Kisha. You might as well tell me how to get there myself."

M scoffed, "I know. That is why I will make the arrangements for a team to go there to save Taki while the others concentrate on finding Daikoku and eliminating her as a threat to Michiko."

Michi was surprised at M's take on the situation. "You agree that I have to stop them?"

"I do not agree on you taking down the EGU. That would cause another power struggle issue that we do not want to see. The EGU helps keep the hierarchy in Hell in place. But I do believe we have to stop Daikoku. Unfortunately, she has the EGU to work at her side," M replied to Michi.

Dillon added to M's statement, "The EGU has other factions that will not take kindly to the disruption of their bases. If this lieutenant is looking to move up in rank, the others will not like his way of moving up or their responsibility to clean up his problems."

M ignored him and continued, "Michiko, take Benzi, your anchor, the creature, Dillon, and Chike with you to defeat Daikoku and the lieutenant." She paused before adding, "You know how important it is to not start an all-out war with the EGU Faction of the East." She directed her last statement towards Dillon. "Mikael, Adam, Bishamonten, and Xeno will come with me to find Takisha," she concluded.

Benzi pouted, "Why does Bisha get to always travel with white eyes?"

"Isn't he handsome, Benzi! All these fine angels Taki was around by herself! They lucky I got Niko, because, hmm. Hmm. Hmm. Is all I can say!" Michi squealed and laughed with Benzi.

Adam glanced at Niko. "How bro? How?"

Niko shrugged his shoulders. "She's cute."

M sighed and rolled her eyes. "I thought Mikael coddled Adam. Please do not blow Otherside to Hell, Michiko." She looked at Michi and then Dillon. "I will find Takisha and we will all meet at the Castle of Angels. If needed, have Michi find Adam or me for help."

Mikael walked up to Dillon while everyone else was saying their goodbyes. "Are you okay with this plan?"

"Yes. I wasn't going with your group. This is the best plan if you want my help," Dillon sighed.

Mikael chuckled. "I know. I was checking to make sure you were good with going with her plan—"

Dillon interrupted him, "I know how to be cordial for the sake of the mission. Now, stop holding us up and we will be in contact when it is time," he said, walking off to stand next to Bisha.

Adam shook his head, "He is so damn mean and antisocial."

"He wasn't always like that," Mikael said.

"I'm tired of hearing that. I mean come on. What happened then?" Adam said to Mikael while waving at the excited Michi as she kept waving at him.

Mikael looked at Adam and smirked. "You are just as silly as she is," he said, watching the other group disappear for their mission. "That, my boy, is a story no one likes to tell. One day I guess I will have to tell you if things keep going the way they are."

"What are you talking about there, Mikael? Are you ready? We have a stop to make before we head to Hell." M walked up to the two men.

M looked up at Adam. "Where we are going, I do not need you to lose focus on why we are there. This place isn't Otherside. We will have to fight for our existence to retrieve Takisha. We will stop at Lucy's shop, as this was considered a neutral meeting place for the last of the information we need. Tell me now if any of you need to change clothes. I tell Takisha all the time she can be dressed decent, even when handling business." She looked Adam up and down. "And do you all need to get more weapons or anything before we start on this journey?"

"I'm ready! I was able to reup when we got back here on my weapons so, I'm good. Baby G here is not putting on no suit, Mel. I'm good with my uniform, not a scratch on me from earlier. I haven't been this excited about going there since I was a kid," X said, excitement pouring from his voice.

Mikael shook his head. "I remember those times. Like I used to say, this is not a field trip!"

"Wait, what? You used to go there when you were little?" Adam questioned.

M interjected their conversation, "This is not a time for reminiscing! I already reached out to Lucy and she is prepping for our arrival. Bishamonten, come. Your fighting spirit will be needed for this trip!"

BAD GUYS MOVE

"Well, what do we have here?" Lieutenant Zerrick looked down at the injured angel lying on the ground. He circled the young, battered angel, "So, what were you doing out here, little birdie? You know this is too far for your kind!" He stepped on the scout's hand, bending over with his sword in his hand and slowly running the blade through the angel's chest. Eliminating the last of the discovered scouts.

Zerrick stood up. "Is that all of them?"

Daikoku came to his right. "Yes, Lieutenant. He is the last one we caught scouting this area. I believe he is connected to the angel General Xeno, judging by the purple and gold symbol on the scout's chest. Would you like to pursue this?" She was hesitant to ask, as she knew Xeno was connected to the former Queen Melchorde.

"No. We will finish up our work here before our departure back to the Eastern Headquarters. We will regroup once we get there and reassess our plans," Zerrick said, walking through the brush area without looking at Daikoku.

He was leading his men back to the base that was attacked earlier. Once his group collected the information from the basement area and got the remaining EGU soldiers to follow him back to the headquarters, he would begin developing his new plans.

Zerrick knew while he was under the eye of Cressius Crest, his plans of taking over EGU were at a halt. He figured once he got back to HQ, he would get rid of Daikoku, as her plans were beginning to bore him. He began to think that he could claim the Shichifukujin as his own.

He smiled while walking back to the debris of the once large EGU training center. "Daikoku, I haven't asked what you think our next move should be?" he said, curious to what the Shinigami was thinking.

Shocked, as he hasn't asked her opinion on anything since their encounter with Michi, Daikoku said, "We need to find Michiko. Once we do that, we can continue with our plans."

Aggravated that she was still thinking that way, Zerrick replied, "And why do you think that should be our next move?"

"That is our goal. To find Michi and get the plans we made come to fruition. Nothing should be considered an obstacle. I have the power to do this!" Daikoku said fiercely while the air around her hissed with power. "I will not be defeated again!"

Zerrick finally looked towards Daikoku. "Ah, there it is. You are humiliated and can't think properly. Michiko is no longer the pursuant. She is the hunter. The fact that you don't believe you are being hunted makes me question your resolve. Come, let's see what else you have to show me." He walked past her to continue ordering his guards around to collect the artifacts and items from their experiments in the basement. He knew once he checked in with his general, he would rid himself of Daikoku and create a new plan of taking over the Eastern EGU and Otherside.

****

"If you two weren't my sons, I would return you myself." Seraphin walked into the twin's prison.

Both Dante and Deuce rose to greet their mother. Dante huffed, "I take it you are here because Grandfather decided to let us loose? His version of punishment is quite disturbing."

Deuce added, "Seriously. He is one sick bastard." He remembered how the last mental brutalizing session was worse and caused him to pass out at the pain.

Dante chuckled, "Yea. Your bitch ass went out like a punk!"

"At least I wasn't screaming for my daddy!" Deuce turned to stare fiercely at his twin.

Dante turned to hit Deuce. "You mother—"

"You both are some little fucking bitches that need to shut the hell up!" Her shout echoed across the room. Seraphin smoothed out her clothes before starting again. "Damn. Still act like fucking children. Like I said, I would kill you both if I didn't birth you two myself." The conviction in her voice sent a chill down both demons' spines.

She whipped her head to the side to move some of the cloud of red hair out of her face. "Now. I came here to tell you two imbeciles that Father has granted my request to let you two go. Of course, under the terms that you will capture and return your Aunt Melchorde back to the Golden River Realm to answer for her crimes."

Both males folded their arms in front of their chests and cocked their head to the left with furrowed brows. Dante responded first, "Mother, as much as I want that bitch dead myself, after that last fiasco in Earth Realm, I do not think we can defeat Melchorde."

Deuce added, "We all know Aunt Mel is not coming back here. For once, I agree with this one here." He pointed at his brother.

Seraphin rolled her eyes and moved to sit in a chair that was in "I know for fact that Father knows you two will fail. The best thing you two can do is get more information on these gods returning. I believe that is what he is going to use you two for anyway." She paused, then stared at them. "I think Father knows of my plans for you two. We have to be very careful on making sure that we move in the best INTEREST," she emphasized the word with air quotations, "of the family at all times."

The twins understood what their mother meant, as they knew their release was temporary as long as their grandfather could use them as he saw fit while also watching the twins' every move.

Dante pondered for a second. "Well look, I got an acquaintance in the EGU over East that can assist in giving me men and access to lots of information. He owes me a favor anyway."

"I think we should check on our friends in New York. See how Taki and that fire boy are doing," Deuce said while remembering his fight with Taki, getting lost in his thoughts.

Dante rolled his eyes while throwing his hands in the air with frustration, "See, you always thinking about the wrong shit! Why—"

"Wait, no. He's right, Dante. I think that is a great idea," Seraphin interrupted Dante's outburst. "I have a job for you anyway that is connected to your idea. We might as well use Father's plans for you to our advantage. Regardless of what, our plans may be delayed, but definitely not over."

She stood up. "Number One, go and get the EGU under your belt. That will help us in the long run anyway. Don't screw this up! We don't need any issues with the Cressius Crest. You know they are out there trying to consolidate their own power."

Dante responded. "Mother, I will get it done. Don't worry about them. If I do run into any issues, I'll just call lover boy here to get his future wife and make the family play nice."

Deuce retorted, "Oh please, don't make me. I didn't want to marry her then and most definitely don't want her now. She's fucking crazy, Mother. I am good to do whatever for the cause but that."

Seraphin smirked at the memory of her son not wanting to partner with the Cressius Crest's youngest family member. The girl was just like the twins, the first and last birthed in darkness naturally from the Fallen. Dante couldn't stand the girl, and the alliance didn't last long once the relationship turned sour. Good thing was Cressius Crest knew they were no match for Gilden Crest.

"Well Number Two, I won't promise you won't have to play nice. For now, make sure you have your twin's back. Always. Hmm." She raised her right eyebrow while staring at Dante.

He looked down. "Yes, Mother. Now, what else is it you wanted me to do?"

"Dante, is there anything else you need? Your brother and I will be going to make a visit to your Aunt Jade before he starts his mission." She reached up to touch the oldest twin's, "I love you, my son. Bring hellfire with you everywhere you go."

He bent his head down to have his forehead touch hers. "As hellfire will burn everything in my wake," he said, disappearing from their sight.

"Okay, Number Two, just wait until I show you something that I stumbled across! Your Aunt Jade will be shocked and it will start your journey in finding out more about the god situation. From what I learned there is another one that is causing chaos for the Cressius Crest over in the Eastern Region."

Dante looked at his mother. "Another God? Hmm. That's interesting."

"That's what I said. Father is still gathering information, but there isn't much out there that is verified. So, find out what you can. I have a feeling that my little surprise may be connected to all of this. Come, let's go say hi to Jade."

"So, we're really going to Hell?" Bisha asked X.

"I guess so. I haven't been in a really long time. So, hopefully it smells better from what I remember," X replied walking down the street to Lucy's shop. "Mike, any idea where Adam and Mel went? I've noticed them two sneaking off lately. Should I be worried?"

Mikael walked alongside Bisha and X on the dark Brooklyn street that Lucy's shop was on. "I don't know. That's not the first time I've witnessed that either. It has something to do with the fact she can make him disappear when he's not in his right state of mind."

"True, but come on. Now they got us waiting outside like we creepers," X replied.

Mikael responded, "No one said we couldn't go inside." Reaching the store front, he grabbed the handle to the doorway. "Come, I thought you would be happy to see your girlfriend." He laughed while walking in as Bisha followed, leaving X standing outside.

X followed after a moment. "Don't get cute. She ain't giving it up yet! So, I ain't claiming it!"

Lucy joined the group. "I keep telling you sexy white eyes, you're not mine anyway. Be patient." She winked at X. "Bishamonten, it is my pleasure to see you on this side. I'm surprised to see you here with Mikael and X."

Bisha smiled. "Luciana, what a pleasant surprise." She bowed. "I know you already knew you would see me. But that was a good fake surprise."

Lucy laughed. "Aww, man. I thought you would have believed me."

"Your aura altered, so I could tell you were lying." Bisha chuckled back.

"Well darn it!" Lucy snapped her fingers. "I taught you that trick! Don't be using my own stuff against me. That's me getting lazy being around humans so much. My only "Other" excitement arises when these angels and gods come to play with me."

Mikael smirked at her. "Well, I am glad we bring excitement into your life, Luciana," he said, repeating Bisha's use of her full name.

"I knew that wasn't going to get past you, Mikey!" She laughed as she locked up the shop's front door and began to lead the group to her back room. She walked around the glass counters, leading them through her orange and red beads.

X followed last in the group and noticed the strong aura coming from the crystal ball that sat on the counter. He saw the clouds and lightening were darker and stronger than before. He called out, "Hey Lucy, what's up with your ball over here? Looks like it's about to break." He stopped and walked up to it to stare curiously.

Lucy returned from the back, leaving Mikael and Bisha sitting at a table. "What are you talking about?" She walked up to the ball and noticed more activity than usual. "You know, I've had that thing over three-hundred years and never saw so much activity as I've observed recently. I don't know. This freaky little thing's been drawn to me ever since I found it in this creepy bazaar in Otherside."

X stood up from leaning over with his brows furrowed. "You've been to Otherside?"

"Duh, I'm a demigod. Of course, I've been to Otherside." She laughed at his question.

X leaned back on his right leg while folding his arms. "I mean, I just told the rookie that no humans been to Otherside. It looks like you've made me a liar."

"Get with the times. Otherside is booming in business with Earth Realm dealings. You angels don't know the half of what's going on. I will admit, I don't go often. It takes a lot out of me to get there. I built this place here because it helps me get to Otherside when I need to," Lucy said.

X asked, confused, "Wait. What? You built this place?"

Lucy sighed. "Yes. This place is over one of the rifts to get to Otherside. I created a barrier around this place to protect it from people that shouldn't have access to Otherside. Like you know, if they are not connected or touched, they can't cross anyway. I discovered a while ago I can cross. The trip takes a lot of my energy, going and coming back. You witnessed the aftermath before."

X considered what Lucy explained. "Oh, wait. When I found you passed out that time? I remember that. It felt fucking weird in here and I could tell you were drained."

"Yea. I had just come back from Otherside. I did a roundtrip and it cost me. I was lucky you found me. I still can't get over how I was able to go the Castle of Angels and not get fatigued."

X walked up to Lucy to stare into her eyes. "That's because I took you there. My power healed and helped you over there. Don't worry about the small details. Quit playing with me like you don't know how I really am." His white eyes looked as if they were staring into her soul.

Lucy enjoyed his banter and flirting. After her vision last month, she knew she could no longer tease or play with him any longer. She thought to herself, *if you only knew, handsome. She is going to bring more than you will ever need. I doubt I can withstand her tie to you.*

"And there she goes again. As soon as I get close to you, I lose you. It's all good." He stepped away. "Come on, chica. Let's wait for Mel and Baby G so we can get this trip to Hell started."

****

Michi grabbed the demon in front of her. "Where is your lieutenant?" she growled, causing the demon to tremble as she was fully gold.

Group One had already recuperated and started on their part of the mission. Michi and Niko had reached the inside of the target base that the group had decided to attack, leaving Chike, Dillon and Putzin in the front of the building near a warehouse fighting other EGU soldiers.

By the time they made it back to the Castle of Angels, they had a chance to regroup and Dillon had his scouts collect some information on where they would start to search for Daikoku. They were now in the eastern part of Otherside searching for the EGU Headquarters. Dillon's lookouts confirmed that the angel scouts left behind to collect info on the base that Michi was found had returned to the light. Most likely by the EGU soldiers sent to protect the place found them and assassinated them.

Michi spoke to Niko, "Do you think they are here? I'm actually tired of looking for them!" she said shaking her head. 'Where's Putzin?"

"He's with the other guy, Chike," Niko answered Michi.

"Oh okay. So, come on. They will have to catch up," she said just as a group of EGU soldiers began to descend upon her and Niko. She guarded herself as the group rushed towards her and used her small frame to duck low and used her body as a way to knock the full group of soldiers to the ground.

"I love this! I am really solid gold. I was like a pinball!" Michi jumped up excitedly. "Now where is Daikoku?" She grabbed the collar of a downed soldier. "Where is she!?" she shouted in the EGU soldier's face.

Niko grabbed Michi's shoulder. "Come on, baby girl. We will not find them that way."

Just then, Putzin joined them.

"Hey! The angels and the Shinigami are almost here. They sent a lot of soldiers here. This one is not too busy. That's okay! I will be right back," he said, leaving Michi and Niko to fight the oncoming soldiers.

Michi pissed at Putzin for leaving, but witnessed Benzi and Dillon approaching her and Niko's fight.

Benzi shouted out to Michi as she moved closer, "Where are all of these toy soldiers coming from? What did you find here?"

"Nothing. Absolutely nothing. They are not here. Who told ya'll they were back in Otherside?" Michi said, frustrated, and began to scream.

Niko, not wanting her to go into another fit, said to her, "Michi, calm down baby. It's okay. We will take care of this." He stroked her face and rubbed her back.

"I am calm. I want to find her!" She looked up at Niko as a thought that wasn't hers came to her mind. *I know he thinks he's going to get rid of me. He doesn't know who he's dealing with. I will have his head before he takes mine.*

Niko stared at her, confused, and kissed Michi on her forehead. "Who is trying to get rid of you, Mich?" He pulled her forehead to his. "You're getting lost again."

Benzi walked over to Michi and Niko. She turned Michi to her and saw that her gold eyes stared off as if she were gazing into space. "No, her and Koku have synced. This used to happen when Michi was a little girl and has gotten stronger I see." She held Michi's hand and started a chant.

Michi's eye began to flicker back to her brown color. "You know, I am starting to understand what's going on. Ebisu told me for some reason Koku's powers are syncing with mine. He said I must defeat her."

"Ebby never got along with Koku, so of course he would say that. Honestly, do you know how you would feel destroying a Shinigami?" Benzi looked Michi up and down curiously.

"Benzi, you don't know what she's done. To the others, to angels, to Otherside beings, to humans and whoever else. She is evil. I have to stop her. She killed my whole clan. How can I not put an end to her?" Michi asked and turned to walk away. "Come on. I think someone can help us find these two without us looking all over the east. We will have to go back to Earth though."

Dillon slowly walked around the rubble of another warehouse, stepping over the demolished boxes and storage items. "Who are you speaking of, Michiko?"

"You know, you and M really act just alike. She, and now you, are the only beings I respect to call me that," Michi said.

Dillon shifted himself to fix his tattered clothing and responded Michi's comment, "That is your name. You and Takisha got too used to your nicknames," he scoffed. "Now, who is this person?"

"You will see when we get there. Come on, gang," Michi said, grabbing Benzi's and Niko's hands while everyone else crowded around as they left Otherside to return to Earth.

Michi laughed as Dillon looked around. "Why are we standing outside of Lucy's shop?" he asked.

Michi was still laughing. "Because we need to speak to Chain Face. I don't know what else to call him since that's what everyone else calls him."

"Oh, wow. I get to see him too," Chike responded.

Dillon raised an eyebrow and leaned backwards since he was surprised Michi knew of Chain Face. "I didn't know you knew of this character. I, for one, haven't met him officially."

Benzi was now confused. "Chain Face? Who is that?"

Michi responded, "You'll see. He is coming right about now!"

DIDN'T SEE THAT COMING

Dante arrived at the Eastern HQ and searched for General Krio. He requested an audience with him and the Isis, knowing if he wanted to be able to fight Melchorde and the angels, Dante and his brother would need an army. Why not use an already powerful army? At least that's what Dante thought.

"Your Highness, what a wonderful surprise for you to approve my request. I appreciate your presence," Dante said, laying on the flattery.

Isis rolled her eyes as she rested her head on her left fist. "Now, if those words were coming from your twin, I would believe them. What do you want?"

"I am asking for permission to work with General Krio with an issue in your territory. Nothing that involves your family or interests. But certain actions can happen in your lands, and I want to be clear that these acts are not acts of war on behalf of the Gilden Crest," Dante stated confidently.

She called out to one of her servants, "Have General Krio come here," then got up from the couch. "How is your twin anyway? It's a shame what happened." She smirked.

Dante chuckled at the attempted seductive look Isis gave him, "I am not my twin. I'm sorry you scared him off with your antics."

"Hm. Scared him. He was the one that was hollering all the time. I think he wasn't…" She paused. "Used to being with a woman that was just like him." She was now standing next to Dante whispering in his ear just as General Krio walked in with a few of his soldiers with him.

Dante was happy to see Krio, as the general was one of the few demons the oldest twin called a friend. "Krio! Hellfire brings the pain!"

"Bringing the pain is my duty, so help me hellfire!" Krio stated back and pulled the twin into a hug, a saying the two started during their training days. He introduced his soldiers, "Dante, meet a couple of my most trusted lieutenants, Zerrick and Laurel. I promise they would give your Riot Hell Squad a run for their horns."

Dante laughed, "I doubt that very much, but I didn't come here to catch up. I need some help."

"Oh wow. Prince of the Underworld coming to me for help?" Krio playfully responded. He also knew if Dante blatantly asked in front of Isis, then he had to be serious. "Well, you know I owe you my allegiance, but at this time I'm assisting Your Highness here in the rebellions in this region. I am unable to leave my station."

Dante smirked. "That is why I asked for Ice Royal's presence. To see if she would think our issues align and whether we can assist each other," he said, moving to sit across from Isis in the large arm chair that sat across from the long couch Isis and Krio were sitting.

Dante continued, "As you both know, the bounty for the former Queen of the Golden River Realm, Melchorde, has been put on hold by the leader. At this time, it is ordered by my family head that only members of the Gilden Crest can claim her." He paused to observe their reactions.

Both the general and Isis sat emotionless and quiet.

"Unfortunately, she has become a bigger problem, as she has associated herself with our new enemies, a new god and a former demon captain, Trystan," Dante concluded.

Isis sat up. "That's interesting. I heard about his treachery. Didn't you have something to do with that as well, handsome?" She raised an eyebrow.

Dante replied, "My brother was in his training group. Unfortunately, I had to help him, and that caused Trystan to reveal his true intentions for my twin. Glad I was able to save him." He added on the big brother protection.

"Well, it sounds like the Gilden Crest has some problems they need to handle. How do our problems align? I don't see the connection." she said to the twin.

He leaned back. "Well to my understanding, there is a second god attacking your bases as we speak, correct?" He grinned, raising his left eyebrow.

Isis squinted her eyes at Dante. "It seems you are well versed in the issues at hand in this area."

"Of course, I am. I have a lot of information that I think will help the both of us. Like I said, it is confirmed that another god has returned to our realms. I had first hand encounter with the first god that has caused you issues. I believe he maybe the Sun God. I am working on getting more information on the second one as well. I believe your Lieutenant Zerrick back there has failed to capture her numerous of times." Dante stated as he looked back at Zerrick.

Krio leapt up from the couch and glared at Zerrick, "Excuse me? Zerrick, you know of this second God?"

"Well, goddess, it's the Shichifukijin that is amongst us. I am surprised your lieutenant hasn't told you since he thinks he can use that power for himself," Dante said, sitting back to look at the general and the lieutenant glower at each other.

Isis stood up. "Everyone but Dante and General Krio, out!" she ordered.

****

Jade paced back and forth staring at her sister and nephew in shock at what she just heard. "You both are risking a lot with what you did. Seraphin, how stupid could you be!" she yelled.

"How dare you! That's exactly why I didn't want to tell you! How stupid could you both be! How could you not know!" Seraphin scoffed back at Jade.

Deuce stood and watched his mother and aunt go back and forth over the events of the past few months.

He interrupted the two women, "Wouldn't it be better to take her back to that shop in New York? It's considered neutral for 'Others.' We can also start the second part of our plan. Mother."

"What shop?" Seraphin questioned. "I am pushing my luck by being here anyway. I just wanted you to know." She turned to Deuce, "Bring hellfire with you everywhere you go."

He replied, "As hellfire will burn everything in my wake.", staring at his mother as she disappeared back to their realm.

Jade watched him in disgust. "I hate that damn saying. Makes no sense if you want to take over anything after Hell. Can't have hellfire burning everything in your wake." She huffed. "Fucking cornballs."

"As we will burn all for you too, Aunt Jade," Deuce retorted. "What do you think of my plan? Send Taki back to them unharmed and we will be fine."

Jade looked at him. "Number Two, you really think she won't find out it was her own sister? Also, what you and Seraphin were talking about is crazy. There is no way."

"It explains a lot, actually. I know what I saw. But that's not the main thing. We have to get the Eastern Region back in order. The Cressius Royals are not in the best position with the rebellions in their area. Add the second god to this, and we have more than a full plate of issues," he responded.

"The Shichifukijin. Damn it, Michiko," Jade said out loud.

Deuce looked directly at Jade with a raised brow while he rubbed his forehead. "You know who it is?"

"Number Two, bring Taki in here and let's prep to get her back to her people. We are in preparation for our own war with the Rovin Royals."

Deuce chuckled, "Don't tell me they are still upset at grandfather's stance on eliminating the exterminated Narby Crest? That was over a thousand years ago. Come on, we have better families to conquer."

Jade said, "It doesn't matter. Both need to be dealt with immediately, again. Bring Taki here so we can get her ready to go."

Deuce smirked. "She's right here, Aunt Jade," revealing Taki using his power. She was passed out on the floor near where Jade was sitting.

"I see your little magic trick isn't just a trick anymore? I heard what you two did a few months ago. I'm surprised Father let you two out. I would have returned the both of you. Relatives or not. That was dangerous. You two could have ripped the veil between all the realms. Then what?" Jade said angrily.

Deuce shifted his body side to side with his head down, as he was uncomfortable with his aunt scolding him. "We got major punishment from Grandfather and tongue lashings from our mother. I don't need the gospel from you too!"

"Gospel? The Gospel!" she shouted. "You two think you have what it takes to do what Father does. You have no idea. You two and your mother are too foolish to see that he realizes what you all are up to," Jade spatted back.

"Aunt Jade, I have no idea what you're talking about. All my mother has done was keep the best interest of this family as her first priority. My brother and I assist her with her duties." Deuce smiled at the end of his sentence.

Jade bent down and reached out her right hand, hovering it over Taki's body reading the passed-out Taki's energy signature. "You know, I would believe you if I didn't know who my sister and your father really are. You can speak that family shit if you want to, but I know what ya'll did in Earth Realm was your first plan failing. It's okay. Father will most likely send me to return you all. Get her out of my sight."

She stood up and walked away from her nephew. Angry at what he and Seraphin told her about Taki, angry at them for their lies and attempting to take over Hell on their own. She turned around before walking through the wooden door to leave the area. "You better not touch or harm her, Number Two. You and your mother are really weighing my patience. I do not have time nor the energy to deal with whatever schemes you all are concocting. Take Taki to the neutral zone and then take your ass back to your mother!" She left the room leaving Deuce with Taki.

SO, WHERE TO?

"You agree with my terms, Isis?" Dante said to the general and the Cressius representative.

Krio was not happy with what Dante was proposing, but at the same time, he knew Dante wasn't lying about what he told him about Zerrick. "I hate that I have to find out about my men and their antics from an outsider. Sorry, you're my guy, but this is appalling."

"Believe me, I know. I'm surprised you haven't heard about any of this. I was shocked to hear about the first one, but this second one is too close. The fact that you employ one of the original Shinigami of the Shichifukijin can't be a coincidence," Dante said.

Isis responded, "I have heard some rumors of this Daikoku. That is one of the reasons I requested her to my realm to see if she could help with the rebellion and then our recent Earth Realm issues. To my understanding, she and Zerrick were doing excellent. The past twenty human years, she has been very helpful. But I do know that she was using that time to try to find her own way of gaining more power. She isn't as smart as she thinks she is." She stood up to leave, bored. "To be honest, I don't care about the god issues. It will make things a bit more interesting. Those pansy angels were getting boring anyway. So, you can handle this as you see fit, Dante. Just know you owe the Cressius a favor. Do as you please with Zerrick and Daikoku. Also, the EGU resources of the Eastern Region are at your disposal. General Krio, you continue concentrating on the rebellions with the Vole Crest and make sure that all your connections know to follow Dante."

"Yes, Your Highness. I will take my leave." He bowed to Isis. He moved to leave and spoke out to Dante, "You seriously owe me one, you slick motherfucker." He chuckled and walked away.

****

"Howdy!" Chain Face appeared next to Michi. "I knew you would be here, so I came. Only thing I can tell you is that they are about to attack the Hida Clan. Ask the handsome uncle why would they attack their friends?"

Michi was confused as she looked at the messy stranger wrapped in his dirty blanket. "You can take a bath sometimes, buddy!" She moved to stand in between Niko and Dillon. "Now, why the Hida Clan? I thought the Hida clan was associated with the EGU." She looked up at Niko. "Do you think your uncle will help us?"

"I doubt it, but if he said they are about to attack them, then we need to go now, Michi. Can you please take me to my uncle?" Niko said in a panic.

"Okay! Next stop, guys!" Michi said, ready to leave.

"Oh no, Missy. Don't leave yet. Let's chat for a sec!" Chain Face shouted out. "Now, make sure you listen to those that talk to you! They have a lot of information for you. Also, don't make things harder for your friends. Make sure you are not acting off of revenge. Things happen to learn from them. You and Sunny boy are something special to us, so don't go messing it up!"

Michi pondered on what the man was saying to her. "Well. Tell them to not talk in circles and to let me get my hands on Daikoku. I feel it, Chain Face! She is supposed to be with me."

"I get that, beautiful. But don't cause more problems trying to solve others. That's just going in circles. Get to the root and it will make it all go away," Chain Face responded to her.

He looked over at Niko. "You will not find all the answers that you are looking for, but you will get the closure you need. Everything that happened, she did to protect you." Chain Face wrapped his blanket tighter.

Dillon finished analyzing the being in front of him. He knew he couldn't do a reading on the creature since Mikael told him before that this being could sense when another was reading his aura. "So, are you going to tell us your real name and what you are?"

"Now what fun would that be?" Chain Face responded refusing to look in Dillon's direction. Chain Face whipped his head to look at Chike, he continued, "Your master will be happy with your progress."

Dillon could feel the energy permeating off of the dingy man wrapped in a blanket. "Now, stop with your partial revelations. There were a few of you—"

"Aht Aht, no you don't. Now you can go. Had to stall you for a few minutes. Now you will find the answers you seek for the two that are hunting for you." He disappeared, leaving the group standing out in front of Lucy's shop.

Michi peeked at Dillon. "Who do you think he is?"

Dillon turned to look down at her. "You are keen with your senses. I will reveal that after I have another conversation with this Chain Face. He purposely blocks all energy access to him. I do know all the info he gave you were revelations he's seen, so take heed to what he said."

Niko was still worried about his uncle. "Can we go now? Especially if this guy is right about my family being attacked."

"Yes. Come, Michiko, do you recall how to get to Niko's house?" Dillon asked.

Benzi interrupted his question as she felt a sudden shift in the air, "I don't think it will be hard, but did ya'll feel that?"

Chike spoke up for the first time, "It's been going on for a while. It's weird."

"Let's go!" Michi said as her stomach began to churn with eerie feeling while she held onto Niko.

NEW PARTNERSHIP

"So, do you really think you half breeds can go against the real thing?" Dante stared at Touma with a raised brow and smirk.

Touma was surprised at this demon approaching him in his home, unsure of why the EGU and Daikoku were suddenly following this stranger that Touma had never seen before. "I find it insulting that you are demanding information and my men and I don't know you. I have never had an official agreement with the EGU of the East. I am just acquaintances with Lieutenant Zerrick. So, until I speak with him, I have nothing to say to you."

"I know for a fact that it is your nephew that has her. I know he is protecting her. Tell me where he could be," Daikoku said to the head of the Hida Clan.

Touma stood in his study looking at the two beings in front of him. He understood his position and knew that he would sacrifice a good number of men in a fight with them. He looked out the window, "My nephew doesn't know the makings of this world. It's been a secret to him since he didn't show any signs of being one of us. At this time, I do not know where my nephew is. After that debacle at my other home, I have not had any contact with him." He turned to face Daikoku and Dante. "Even if I did, I doubt very much I would tell you. I am not sure how my family could be of much help. How about you take EGU and demon business out of my area?"

"You are a very defiant man. But you can't believe you can go against me?" Dante scoffed at the clan leader, "Lieutenant Zerrick is no longer with the EGU due to his insolent ways. Now, I am in charge of this faction. I want you to hand over all of the information that you collected on Michiko Tanaka and her friend Taki Mashiro."

"All of the information was given to EGU already. Also, it seems to me that Zerrick was right about you. The next big power and you immediately jumped ship," Touma said to Daikoku, who stared at him.

Dante responded to Touma's taunt, "No reason to be jealous she didn't come to you. To be honest, you probably don't even know who she is. She definitely needs the real thing." He smiled towards Daikoku. "Now, give me what I want, or your pass to be move freely will be revoked. Unless you want to find out who I really am?"

Touma was not moved by the demon's threat. "I do not care to find out who you are. You full demons think that because we have human blood running through our veins that we are weaker. You do not know how many of your kind had to be reminded that this is our realm and your presence here is temporary and borrowed."

"I do not like your tone, Touma Hida. Are you threatening me? Honestly, none of this has anything to do with you. Giving me what I want will leave your family out of something you do not understand." Dante walked closer to Touma's desk.

Touma's guards moved towards Dante as Touma put his hand up to stop them, "No need. I will handle this." He looked towards one of the guards. "Do not interfere. Unfortunately, these two are a lot more powerful than what we want to deal with right now."

"I am glad you recognize that. I am tired of talking. Where is the girl and your nephew?" Dante said, using a bit of power to split the desk in front of him in half.

Touma dashed towards Dante swiftly. "Now, that was disrespectful. I will tell you nothing." He finished his sentence with a swing to Dante's head and a lower kick to the larger man's right leg, causing Dante to fall to his knee.

Touma's guards instantly rushed to surround Daikoku to begin the fight between the Hida Clan and the EGU.

****

"Come on, wake up!" Deuce spoke out to Taki. "Get up!" he raised his voice, attempting to wake the still passed out Taki.

Groggy and not recognizing the voice or his surroundings, Taki asked, "Where, where am I?" She rubbed her head. "What the hell?" She slowly sat up rubbing her eyes, trying to see and assess her environment.

"You're most likely low on energy. Traveling between realms can be exhausting when you're not used to it," Deuce spoke out, standing over Taki in an empty parking lot.

Taki recognized the voice and jumped up then backed up. "You motherfucker!" She looked around and picked up a small rock. She ran towards Deuce, using her right hand to swing to hit him. As he dodged, she quickly used her left hand that held the rock to land a punch to Deuce's left jaw, splattering blood on the pavement.

"Yo, and to say I was about to be nice! I could have left you in these dirty streets!" Deuce said to her, spitting out more blood. "You're lucky I like you. Any other human, I would have killed." He paused and added, "Then again, are you human?" He gazed at Taki intensely.

Taki looked around, attempting to figure out where she was, and saw her tattered clothing. "Look, one minute I was with M and them, then some random creepo snatched me and was sniffing me and shit. Then some bitchy ass woman I met had me locked in a room like I was a prisoner, and now I am waking up to your black ass!"

"What the hellfire did you call me?" Deuce chuckled at the way Taki described him, still rubbing his face from her punch.

She turned to walk away from her foe. Unfortunately, all of the power she had siphoned from Adam was gone and she doubted he could feel her right now due to her being so low on energy.

"Why are you here?" she asked.

Deuce still hadn't decided what he would tell Taki, as Jade was mad that he was involved with returning her. She told him she would stay out of his and his mother's plans.

"I haven't decided yet. I could kill you and leave you for that Sun God to find, or you can play nice and tell me what I want to know," Deuce said.

She gazed at him with an evil smirk. "Tell you what, shit face? I doubt very much I have anything for you!"

"Don't play hard to get. If I told you who you really were, would you help me then?" Deuce smiled back, showing his white teeth. The twins had skin like black leather that sometimes blended with their uniforms. The coiled noodles that were their hair reached Deuce's neck, which he swung back to stare at Taki again.

Taki was curious to what he was talking about but still pissed he had tried to kill her. "You think I will tell you anything? My past doesn't matter. I know who I am today. So, I will pass, thank you very much." She walked away towards the garage exit.

"Do you really think it will be that easy, princess?" he said with a raised brow.

She stopped as she realized Adam still hadn't come for her. "Okay. Come on with the games. Tell me what you want. Obviously, I can't leave on my own."

Deuce chuckled, "You are too funny. Well, glad you realized. Don't worry. You are safe and I will return you to your friends. But you have to do me a favor. I want to be able to follow you at all times. At least while you are with Aunt Mel."

"You know, I know that you are related to M. I'm not surprised though. Your brother kind of acts like her," Taki said noticing the slight differences between the two such as Deuce's shorter hair and no scar on his chin.

Deuce cocked his head to the side, confused. "Really? Most people can't tell us apart at all. Most of the time only my mother and Mel could tell the difference. What do you see?"

"I don't see anything right now, but I notice how your hair doesn't fully touch your shoulders like your brother's and you are slightly shorter without the scar, I can tell that," Taki said, chuckling and then leaning on the column.

Deuce walked closer to Taki to stand directly in front of her. "I can't wait until you find out the truth. Melchorde probably doesn't want you to know. Regardless, let me follow you. I promise I won't cause any issues."

"Why would I let you secretly follow me? For what? Are you crazy! A would fry you like the chicken from the spot down the block from my house. I don't understand what you want," Taki responded.

Deuce looked down at Taki intensely. "To make sure Melchorde eventually comes home. As long as I have you, she will have no choice but to come back."

Taki stood up from the column and looked up at Deuce. "Look my g, that last time you got me was because you stabbed me from behind. Let's not act like I wasn't kicking your fucking ass before you did that bullshit." She paused and then stood on her back leg. "So, let's be clear: I am not nor will I ever be fucking scared of you."

"You're not huh?" Deuce questioned as he began to release some of his demon power. His body grew bulkier, and the beige looking horns started to protrude from the right and left sides of his temples while his hands and feet stretched to larger lengths.

Taki jumped back with a yelp. "What the fuck!"

"I guess your last statement wasn't true at all," Deuce snarled through the larger teeth that showed. "You will get used to this if you don't decide to cooperate."

Taki grabbed hold of the column behind her and began to pull herself up to a defensive stance. "You're still a piece of shit and I will kick your demon ass if I have to!" She slightly trembled due to the power that was permeating off of the creature in front of her.

"You feisty human women are cute. You don't know how many I took as they fought," Deuce said. "I love—"

He was interrupted by a smack in the face by Taki. "How dare you! I don't give a damn what you are, you fucking leather faced dirtbag! Don't you dare casually talk to me about raping women!"

"What? Rape? You mean to share sexual favors with humans? You disgust me! Don't ever insult me!" Deuce replied with repugnance.

Taki stood back. Head cocked to the side with her hands on her hips. "Then what you mean *took*? You just said took as they fought!"

"Oh. I meant sacrifice. You don't know how many people sacrifice the women of their lives to get what they want. Humans are pathetic." He smirked at her. "Don't ever think I would do such a thing with humans. That is for the special breeds to create the half-breeds for us. That is all."

She stood shocked. "You are fucking disgusting."

"And you are going to help me, or that little room you remember will be the last place you'll see." Deuce smiled again.

Eyebrows raised in shock, Taki responded, "You piece of shit. So, you *do* have something to do with me being kidnapped? You motherfucker."

"I actually don't, but I figure why not use it to my advantage while I can. All you have to do is allow me to be your shadow. No one will know. Not even Aunt Mel," Deuce replied to Taki's insults.

Taki began to pace back and forth in front of the twin. "What the hell? That's nasty! I do have a boyfriend and I'm a girl, I use the bathroom! How the hell can you be a damn shadow! Adam will know.

There is nothing that can get past A now. His powers are out of control.”

“You humans always think of the smallest of details. Like any of that is important.” He scoffed and continued, “That’s another thing. I want to assess your boyfriend and see what we demons have to deal with now that the Sun God is back.”

Taki still paced. “You’re basically asking me to be a spy for you! You have to be out your fucking mind. I don’t give a shit where you take me. I am not letting you spy on my people! You obviously got me fucked up!” She kept pacing, feeling light headed and sweaty.

“Loyalty is what you all call it, right? Well, okay. I’ll let you believe that. But now, you have no choice—” He looked and noticed Taki had stopped pacing and her face looked grayish with sweat forming. “Taki!” He called out as he caught her, stopping her fall to the ground.

Taki began to scream uncontrollably as the blue flames formed around her, causing Deuce to let her go. He jumped back as he watched Taki’s body begin to burn with blue flames engulfing the area around her. The energy in the air began to cackle as Taki’s screams got louder.

Immediately feeling the shift in atmosphere, Deuce disappeared, leaving Taki to her rescuers.

He watched in the background as M and Adam had come to Taki when they felt her power explode. He thought, *What the hell was that? That did not feel like the Sun God’s power?*

THE HIDA CLAN

"Oh snickers!" Michi yelled out as she and the rest of the angels, Benzi and Niko all came into a big melee. Niko had requested Michi to take them to his uncle's clan's headquarters.

The Hida Clan's main building was located in Staten Island in an area not too far from the Bayonne Bridge. Touma always wanted to keep their activity lowkey, as the clan's front was local business men that only participated in low level crime.

Michi looked at Benzi. "We have to find Touma Hida!" She grabbed Niko while Benzi followed Michi with her own power.

Dillon looked around at the EGU fighting with what looked like half-demon creatures to him. "Are these half-demons?"

"I believe so, General! Remember, Michi's anchor is connected to them, so I will guess that they are all half breeds," Chike responded.

Dillon replied with disgust, "This is blasphemy. They should not exist. Especially in Earth Realm. This is a hazard to humans." He marched to a halfling, "You are not supposed to exist!" He used his sword to hack at the halfling while throwing his small knife at the EGU soldier's head to meet its forehead.

Chike was surprised at Dillon's sudden outburst since he knew Niko was a halfling. He wondered what made him think there weren't others. "Dillon, we have to find Touma. This is a distraction. We have nothing to do with this."

Dillon, after taking out about a dozen EGU and halflings in the common area of the first floor, said, "True, but how did they exist and we didn't know?"

"I was taught that the halflings are the ones that keep the demons and Otherside's creatures connected and in Earth Realm. Unfortunately, neither the demons nor Otherside beings are playing by the rules anymore," Chike answered.

"Let's find Michiko. We can't let her out of our sight. We will discuss your teachings later." Dillon motioned for Chike to follow him as Michi appeared right in front of him.

She grabbed Dillon and Chike. "Let's go, slow books! I found Touma! I saved him, but his clan is gone," she said, causing them to appear directly in front of a fallen Touma.

Touma coughed as he attempted to sit up. "Niko. What are you doing here and with the Tanaka Clan's princess? I guess what those assholes were saying was true."

"What assholes?" Niko questioned as he attempted to help his uncle stand. They were all now standing in Touma's office where Daikoku and Dante forced him to submission.

"Unfortunately, they took over the Hida Clan and now he and Daikoku are out using my resources to search for you and your girlfriend here," Touma said, pointing to Michi as he stood up with the help of Niko.

Niko shrugged his shoulders while shaking his head, he asked, "Why me? What do I have to do with it?"

"They mentioned you are protecting the girl. I guess they figure if they find you, they find her," Touma responded as he began to search his office for something.

Niko wanted answers from his uncle but knew this wasn't the right time. The only words he could muster was a question that always plagued him: "Did she ever love me?"

Touma spun around quickly, shocked at what his nephew was asking him. "Boy, you don't know the story. That's why we are here."

Michi interrupted the mini family reunion, "Well, I'm right here! Why did they run! I'm looking for their asses!" She clapped with joy. "I got it right again!"

Niko shook his head and smiled as he walked over the broken chairs and table to reach Michi and grabbed her hand. "Yes, you did, baby. But let's find out what my uncle knows before you start wanting to go looking again."

Touma spoke towards the couple, "When did this happen? I see that look, Niko. And she activated your demon powers."

Niko looked directly at his uncle. "Uncle Touma, Michiko Tanaka is the Goddess of Luck, the Shichifukijin. I am her anchor. We're still trying to figure out what all of this means, but that's what it is. Also, I am helping Michi find Daikoku and Lieutenant Zerrick to stop them from trying to kill Michi so Daikoku can become the Shichifukijin herself." He stopped and looked over at Dillon and Chike. "Anything else to add?"

Dillon said, "Besides these beings that shouldn't have been created?"

"Um. No. You summed it up good," Chike said, nudging Dillon for his rude remark.

Dillon was not backing down. "I will have to consult with the higher ups about this."

"I think they know already," Chike said, shaking his head at Dillon's traditional angel mindset that his teacher had told him about.

Michi interrupted everyone, "That was a great summary, but what are we doing now to find them?" She stepped towards Touma to gaze intensely. "Where did they say they were going?"

Touma looked back at the petite woman with raised eyebrows. "They were going to Taki Mashiro's last address to see if you were there. We've been keeping tabs on you for the EGU for at least a month before you disappeared. We were just told not to make contact. My assistance for the EGU was for my friend Lieutenant Zerrick. Which I believe has returned to the fire." He put his head down to mourn.

"What? They killed him?" Niko responded, surprised.

Touma answered instantly, "Lieutenant Zerrick is no longer a threat to you. You have a new threat that Daikoku has aligned with. My men confirmed his name is Dante and the EGU of the Eastern Faction have given him all reigns. He has control on this side until the matter with Daikoku is solved."

Chike asked, "Dante? Was he dark skinned, tall with a chisel chin and coiled shoulder length hair?"

"I know it's him by the chiseled chin comment. His chin and cheekbones were so perfect he could model for Vogue," Touma said to Chike.

Niko was shocked by Touma's description of Dante. "Uncle Touma, that is a surprise you would say that."

Dillon interjected, "He is the youngest child of Seraphin, Princess of the Golden River Realm. His grandfather is Belial, the leader of the Gilden Crest."

"He's what? He is breaking all of the Royal Fallen Families' creeds! I have to notify my family of this defiance!" Touma said, wondering who gave the order for the Gilden Crest to attack the Hida Clan.

Dillon spoke to Touma for the first time, "Gilden Crest is not part of the Eastern EGU Faction. He is obviously working with another Royal Fallen Family."

"The leading Royal Fallen Family in the Eastern Region of Otherside is the Cressius. They are currently at war with the Vole Crest due to the Vole Crest wanting to take over the Eastern Region. This is causing some of the Otherside beings to choose sides or run to the Angels," Chike added.

Dillon clenched his jaw and side-eyed Chike at how much he knew of Otherside matters. "Xeno was telling me that he had to verse you on Otherside affairs since you were a new recruit. You sound very rehearsed in the affairs of demons and angels. We still don't know who your master is."

"No, but ya'll know I am on your side. I'm an angel. So, come on D, don't get weird on me now," Chike replied.

"So, that's it! The Cressius is using Dante to defeat the Vole. Just so that bitch Isis doesn't have to get her hands dirty," Touma said to Chike and Dillon.

Niko spoke out, "What does all of this mean? You just spoke about individuals we have no idea about."

"This universe is much bigger than you think, nephew. There are rules and hierarchy that are followed to make sure the universe flows the way it's supposed to," Touma said. "I will say again, now including the Gilden, they are breaking the creeds that bind the rules of Hell and Otherside."

Michi spoke to Touma, "Can you help me find her? They will make all of our lives bad if either one of them gets what they want." Michi looked up from picking the polish on the nails. "I so need a mani," she pouted and added, "What does this Dante want? Taki told me about him and his brother. He's a twin."

"There's two of them!?" Touma shouted out.

Dillon spoke out, "Yes. Did I forget to mention that he is an identical twin to Deuce? Number One and Number Two is what their aunt used to call them."

Chike said, "Well, this is interesting. So, now there is a three-way war with the Royal Fallen Families with Otherside, with the angels and humans in the middle?"

"Earth is our playground. The humans are not even a factor in this war," Touma answered the angel.

Dillon responded to Touma, "You are not full demon. How are you involved in a war that you were never a part of?"

Touma laughed at Dillon's question. "That is the problem with you angels. Just stuck. Do you really think that the Angel vs Demon, good vs evil fight still exists? This Earth Realm is so full of gray that we thrive without recruiting. We demons, yes even we halflings, have plenty of human affairs and Otherside connections."

He stopped moving around and bent over to punch a hole in the floor. He picked up a phone from the created hole. Placing the phone to his ear, he spoke in Japanese fast and intensely.

He hung up. "Let's go, Niko. You will meet your real family. Others," he said speaking to Benzi, Dillon and Chike, "outsiders have never seen what you've seen in over a thousand years. I am a third generation halfling and take pride in my heritage. My grandfather led this clan during the Hellfire Wars about a thousand years ago. We are the few of the halfling clan to have survived."

Dillon questioned Touma, "The Hellfire Wars?"

"Yes. This war involved around fifty Royal Fallen Families. We still don't know what started it. At least my family doesn't, but there was a time where all the Hell realms where fighting to unite Hell to take over Otherside," Touma said to Dillon.

Benzi spoke up from listening, now joining the conversation. "For some silly reason, Dillon, a lot of the Royal Fallen believe that if they unite Hell and Otherside versus Heaven that they will have a chance to take over Earth Realm."

"That is pure blasphemy! No being, creature or wretched demon should ever think such wickedness," Dillon responded.

Benzi laughed at his tensed emotions. "I get it. But you can't stop someone from believing. Just like we can't get you angels to start thinking in current times."

"Benzaiten, do not test my patience today." He scoffed then walked to a corner of the office and stood alone.

Benzi yelled out, "Come on, Dills! Don't always be the salty one. You're worse than—" She immediately stopped speaking as she saw the murderous glare from Dillon along with a chill that crept up her spine as her eyes met his. Benzi mimicked zipping her lips. "I will be quiet now."

Chike was confused at their exchange. "Touma, do you mind explaining to me where we are going?"

"You're good. Let's break the ice in this motherfucker. I can't believe that bitch is pulling this shit!" Touma replied to Chike. "FYI,

I am connected to the Lohmer Crest, they are my ancestors. Now we are going to Otherside to have a chat with a family member there to make sure I am not starting a war that could lead to another Hellfire War."

Michi finally got out of her head and joined the conversation. "Well, I don't care if we start a war or not. Dante and Daikoku are going down. Dante should have minded his business!"

Niko stood next to Michi. "Yes, baby. Let's do this right. We will not do what we did going to Otherside, okay?"

Touma looked at Niko inquisitively. "You've been to Otherside?"

"I have. Michi and I were searching for Daikoku and Zerrick. I told you, I am helping her end this," Niko said to his uncle.

Touma was proud of his nephew but a little jealous, as he always wanted to show him. He was very fond of Niko, but wouldn't allow himself to get close since he didn't show signs of being a halfling. "Okay. Let's get to the basement. We have access to our own rift."

Dillon's eyebrows raised but he stayed quiet. Benzi shook her head and called out to Michi, "I hope we do not get involved in all the bullshit that's going on in the universe!"

LUCY'S HELP IS OUR DUTY

"Well, it looks like we are still waiting on those two. Let me try to call Baby G and see where he and M are," X said to the group as they sat at the table where Lucy used to do tarot readings for customers.

Bisha spoke to Lucy, "So, tell me. How did you get involved in all of this?"

"Looks like reunion stuff will have to wait. They are here," Lucy said to Bisha. She got up and walked through the beads of her store. "You shouldn't be able to do that in here."

Adam, M and Taki were in the main area of her shop. M responded to her, "We traveled here by Adam, so I take it your barriers can't stop the Sun God."

"We found her on fire in some random garage in the Bronx. Out the blue, I was able to feel her pain. She's passed out now, so we need to regroup at the Castle. I attempted to heal her, but there's nothing physically wrong," Adam said to the group as he watched Mikael, Bisha and X walk from the back.

M answered him, "She's passed out due to her traveling through different realms multiple times. She should have never been in Hell. And we still don't know who took her!" She was just as frustrated at the situation as Adam.

Mikael asked, "Did you assess the location you both found her?"

"I did what I could, but I was more worried about Takisha here," M replied to Mikael.

Mikael replied and looked at Bisha, "No problem. Bisha and I will go do some investigating. No way she was just left like that."

Adam spoke through gritted teeth, "She probably burned them. Somehow, she was able to tap into the blue flames we saw before."

"What?" Mikael asked.

"Elaborate," Dillon said.

Adam kept Taki in his arms as he spoke. "A few months ago, at M's house, when Kisha was mad at me, she had an episode where she controlled blue flames and burned M's whole dining room. Including melting the gold silverware. M said it was real gold too. That wasn't the scary part. I didn't recall her siphoning any of my power.

So, we are not sure where the blue flames came from. Usually when she has my power, she doesn't control the fire. She subsides it."

Mikael spoke after Adam. "We are all still confused on how this god and anchor thing works. She obviously siphons your powers, but we don't know what she can do with them. Stop treating her like a porcelain doll and let us get to the bottom of all of this."

"You want me to allow ya'll to make her some fucking science experiment?" Adam retorted. "Look, we will figure it out. For now, let's be happy we don't have to go to Hell." He breathed into Taki's hair.

M responded, "Very true. Let's reconvene at this one's home while Taki rests." She pointed to Adam. "We can confirm with the other group if they found Daikoku and solved that problem."

"We still haven't solved our problem yet," Bisha said to the group.

Lucy added, "Right. I had made arrangements for you all. I think it is too late to cancel." As she finished the shop's phone rang, and she walked over to the landline telephone. "Hello, you're worse than me. Thank you. I appreciate the help though." She hung up. "Welp, we're good. They knew. Don't freak out. They are like me on the psychic level. Not a demigod though," she added at the end to make sure Mikael didn't think she was hiding others like her.

M stood at the counter next to Adam, who was carrying Taki. "You are correct, Bisha. We still have our problem. We have no idea who took Takisha and if they are still after her since it seems she escaped on her own. When she wakes up, we have a lot of questions to ask."

Mikael looked at Lucy. "Anything interesting to share?"

"Please be careful. This is going to end brutally. Sad part is, we can't do shit," Lucy responded.

Mikael glanced over at her with a raised brow, "What do you mean?"

"Just like Adam had to find himself, Michi does too. Unfortunately, she's going to have to learn a lot in a short time. Her journey is different from them all, as she will have to decide who's worth it," Lucy answered Mikael.

Lucy walked up to Bisha and held her hand. "Trust her. She can handle everything she has been taught. She is now the Goddess of Luck. She is no longer a god in training. Treat her as such."

"Thank you, Luciana." Bisha bowed and thought about Lucy's words.

Lucy finally looked at X and noticed he had that longing in his eyes again. "Xeno, please be patient."

X looked over at her. "Man, listen. I don't have all day. You know I'm a busy man with me saving the world, defeating demons and training gods. Tell her ass to come on. Before I fight fate on my own." He licked his lips with a penetrating look in his eye.

"Papi," Lucy whispered, as she was still very much attracted to him.

Mikael said, "Bisha and I will go and investigate now. We will meet you back at Adam's. I'll also try to contact Dillon or Chike to see how things are going on their end."

X glanced at Mikael with an evil look and flayed his hands in the air. "Fine. I'll go with Baby G and sexy chocolate to the crib and call the others. I'll be bored around these lovebirds by myself." He said, squinting his eyes over at Lucy.

"I think you will be fine, Xeno," Mikael said to him. He pushed Xeno to stand next to Adam as he stood by Bisha. "We will meet back up later as soon as possible. Be safe, and may the light always follow you."

****

"Look at this here. Nothing but humans. Do you morons have any idea where this Taki character is?" Dante yelled out at the EGU lieutenant that had given him Taki's address.

"Unfortunately, she hasn't been seen around these parts in a long time," the lieutenant spoke to Dante.

Dante walked up to the lieutenant as he stood in front of him on a rooftop in Manhattan. "Did you find any more information on Michiko?"

The lieutenant shook his head. "Last known location was in the Eastern Region of Otherside. I am not sure why we are in Earth Realm."

"Because this is where I want to be, asshole." Dante kicked the lieutenant off the roof, causing him to slam into a parked car below and immediately disintegrate, returning to the fire.

"Now any other questions on what we are doing?" Dante looked around at the other EGU soldiers that were in his presence. He watched as all shook their heads in unison. "Good."

Daikoku opened the rooftop door and began to approach the area the soldiers and Dante stood. "Any luck? I believe I may have some. She is still looking for us. I believe you may have had Touma Hida join her side." She spoke as if she didn't believe Dante had to humiliate Touma and take the clan the way he did.

"He can't do shit without his clan. I'm in charge," Dante huffed. "If he does side with the angels, he will be the laughing stock of Otherside and every realm in Hell."

Daikoku stood in front of Dante to take a good look at him. During their time together, he had been very progressive in trying to find Michi and taking power in the Eastern and Western Regions. If she didn't know any better, she would think he is accumulating power for himself and not the Gilden Crest.

"Why are you helping me? A being of your stature doesn't seem like the type to help a Shinigami," she said as she and Dante stood at the edge of the rooftop. Her orange, red and black kimono glistened in the moon light as she admired the stranger that was helping her.

Dante turned to her, still dressed in his black leather EGU uniform. "I'm not helping you. I am helping myself. Assisting you is putting my plans in motion. Just complete your task and you will have free reign."

"Oh really? That is a tall order. How do you know I won't betray you?" Daikoku seductively said while moving in closer to Dante.

Dante raised his right eyebrow. "I am not interested in your personal gifts. You women of power always use seduction. I am not interested. My partner will know how to bring me to my knees without me seeing her naked first."

"Well. I thought we both could have some fun. I am a very sexual creature and like to share with my partner as well." Her eyes moved towards a female EGU soldier.

Dante noticed her look. "I'm good, love." He bent down and whispered in her ear, "If I decide to fuck you, it will be just us. I doubt you want anyone to see how you will submit to me." He stood up and walked away. He stopped to speak to the soldiers, "I will return. I have a little trip to make alone. For now. I want a definite location of Taki Mashiro and Michiko Tanaka. Once found, let me know and we will continue with the plans to assist with the rebellions against the Cressius.

"Okay. How long will you be gone?" Daikoku curiously asked.

Dante replied, "Don't get any ideas, Ms. I WANT TO BECOME A GOD. Don't think my help is free. Like I told you. You might be able to help me." When he finished, he used the door on the roof to leave Daikoku on the rooftop.

Again, another creature in charge of her getting the power she deserves. "I will not allow anyone to get in my way. Zerrick paid the price for getting ready to cross me. I will not allow this one to fuck me over either," she mumbled under her breath. "You all are dismissed. Regroup back here in approximately an hour." She watched as they all began to descend through the door, leaving her on the roof alone. Daikoku opened her kimono and revealed the all-black jumpsuit that showed her small curves. She enjoyed the breeze for a minute before looking at her watch. "Time to hunt.

AND SO, IT STARTS

Daikoku walked into her quarters that she built long ago. This castle rivaled any EGU stronghold in Otherside, equipped with the latest Earth Realm technology and with enough space to house an army. This place has been her sanctuary for over two thousand years. A place that sat on about fifty acres of land on the ends of the southwestern area of Otherside. A quiet area that not many creatures, angels or demons care to be, so Daikoku used it to her advantage and created her own stronghold, unbeknownst to outsiders.

She has built her own small army and trusted people throughout her years with Tor Crest. Her latest work with the other families has expanded her reach and helped her achieve a lot of ground on finding Michi and possibly getting her own piece of Otherside. She'd grown **tired** of being treated as a Shinigami within the hierarchy of the Royal Fallen and the places of Otherside that had their own pecking order. *I will take what's mine. I've worked too hard this millennia to let a brat take it.*

"Your Highness, you have returned. Your men await your order." Her trusted companion, Bridel, came through the entranceway of the massive bedroom. Red, gold and black were the colors that stood out the most. A good portion of the large furniture and decorations were covered in real gold and red stones.

Daikoku stared at herself in the mirror, eyeing the jumpsuit that hugged her petite body. "I just came from the East, and those morons have no idea what is going on. They are so worried about the petty bullshit that they don't see they all are about to lose everything."

"Did you find Michiko?" Bridel asked.

"I did and lost her. The little bitch almost absorbed me. I still don't know how she knows that power. It's okay. If my plan works against the East, then I will have the power I need to grab Michi and take her to become the Shichifukujin myself. She doesn't deserve all that power. It is I that can properly wield and be the true Goddess of Luck!" Daikoku slighted panted after her rant.

Bridel, seeing her master's change of mood, said, "I have some good news. All the plans for the strongholds that will be attacked and headquarters are set. They won't understand what is going on. By the time they do, it will be too late. Everyone is in place to attack."

"Great. Thank you. I am going back to hunt while I can. That Dante thinks he's smarter than me, but I will let him think whatever. By the time he looks up, I will be leading the Cressius and the Eastern EGU." Daikoku turned to look at Bridel as her eyes glowed fiercely causing the Shinigami to seductively walk towards the other woman and kissing her passionately.

****

Michi looked shocked at the large men that walked next to her, Touma and Niko and Bisha. She whispered to Niko, "Where did that little demon go? I haven't seen him at all!"

"He said he would be back and never returned when we were at the last stronghold," Niko replied.

Michi squeezed her eyes and closed her fists. "Oh! I am so going to kill that little horned demon!" she shouted walking next to Bisha.

"Sorry we had to ditch the Angels. We could not bring them here at all. They would have been attacked onsite," Touma spoke to the group. "Now. Please let me speak and do not act weird. We are speaking to my official family of Otherside."

Niko looked a little surprised and questioned, "So, what are they going to do for us?"

"Unfortunately, I have to tell them what happened and see if they can do anything about me losing my title of clan leader. I am also here to ask for help against Daikoku and Dante. They officially attacked the Hida Clan while murdering a friend."

He began to lead the group down a large hallway. The walls were covered in blue and gray pictures that depicted different beings. "These are pictures of my ancestors. Feel lucky. Not too many see these."

"Wow. I'm glad I get to experience this. I really thought you guys were two-bit Yakuza weirdos," Niko replied.

Touma chuckled at his nephew. "You don't know the half of it. We've been a part of this universe for a long time. Involved in every aspect of its creation. It is said that we are relatives of the most powerful Fallen. We are not sure how true that is, but our family has built its own legacy. As of now, our connection to the Lohmer Crest keeps our connection here since not everyone below was good with the demons mixing with humans. Let alone letting them cross to Otherside."

Touma stopped walking and bowed in front of a large doorway that led to another dark large room. As he began to walk into the darkness, lanterns began to illuminate the walls. The group consisting of Benzi, Michi, and Niko followed him and stopped at the exit, as Michi and Benzi were not allowed to continue.

"Hey! What is this? I can't get past the entranceway!" Michi called out.

Benzi added, "Neither can I."

"Wait a second," Niko inquisitively stated. He let go of Michi's hand and continued to walk through.

Touma called back, "It looks like our family doesn't want them involved. Stay here and we will let you know what the next move will be."

"I'll be right back, baby. Don't worry. We will get back to it as soon as we can," Niko said to Michi, kissing her forehead and following Touma.

Michi watched as Niko and Touma walked away, observing the lanterns disappear as they vanished in the dark.

"Well, this sucks. I was hoping to get a bath and some new clothes. I am so in need of a manicure and a pedicure," Michi spoke in Japanese.

Benzi clapped her hands, responding in Michi's native tongue, "Michi-ban! Me too! No one else believes me when I say that this is not okay. I need to get right before the next fight." She placed her hands on her hips and looked down at her disheveled clothing. "I've had this kimono on for two days! This is so unacceptable! All they do is fight! If we have to stay with these angels, they better get us spa services around the clock."

"Tell me about the angels, Benzi. Not the training version. Be honest with me. Ebisu told me to say that." Michi sat down on the floor next to the entrance.

Benzi chuckled, joining Michi on the ground. "Well, if you put it that way. They're selfish pricks that think of their mission above all else. At the same time, it is due to them that the light is still able to shine. Complete darkness cannot be all. Balance is everything, and neither side likes to acknowledge that."

"My books kind of speak of the universe that way. What is the mission they put above all?" Michi asked.

Benzi stood up. "Come, let me show you something. The reason why you can see through Koku's eyes is because we are one. I will show you through my eyes what I have seen. You don't have control over what you see. We will have to train you for that."

"It would have been nice for you and Bisha to warn me before. That used to happen when I was a kid," Michi responded, standing up to hold Benzi's hand.

Benzi scratched the top of her head while scrunching her nose, "I've never witnessed you do that. What have you seen?"

"Well, recently just Daikoku speaking with others. She's weirdly sexual!" Michi blushed.

Benzi snickered, "Weird and sexual shouldn't be in the same sentence. She is a bit different. Always strong headed. I would say she gives Bisha competition in the areas on bitchiness and strength." She cocked her head to the side. "You said Ebisu told you to ask me. So, you have the power to still see them individually? Wow. I'm surprised."

Michi held Benzi's hands tightly. "Benzi! I met Fuki! I see why you nicknamed him that! Jinny is funny too! He hates when I call him that though," she said staring into the air. "Hotei misses you. He said he would have loved this era in time."

"Wow. I miss him too. I am so sad at what happened. I saw it. I'm sorry." Benzi's eyes gleamed with love and tears. "He was my heart."

Michi continued to hold Benzi's hands. "Show me, please."

The two women stood in the hall as Benzi began to mentally project to Michi different parts of her existence from times before the Days of Hunts, during the Days of Hunts and the post war times to the present. Benzi showed the days of when the Shinigami assisted the humans and when they playfully sat around amongst each other and other angels and Otherside beings. The story began to show the tireless battles with the Angel Army and how Fukurokuji attempted to save them from defeat time and again until his defeat by Daikoku and the Angel Army. The mental projections continued with scenes of how Benzi and Bisha were able to survive with the Royal Fallen and Otherside as left over survivors. Some days good and others really bad.

Benzi and Michi still locked in place while Benzi continued to show her past to the goddess. Prior to finding Michi, Benzi and Bisha had become mercenaries for high-level demons and Otherside creatures. They gained enough notoriety for the thoroughness that they ended up the personal mercenaries for the Rovin Crest. They learned of Michi's birth through one of their assignments over twenty-five years ago. Bisha was in charge of eliminating the head of a Royal Fallen, as they were deemed a threat to her associates. After completing her assignment, Bisha told Benzi they needed to find the Tanaka Clan. She felt the birth coming.

Bisha had a vision of all seven of the Shichifukujin being birthed into one being. A being she didn't recognize but had an energy that was so familiar. She noticed the Tanaka's clan symbol in her vision and decided to go to them. To her surprise, the wife of the leader of the Tanaka clan was expecting and almost due to give birth anytime.

Benzi and Bisha decided to see if the vision would come to fruition and immediately noticed the pure energy that Michi wielded from the womb, a surprisingly alert baby at birth along with the ability to communicate mentally. Michi became their precious little god in training. The two Shinigami were able to convince Ebisu and had him come join them with the Tanaka Clan. The three Shinigami remained loyal to the clan for the sake of Michi and left Otherside to protect the young one.

Benzi's projection continued as the story showed the times that Daikoku popped up. There had been rumors about Daikoku and the things she did for the Tor Crest. Bisha had heard the gruesome and hellish situations Daikoku led with the associates she worked for, such as leading the Cressius's agenda with uniting Hell under their crest. Unfortunately, due to Daikoku's ambition for power and wealth, she was easily persuaded to work with demons and the darker creatures of Otherside after the Days of Hunts.

The Days of Hunts caused a rift in the seven Shinigami, as not everyone agreed with the way the gods were being purged. Fukurokuji, considered the leader of the seven, had realized that they had served their purpose and accepted his defeat, allowing the angels to defeat him. As he was their leader, he expected the others to follow, but to his surprise that did not happen. It was Daikoku that had led the angels to his location. She had made a deal with the angels for her safety, and she would lead the angels to the other six Shinigami.

By the time the Angel Army had attacked Benzi and Bisha, they were aware of the attack on Fukurokuji and Daikoku's betrayal. What they hadn't expected was her defection to the Tor Crest. It was Daikoku that defeated Hotei. Just as Benzi assumed, Daikoku had absorbed him, and his connection with Michi still existed. By a miracle, only Benzi, Bisha and Ebisu survived the last attack on them from the angels and Daikoku with the Royal Fallen. The three surviving Shichifukujin agreed to separate to not be caught by the angels or Daikoku. This led the three of them being separated until they were drawn to the Tanaka Clan during the birth of Michi.

The tears flowed down Michi's cheeks as she spoke, "That was beautiful, Benzi! I can't believe I just saw my own birth. It was wickedly amazing and lovely to watch. Especially watching through your eyes!"

"Michi-ban you don't know what it's been like to be Benzaiten. I can say I realized my true calling when you came into my life. I will forever be grateful." Benzi wiped the tears from her face as she held Michi in a hug.

The lanterns behind Michi began to light as Niko's and Touma's silhouettes began to manifest from them returning. Benzi said, "Looks like we will have to continue this conversation later. They are returning."

"I know. I felt them coming. I just wanted to bask in this feeling a little bit longer," Michi said as pieces of Benzi's life story played back in her head. She turned around still wiping the tears.

Niko rushed to her and held her face, planting light kisses on her cheek and forehead. "Baby, are you okay? I felt you while I was in there. You had me a little worried. What's wrong?"

"Hey, handsome I'm okay! Benzi just showed me something else I can do while also showing me the most beautiful things ever! I should show you! Let's—" Michi excitedly clapped her hands and reached for Niko's temple.

Touma interrupted her, "That will have to wait, Ms. Tanaka. My conversation with my family did not go as I thought it would." He spoke with his head slightly down. "There is nothing I can do to assist you. I have lost my seat as head of the Hida Clan of the West."

"Uncle, you still haven't told me what that means. They were really assholes! I can't believe they can be so damn stupid," Niko said towards Touma. He looked down at Michi. "We have to get out of

151

here. They started speaking some weird language I couldn't understand, but I doubt they have good intentions. Let's just say my demon senses were going off."

Touma looked at Niko with a long sigh and shook his head at the decision that the Otherside family member had made. "I do apologize, my nephew. Unfortunately, there are things you don't understand on this side. We are still reeling from the mistakes your mother made, so we are not trusted as such. Again, my nephew, I do apologize, as I will never hurt you. But I must do what is necessary for the family." He finished his sentence as the panels in the hall began to slightly turn, revealing EGU agents.

"Uncle! You motherfucker! You led us to a trap!" Niko yelled out, using his right arm to move Michi behind him as his head whipped around.

Michi moved back to stand at Niko's side. "Are you kidding me, Touma Hida? You already know who I am and what I am capable of. Do you really think you demons can stop me? I AM THE SHICHIFUKUJIN!" she said as her body turned gold and the power around her began to shake the room with the hanging pictures and the wall panels beginning to crumble around them.

Benzi stood behind the couple and watched in awe as Niko held Michi's hand, absorbing some of her god powers and turning into his demon state. This time his skin turned an all-goldish color with red hues that pulsed throughout his body. She stood shocked by his look but felt the pure energy that radiated between the two beings. "This is the Shichifukukin with their anchor. Well, I guess I can only do what I was created to do. That is to always serve the Shichifukujin," she said, turning her back to the couple to face the EGU soldiers behind them.

"You got our backs, Benzi?" Michi called out from behind her. "I am about to turn the front of us inside out!"

Benzi pulled her whip from her waist. "Princess, I will forever have your back. Now, as Taki say, let's fuck this shit up!" She rushed to the two guards that stood in front her and began attacking as she felt the fight behind her had begun.

Michi attacked a group of EGU soldiers with her smaller frame by swiftly cutting them up using the tips of her finger nails as blades since her body was solid gold. The group of soldiers immediately dropped and disintegrated into dust. Niko rushed through another crowd of EGU and attacked his uncle with his large claws ripping the suit of Touma. Starting the fight between the group with Michi and the Hida Clan's Otherside connections.

DEUCE'S PLANS

Deuce paced back and forth outside of Lucy's shop, as he was unable to enter due to the barriers placed by the demigod. "Fucking bitch! I thought being her shadow that would work! This one must be old school." He continued to pace as he felt his other half. "So, how are your plans going?"

"Good, actually," Dante responded as he appeared next to his twin. He stood on the side of the storefront and watched as Deuce continued to pace. "So, why are you worried? Your plans are not working out? What are you and Mother up to?"

Deuce looked at this brother, unsure of what he should let him know. "I'm supposed to follow the human girl to get to Aunt Mel."

"Don't call her that! That bitch betrayed us! She is no aunt to us ANYMORE!" He growled the last word, causing the air around them to stir. Dante wiped his leather uniform down in an attempt to calm himself. "Why are you frustrated?"

Deuce stopped pacing and looked at his brother as he felt the fury roll off of him. "You seriously have anger issues. I get it, but shit. All of this is giving us the opportunity to set our plans in motion again. So, calm yourself Number One." He leaned against the building and felt a shock of pain through his veins, as the brick had protection as well. "Who is this woman that owns this building? There is no way she is that thorough with protection barriers."

"She obviously is. I thought this was considered the neutral zone, but it is heavily protected against high-level demons," Dante said as he felt a shift of energy in the air.

Chain Face appeared in between the twins. "Whatever you do, do not follow the plans of your mother. She will be your demise."

Dante immediately grabbed his sword to swing at the mysterious man. "Who are you! How dare you speak of us as if you know us!'

"I am interested in what this stranger knows, brother. This one here is different," Deuce said, unable to read the energy coming from the being that stood in front of them. He looked at the dirty blanket that was wrapped around the stranger. Strange chains peeked from under the blanket that showed on his face, arms and feet.

Dante scoffed, "What can this dirty motherfucker tell us! He—"

"You are rude and that's why you will probably return to the fire!" Chain Face said to Dante. He turned to look at Deuce. "Make your own choices. Do not allow the ignorance and arrogance of others to lead you to your return." He disappeared from in front of the store.

Dante leapt towards the empty space. "You stupid motherfucker!"

"You know he is more powerful than he pretends to be. What he said is interesting, as we have been led by others all of our existence," Deuce said, pondering.

Deuce snapped his figures at his brother. "Don't let some stranger get you thinking! We were born to take the Hell Realm and the Otherside and lead them to take over Earth Realm. It is our duty and reason for existence to lead the demons against the angels in the next war."

"I know, brother. I know. Do you really want that? Is that something you wanted or was it drilled into us from our birth?"

Dante grabbed Deuce by his leather vest. "You will not falter! This is what we were born for! Stop second guessing! Follow this human bitch and capture the traitor so we can present her to Grandfather!" He released his brother. "I am going to continue my plans! You better get your plans together before I end up ahead of you, like always," Dante concluded and disappeared from Deuce's sight.

****

Taki rushed to sit up, as she was unsure how she ended up passed out. The instant movement caused her head to hurt and the last thing she remembered was the strange woman and the creep that was sniffing her were talking to her, and then next thing she knew she was in a garage talking to the twin that stabbed her previously. It was during that conversation she blacked out and only remembered a strange warm blanket sensation that had covered her body. And now she was waking up in another strange place, or so she thought.

"Where the hell am I now?" Taki felt around the dark to attempt to find some lighting. She was confused by the familiarity of the environment. She attempted to get up from the large cushion and the light turned on, instantly blinding her for a second. "What the fuck?" she yelped.

"Oh shit! Baby girl!" Adam switched off the light to the bedroom he and Taki shared at his penthouse. He hurried to her and grabbed her into a bear hug. "You had me worried! You wouldn't wake up. Wouldn't respond to me healing you. Nothing."

Taki was surprised at where she was and that Adam was in front of her. "Oh shoot! I'm home! I'm home." She squeezed him tighter. "Wow, this is surprising. I was just saying I was tired of waking up in weird places. At least this time I woke up at home!"

"Home. Uh? I like that sound," Adam playfully said and stepped back to assess Taki for any injuries.

"Don't make this about my mailing address, Adam. You have no idea what I've experienced in the last twenty-four hours," Taki responded and started swatting his hands as he checked her for injuries. "I'm fine, A. Where are M and the rest of the them? I was with her, X, Chike and Bisha."

Adam raised her arms and placed his hand on her chest while using his other hand to check her head for a fever. "Look. We don't know what happened to you. I want to make sure you are good. Stop playing with me!" He stared at her as the flames in his eyes danced harder.

He finished his assessment and stepped back, satisfied, "You look fine. And everybody is in the living room right now. I came in here to grab something, now you made me forget." His dancing flaming eyes turned to stare in thought. "Oh! That's right. They wanted me to grab your phone," he said licking his lips while gazing at Taki. "You know, they are in there talking. We have a couple of minutes." Adam began to take his shirt off.

Taki was standing on her knees on the top of the bed dressed in only a blue and gold push-up bra and panty set. She looked down at herself to see why Adam was staring at her. "Cut it out. We don't have time right now," she playfully responded as he dove in and began placing soft kisses on her neck and shoulder. She chuckled, "Come on, A. Let me shower real quick and throw something on so I can tell you all what happened. I would hate to have to repeat myself."

"You're starting to sound like M. You need to hang with me more. Before you start acting like her too," Adam said as he began making movements like a robot. "Okay. I will let everyone know you're coming. We need to get in touch with Michi too," he said before leaving their bedroom.

Taki jumped off the bed, startled by a vibration of what sounded like a phone. She grabbed the phone from out of her hoodie that was on the floor. "Hello? Whose phone is this?"

"You thought you would be rid of me that easily? I told you. You have to help me. If you won't, you will never see your friends again," Deuce's voice came through the speaker.

Taki huffed, "Your threats are not palpable. I told you I will not betray my friends. I told you whatever past info you have on me doesn't matter!" she yelled into the cell phone. "Leave me the fuck alone, creep!" She disconnected the call.

"What the hell does he know about me and how is he trying to get to Mel? I won't mention this to anyone just yet," Taki spoke out loud, removing the rest of her clothing to go shower.

LUCY'S AGAIN

Lucy paced back and forth as her latest vision caused her much confusion. "I don't understand. Why am I still involved?" She sat down on her stool as the bells to her shop rang, snapping her out of her deep thoughts.

"Hello! Can I help you?" Lucy spoke out at the strangers while they laughed and giggled walking into her shop. "Looking for something?"

The blonde woman spoke first, "Have anything to make my husband stay awake when we're having sex?" She began to laugh hysterically.

The lighter, blonder, straight-haired woman spoke to Lucy, "I am looking for something to make a man fall in love with me!" She clapped her hands with joy.

A dark brown curly haired woman that was with them interjected, "Look. Can we get the fuck outta here! I feel so weird in here and ya'll don't need no damn love potions." She started to push her friends towards the exit.

Lucy immediately felt a rush of energic power calling to her from the woman that spoke. "Hey! What's your name, beautiful?"

The brown-haired woman looked back. "I'm sorry. My friends are intoxicated. I will get them out of your hair," she said, holding her inebriated friends on each side of her as they giggled and attempted to get away to look and touch things in the shop.

"That's okay! I see they are curious souls. But what are you looking for?" Lucy said, intrigued by the human woman in front of her. As Lucy began to do a reading on the woman, the crystal ball on her counter began to shake on the stand. The sound of thunder and water began to get louder in the store as if a storm was coming. Lucy looked at the ball unable to make sense of the situation. "I'm sorry. I have to close the shop early tonight." She walked around the counter to begin getting the women out of her store.

The women were still being silly and fighting their friend to leave. The lighter blonde woman rushed towards Lucy and grabbed her hand. "Are you a psychic? Can you give me a reading? I saw it on your sign. You do that, right?"

"Oh, my god. I am so sorry!" Lucy said as a quick vision of what the woman that grabbed her would go through. "I will pray for you." As she went to release her hand from the woman, the other blonde woman ran towards the back of the counter and the brown-haired woman followed, attempting to stop her.

"What are you doing, crazy girl! You and alcohol don't mix!" Lucy yelled out as she watched the brown-hair woman attempt to reel her blonde-haired friend from her drunken shenanigans.

The brown-haired woman grabbed her friend by the arm and then the crystal ball caught her attention as she watched the mini storm that warped around the inside. She suddenly began to become drawn to this object and started to approach it. But she stopped at the sound of the shriek from her friend. The darker blonde friend had burned herself on an object that suddenly sparked fire when she touched it.

Lucy walked over to the screaming woman. "You are so rebellious and that is why things are the way they are in your life," she said to the woman, grabbing her hand and rubbing some ointment on the burn and adding her power to the ointment to instantly heal the woman's hand. She added, "The sign clearly says DO NOT TOUCH!"

All three women stood frozen with wide eyes and mouths gaped open while they stared back at each other and the now healed hand. The brown-haired woman attempted to move around her friend to return to going for the exit. As she curved the corner of the counter, the brown-haired woman's elbow touched the crystal ball and caused the ball to begin to fall.

Lucy turned as a vision completed in her mind immediately after healing the blonde woman and revealed who the brown-haired woman would become. "No!" she screamed out watching the crystal ball fall to the floor and shatter, releasing the storm inside.

All four women shocked at first, began to run for cover as the clouds, the thunder and rain began to rise to the ceiling, causing a thunderstorm inside of Lucy's store. The thunder cracked so loud it shattered the windows. The storm clouds covered the whole store, making visibility practically impossible.

Lucy stood in front of the three women huddled together and screaming for help as she watched a large dark figure begin to form in front of them. "What in all god's name is happening now?" Her powers began to react to this being in front of her. Her hands began to glow a white color with a blue hue that formed around her hands. "Oh my." She stared at her hands and then felt the shift in the air. Lucy immediately looked up and noticed a pair of piercing caerulean eyes staring at her from afar. The being looked large and was covered by the smoke.

The eyes looked around and then let out a large bellow that shook the building and shattered all the glass in the store while Lucy and the three humans lost consciousness.

****

"I do not trust this half-demon. I had my associates gather more information on this Hida Clan. Let's just say he told us what we needed to know. What he didn't reveal is once his title is lost, they will not help. They are bound by their clan's bylaws to follow the new leader. I believe Michiko and Benzaiten are walking into a trap," Dillon spoke to Chike as they continued towards a dark building. "That is why I had my associates send me the coordinates to the base of their Lohmer's connection. We will make sure whatever plan they have for her will not succeed."

Chike looked over at Dillon as they stopped at the beginning of a path towards the building. "Do you think we have enough men to handle this?" he said, looking back at the twenty angel soldiers they had accompanied them.

"I believe the half-demons are underestimating the new gods. We are just making sure the gods have support," Dillon said as a large blast from the building interrupted their conversation, causing debris and the after effects from the blast to make them all run for cover.

Chike stood up from diving for cover. "What the fuck was that!"

"Seems as if my calculations were correct. That is most likely our lovely Michiko showing the half-demons why they should have never underestimated her," Dillon said just as a few EGU soldiers began to descend on them, starting their fight.

Chike yelled out his orders for his men, "Destroy all EGU soldiers and try to not kill the half-human half-demon beings" He yelled while the angel soldiers defended themselves. "Dillon, where do you want to start looking for Michi?"

"I don't think we have to look for her." Dillon nodded toward a battle going on in front of them. "It looks like Michiko and Benzaiten are fighting the Hida Clan ahead of us."

Chike unleashed his wings and rushed towards Michi after spotting her. "Hey Michi! Dillon figured they would betray you." He jumped at Michi's back as she was surrounded by EGU soldiers. She held the collar of Touma Hida. Chike looked down. "A hostage?"

"No. He just deserved that ass whooping I just gave him! Where's Niko?" Michi said to him.

Chike chuckled at Michi's slang and then assessed the EGU soldiers in front of him. He threw two small bombs that knocked them off their feet then rushed in during their disorientation and began illuminating them.

"That is cheating!" Michi called back to Chike.

"Nope. Just gets rid of them faster! These motherfuckers are like roaches." Chike responded with a chuckle and then ducked as he sensed a presence creeping from behind. Still ducked low, he used his right hand equipped with his short sword to stab the EGU soldier, causing the demon to fall.

Dillon caught up to the fight and saw that his help was not needed but noticed how Michi was still fighting as she held the collar of the former Hida Clan leader. "Michiko, I thought we had an extensive conversation about torture. Especially towards humans."

"He's not human, Godfather! And technically I am not torturing him. Not my fault his guys aren't landing hits on me but instead on him." Michi smiled and used the passed out Touma's hand to stop a hit from an EGU soldier.

Dillon shook his head. "Where is Niko?"

"I don't know. We got lost fighting in that small hallway! That's why I blasted it open," Michi responded as she attempted to continue to fight the oncoming soldiers.

Dillon looked around the melees of fights that consisted of EGU soldiers versus the angel army with Chike and Michi assisting. "Hey! Look out!" he yelled out at Benzi as she stood where Dillon noticed a shift in the environment.

All of a sudden, a large energy rift began to open, revealing a dark figure as he held on to another figure. Dante stepped through holding a downed Niko. "Hey Goddess! Does this belong to you?" he yelled out towards Michi standing about 5 feet from her.

Michi kicked the last EGU soldier she was engaged with away from her and looked at the scene of Dante and Niko. She realized what she was looking at and her body instantly turned gold and appeared next to Dante using her left hand in a darting motion towards the hand that held on to Niko. "You!"

"Hey! Hey! Don't hurt your boyfriend." Dante blocked all of Michi's swings while still holding on to Niko. "Okay! Not bad, Luck!" He dropped Niko as Michi's aggressive attacks grew faster. "Quit, little girl! I wanted to have a conversation. That's why this one here is knocked out! Didn't want to talk." He leaped back far away from Michi to stop exchanging blows.

"Scared Twin! Don't think I don't know who you are, Dante!" Michi confidently responded as she searched around for Dillon and Chike.

Dillon appeared next to her and whispered, "Concentrate on getting Niko. I will engage with the demon."

"No! I will kick his ass myself. You get Niko out of here and I will meet you all back at the safehouse," Michi said to Dillon.

Dillon scoffed, "No, I will not. Stop with your rebellious ways and—"

He was interrupted by Dante. "Look. I came here to speak with you, Michiko, about what you need to do. You know that Daikoku is working for me now and requires your power. Just surrender to me and I will let your precious half breed live," he said dangling the passed-out Niko in front of him.

"What? Why are you helping that bitch!" Michi hollered out to the demon. "You have nothing to do with this!"

Dante dropped Niko and stood firmly. "Let's just say she has the same interests as me at this time. So, I will assist with her goals. That includes taking your power. So, make this easier for me and just surrender. I am in no mood."

"We care not for your mood, demon. Return the half breed and we will let you leave in peace," Dillon responded.

Dante looked at Dillon. Realizing who he was, Dante disappeared then appeared in front of Dillon throwing a punch to his face.

Dillon ducked and stepped back, turning around and then swinging his left hand, landing a punch on the demon twin. "You can't beat me, Number One. Another thousand years wouldn't help."

"Fuck you and that bitch!" Dante swung, landing a hit on Dillon's jaw and then finishing with a blow to the gut that caused Dillon to hunch over. "Whew, let me calm myself. Look, Luck, if you want your little boy toy back, surrender. I will give you two days to make your decision." He appeared back in front of the unconscious Niko. "I will return to you. And don't worry. No matter where you go, I will find you." He picked up Niko and created the split in the area again. Walking through it with Niko, he disappeared.

Dropping to her knees, Michi screamed at the top of her lungs. "I am going to kick his demon ass!" Her whole body was solid gold and everything in her area began to turn to gold.

"Michiko, get yourself together." Dillon walked over to her and held his hand out just as his feet and legs began to turn to gold.

Michi slowly breathed and attempted to calm herself. "Okay. Godfather, you are right. You are right." She huffed and began releasing her hold on the area around them, including Dillon. "I am so sorry, Godfather!" She stood and then bowed to him.

"Michiko, please stop calling me that useless human title," Dillon responded.

She jumped up and searched Dillon's features. "You know. You are a very handsome man, my godfather! You just need some love in your life and you will be okay!" She skipped over to Benzi. "Usually I would be all, ARRGH!" She mimicked the sound of a monster and moved her hands like fake claws. "I know for a fact they will not harm him because they want me. Also, I am going to get my Niko before they can even start their plans. So, I will not worry." Michi looked at Benzi. "Right? No worry?"

Benzi moved in to hug Michi. "It's okay to feel, Michi-ban. You are right. We will get him back before they can do anything." Benzi looked at Dillon. "Any ideas?"

"Yes. Destroy Dante," he said as the air around him seethed in anger. The vein in his forehead pulsed. "Let me contact Mikael. We have to regroup and figure out where they are holding him. Once we do, we will attack and abolish them all!" he said, squeezing his fist tightly.

Mikael looked at Bisha. "Do you feel anything over there? I am picking on up on high-level demon activity."

"We are in agreement. It seems like a demon barrier was placed here previously," Bisha said to Dillon. "I mean high-level, maybe Fallen level power."

Mikael began to walk around the garage area. "Yea. I can tell that too. But this place doesn't look like a base of operations or that there is a rift close. So, why here?" he questioned just as he felt a familiar energy signature. "Come, follow me! I've only felt this once before," he called out to Bisha as he ran towards an area that had black scorch marks all over it.

"What is this? This feels very different. I've never felt anything like this before," Bisha said as the hairs on her neck began to stand and a chill ran down her spine. "What is that?"

Mikael was perplexed as to why this energy signature was so pertinent in the garage. "Bisha, what I am going to share with you, no one outside the circle that was involved with his birth has heard." He bent down to touch the floor's smut and rubbed the residue between his fingers.

"Mikael, just tell me what you know about Taki? We already knew she wasn't human," Bisha said, rolling her eyes.

Mikael's eyes rose and then he smiled. "I guess you didn't know it was my godson that caused those previous issues with Takisha. She should no longer suffer from what Adam described."

"That is not what I am speaking of," Bisha responded as she watched Mikael, who still kneeled. "Benzi, Ebisu and I always knew Taki wasn't human from the first time we met her. I'm not speaking of her issues that she suffered from back then. I could tell that wasn't the main subject at hand. I believe Adam's power masked the real dangerous situation at hand with her. The only problem is I can't fully read her either. Her powers are very unique. In all of my existence, how did I run across the reborn Shichifukujin and an unknown human-like being that can possibly wield the power of gods?"

Mikael stood up. "That is beyond me. Who would have thought I was raising the next Sun God? I am attempting to understand the Ultimate High's movements, but I am as lost as everyone else. I'm starting to feel like a human. I really don't know what to do."

"That is the blessing of free will, Mikey!" Bisha said. "Now finish telling me what you said I can't tell anyone."

Mikael moved his mouth to talk, but his phone began to ring. "Hello, Dillon. I'm in the middle of investigating—" He stopped mid-sentence to listen. "Okay, let me finish up here and see if I can get a grasp of what happened to Taki." He moved to look at the other areas that were scorched, not sure if he should reveal his thoughts to the Shinigami.

"What's going on?" Bisha called out as she noticed the energy flux around Mikael and his facial expression showed an overwhelmed look.

Mikael disconnected the call and paused before he began. "It looks like Niko was taken by Dante and Lieutenant Zerrick is no longer a threat," he said, shaking his head.

"Wait, what? The twin? He's a menace. Him and his brother. They always somehow got involved in my work. I've run across them more than once." Bisha stared at Mikael.

Mikael looked at the Shinigami. "What we're doing all that time. Benzi won't tell what you both did to survive."

"Really, it's none of your business. But as a former friend, it wasn't all great, Mikael." Bisha cocked her head to side and stared up at him. "You have no idea, but that's okay. All of that led to us finding Michi."

Mikael looked at her. "Well, I'm glad you both survived. Now, we will continue this conversation later, as we all need to put our minds together so we can find Niko before Michiko starts another invading spree."

****

Lucy stared, stuck in her thoughts, as she couldn't believe the story. She could only listen to the stranger that destroyed her shop. She gave the tall stranger a blanket, as he was naked and full of energy. He was hungry and ate all of the food she had available, including the mints scattered across the floor that sat previously on her glass counter.

"I have a place we can go to ask questions. I can't believe what you just told me. There is no way. And I'm the psychic here. How could I have not seen this coming?" she said to the silent stranger. "I'll be right back." Lucy walked back to the front of the store to continue giving her statement to the human authorities to cover what really happened. She decided on a burst pipe with some carbon monoxide exposure for the explosion that caused all the glass to break. Lucy wasn't a scientist, but she made the story sound good.

Lucy walked over to the three women that were huddled together next to an ambulance. "Are you ladies okay? That carbon monoxide can be a bitch! I wonder if I can get free rent from the landlord because of this. My inventory is ruined and my store will take a lot to reopen."

"Awe! I am so sorry! We must have passed out from the poison as soon as we walked in. I was so intoxicated earlier, so I'm glad I just passed out and missed all the excitement," the lighter blonder haired woman said, looking around nervously.

The brown-haired woman spoke out, "That wasn't no damn carbon monoxide! Someone did this! Lady!" she shouted, staring at Lucy with tears in her eyes. "You saw it! You saw it too! I saw you looking scared just like I was!" she screamed out as an officer came to speak with Lucy.

"Hey, I'll be right back." Lucy walked away, glancing back at the woman. "So, we have another one already?"

The brown hair woman glared at Lucy while Lucy spoke with the officer. Her body had a tingle that ran down her spine that made her feel weary about the whole ordeal.

Lucy turned back around to return to the women. "Look, keep in touch. Please let me know if you all are okay," She said to them.

The darker blonde woman looked at Lucy. "This was a creepy experience. I rather not keep in touch,"

The brown-haired woman looked at Lucy. "You know this wasn't no pipe or whatever they are saying it is! You creepy witch!"

"Okay. Goodnight, ladies! Sorry for your experience tonight," Lucy said as she walked away and returned to the back where the stranger was sitting. She noticed no one had approached him since all of the activity in the building. "Are you okay? I see everyone is ignoring you."

He responded, "I chose for these humans to not see me. So, in their eyes there is nothing sitting here. You're technically talking to yourself."

"Is that so? Seems like you can communicate well," she spoke with her thick accent.

The stranger moved his gaze to her eyes. "I've listened to you for the past 300 years, of course I will understand how to talk to you." His caerulean eyes pierced her soul.

"What are you?" Lucy said, lost in the blue eyes that made her want to dive deep in their warmth, and electrifying sensations surged through her body. "Wait a minute, wait a minute. This can't be?" She realized what her vision had showed her earlier. She stood up slamming her hands on the table. "What the heck is going on? Why am I involved this time?" she said, grabbing her phone to call X.

TAKI'S UNREVELATIONS

Taki walked out into the living room area that had the sunk-in look with the beige and earth tone colored furniture. She noticed X sitting on the stool at the kitchen island while Adam sat in a chair closer to the French doors that led to the balcony.

Adam was smoking his weed cigar and noticed Taki come from the back. "Hey beautiful. Are you okay now? Shower did you some justice?"

"Yes. Where are M and Bisha?" Taki answered him. "Don't worry, boo, I'm fine."

Adam strode towards her, placing his hands on her hips. "You know I will always wonder if you're okay. Especially with all of this. I feel so bad about bringing you into all of this," he said placing, a soft kiss on her left hand. "I know what this hand needs," he said teasingly.

"Stop playing, A!" Taki said flirtatiously. She placed her hand on his chest and looked up at his dancing flame eyes. "You know this is creepy as hell. I will never get over your eyes. But at the same time, if you look at me regularly now, I'll probably feel a way!" she said, walking away from him towards the kitchen.

X turned the stool around to face the couple. "I stayed here to listen to this corny shit! Get a damn room!" he said, laughing and getting to the refrigerator before Taki. "What you want? I'm hungry!"

"I just want a water. Throw me one," Taki said as she sat in the stool next to where X was sitting. "So, again, where's M? I don't want to have to repeat this story a thousand times."

Adam walked over to the kitchen area and stood near the corner of the room but still faced Taki and Xeno. "She said she would be right back. She hasn't been gone long. Uncle Mike is out with Bisha looking for anything at the place we found you to see if we can find out who took you. But I haven't heard from Michi or Chike since we separated."

"Well, that sucks. I was hoping Michi was here too. I think Bisha and Benzi know who took me! Then some weird ass lady. Like I told you. I had my own little adventure." Taki drank from the water bottle that X had handed her.

M appeared just as Taki finished her sentence. "Well, I am glad to see that you are up. Ready to tell us of this adventure?" She placed a bag on the island that Taki and X sat at. "Eat. I grabbed some lunch from our favorite place in Yokohama."

"I will never get over this whole we get to travel where we want to thing!" Taki said excitedly as she reached in the takeout bags. "So, let me tell ya'll what's up while it is fresh on my mind."

M stood next to Adam watching Taki. "As your dilemma is important, I found out some disturbing news myself. I believe Daikoku is about to make a move against the Eastern EGU HQ. I received information that there is a faction of the EGU army that is about to attack multiple EGU strongholds. There is only one person with that kind of power."

"But I thought that Zerrick dude was the one that was doing that?" Adam asked.

M walked to the other side of the island to be able to look at Adam, Taki and X. "That is no longer the case. We have a past enemy we have to deal with now. I have confirmed that it is my nephew Dante that now controls the EGU of the East."

X jumped up. "What the hell! Them brats get on my nerves! Damn. What do they want now?"

"I think they are using the Cressius to gain additional power in Otherside. He knows this connection will not be honored in Hell," M said to the group.

X sat down. "What do you mean, Mel? If Brat One knows that then why is he helping another family?"

"I don't know, Xeno. I—"
She was interrupted by Adam. He moved closer to the island, placing his hands on the counter. "He is using Daikoku to get rid of the Cressius while probably thinking of getting rid of her once that happens so he can take control of the East, while most likely his twin is working on the West."

"Well, Baby G! You have been paying attention! Didn't think you would think that deep about it!" X said.

M looked at the Sun God slightly impressed. "Well, if that is his goal, then we need to stop him. At this time, Cressius and Vole Crests are engrossed in a battle that has been going on for a couple decades. Him getting involved and taking control would start a larger confrontation with the other royals."

"Well, where do we start? Do we have a way to get in touch with Michi? I attempted to reach out to her the God way, but I'm not sure what's wrong," Adam said.

X added, "We need to see what Mikael and Bisha found. I imagine they haven't been gone this long to not produce something." He ended his sentence just as Bisha appeared with Mikael behind everyone.

"Hello! It seems we made it just in time. We have very little to share about what we found," Mikael sat on the couch placing his elbow on the armrest while using his right arm to rest his head.

Bisha stood next to Mikael, her eyes only on M. "It seems that we have another unknown enemy on board. We found the residue of a very unfamiliar energy signature. While the scorched area was on par with what you all described as tantrums from Adam." She looked around for a seat and opted out to take a seat in the living area.

"There are a lot of unknowns in this situation," Mikael added. "Unfortunately, besides the unfamiliar energy that Bisha here is speaking of," he stared directly at X, "we will discuss the small details later, but I came straight here to let you all know I spoke to Dillon and we should be hearing from them very soon."

Taki stood up. "What do you mean! What's wrong, Mikael?"

"Unfortunately, Dante has kidnapped Niko and is requesting Michiko's surrender for his life." Mikael folded his arms. "Michiko wants to search for Niko so she can rescue him. Dillon is attempting to get her to come here to regroup with us so we can make a plan for how to save him."

M leaned on the counter. "We were about to hear from Taki about her escapade and now you are telling me we allowed another one of us to be taken? I am starting to question the resolve of the angels, as two of them were left with Michiko."

"Yes, and the two angels made sure that Michiko was safe and in control of her power," Dillon spoke out as Michi's group emerged.

Chike, Dillon, Michi and Benzi all materialized in the large living room, all looking slightly disheveled.

Michi instantly ran to Taki, hugging her as if they hadn't seen each other in years, and began speaking in rapid-fire Japanese. "I missed you, friend. They took my Niko! Fucking bastards!" She laid her head on Taki's chest.

"I know. I just heard, mama! It's okay! We are going to get him back. Don't worry," Taki said, stroking her hair. "I'm glad you're back, though, so I can tell you what the hell happened to me today! Girl!" Taki raised Michi's head and wiped her tears.

X looked at the girls. "Aww! Ya'll cute or whatever!" he said teasingly as he faked sprinkling glitter on them.

"You are an asshole, X," Adam said. "Yo, Michi, let Taki tell her story and then you can tell us what happened." He looked around. "Where is that little demon motherfucker you had with you earlier?"

Michi looked at Adam. "I don't know. We lost him a while ago. He said he was coming back and we haven't seen him since."

"Oh wow. Okay. Well, fuck it then. But I will say, most likely you can find Niko on your own. We need to work on your reading energies from afar." Adam walked over to stand next to Taki.

Taki wrapped her arm around his waist as she sat on the stool. "So, let me tell ya'll since most of you are here."

Benzi interrupted, "Before you do. We have company." Just then, Adam's doorbell rang.

"Well, this is interesting. This person got all the way up here?" Adam said. Looking around, he noticed Chike, Dillon, and Mikael had released their swords and M was standing with her twin swords released. "Ya'll always ready for a fight. I do have neighbors. They are probably being nosey," he said, walking past the large group to answer his door.

He swung the door open. "What's poppin'?" He stood frozen with wide eyes. He rubbed the back of his neck, "Well, this is a surprise. Come on in, the whole gang is here anyway." He gestured for the guests to come in.

****

Deuce lingered back and forth around Lucy's shop and suddenly felt a foreign energy surge that made the back of his neck hairs stand. "What is going on in that damn store?" He attempted to walk through the entrance again but to no avail due to the barriers placed by Lucy.

"Don't be the rebellious one like your brother. You are much smarter than that Two." Chain Face appeared in front of the twin again. "Your mother will be your return. You know the truth about her, don't you?"

Deuce slowly looked back to see the strange, chained face being again. "What truth do you speak of?" He jumped back to put some distance between himself and the being. "You seem to know a lot? Are you a god like Adam?"

"You know what truth I speak of," Chain Face mocked Deuce with a chuckle. "No reason for you to know who I am. Just like it's not time for the others to know either. But what I will tell you is this: you are not supposed to rule anything. It is your job to find out the truth about your family and pick a side." Chain Face wrapped his blanket around himself tighter. "All of you will learn who and what you are. Even this one. She's in for a ride." He paused and pointed his long pale finger with the chains hanging from his fingers and wrists. "But you! You will suffer the most since you can't be easily convinced. What until you find out the truth."

Dante scoffed, "What truth? I was born to rule Hell with my brother!" he shouted at Chain Face. "What do I look like—" He stopped and turned to see a small group of women walking into Lucy's shop.

Chain Face snapped his fingers and placed his left hand on his hip, "Is that what you were told or do you really have a plan for Hell? What will you do differently from the others that tried? What do you plan to accomplish? Have you asked yourself those questions? Probably not since you only know you're supposed to rule. Hmph.", he rolled his eyes. He began to walk away, Chain Face looked at the storefront. "Welp. Time to go. I definitely don't want to be a part of this."

Deuce looked at him confused. "Be a part of what? What are you talking about?" He watched Chain Face disappear just as an explosion happened inside the store, followed by a louder bang that went off, shattering the glass in the store and cracking the brick in the walls. The explosion caused glass and building debris to lunge into Deuce's body. Deuce dropped to the ground.

"What the hellfire," he said through ragged breaths as he attempted to get up. He noticed pieces of brick embedded in his chest from the building was stopping him from returning to Otherside. "Shit. The barrier on the building is preventing me from using my powers," he said blinking hard and attempting not to succumb to the pain that radiated throughout his body. With the little energy he had, Deuce used his working hand to feel around for his cell phone. His hand only touched pieces of brick, glass and a metal pole that laid next to him. He heard a bunch of talking and noise in the background right as he closed his eyes.

Chain Face appeared and stood over him. "Poor prince. You will suffer. But oh, you are going to be so beautiful. This caterpillar will be a stunning butterfly at the end of his road." He clapped with glee as he stalked the laid out and gravely wounded twin. "You may not understand now, but there is a chance you will save her in time," were his last words as Deuce lost consciousness.

THE POINT OF NO RETURNS

Daikoku walked up to the top of the steps and whispered to Bridel, "We will win the day today! No one will stop what we have planned for the future!" She reached the top of the steps of her stronghold to stand over her men, her EGU army, associates and others that had joined her from all over Hell and Otherside for this moment. "Men and women, we have finally reached the point of no return. We are now moving forward with our goal of the Eastern Region takeover. The Eastern EGU Faction, Cressius and Vole Crests will no longer have a hold on anything we do. By the time they attempt to reorganize their ranks, we will have taken everything!" she shouted to the tens of thousands of soldiers that stood before her.

"I have finally reached my goal, and once I have my place as ruler of the Eastern Region, I will complete my goal in becoming the Shichifukujin. We will rule this side of Otherside so we can move freely and independently without interference of the demons or angels! No entity will be able to stop us." There was a round of applause and screams of reverence.

She stepped away and spoke to Bridel, "Is everything in place? I can't wait to see the face of Isis. I am going to have to remind her of her place in the universe." Daikoku looked herself over one more time to make sure she was ready. "Okay, the point of no return." She breathed and began leading her army into the small rift that occupied her lands.

As the large army began to move through the rift, groups started to break off and go in different directions leading to other areas of Otherside. Daikoku exited the rift right at the gates of the Eastern EGU Headquarters.

"Everyone!" she shouted. "We have worked hard to get here, my comrades-in-arms. Together we are going to reshape Otherside for us to rule, and those that oppose us will suffer," she said as her smaller army began to move towards the gates. Ignoring the sounds of the alarm that alerted the EGU Eastern Faction that there was an enemy, Daikoku began her assault as her army began attacking all of the Eastern Region strongholds.

Daikoku had heard about Dante, and he had unfortunately underestimated her tenacity in her ambition to rule. She used him to get rid of Zerrick and made him believe they would be allies. She knew the rules better than he did and knew he couldn't fully take control of the Eastern EGU, as he is not of their lines. He is of the Western Lines of the Royal Fallen. Even if he was the Dante that she had heard about, Daikoku knew he couldn't be working under the interest of the Gilden Crest. So, him ruling was out of the question. Since she would demolish the hierarchy created by the original Fallen Angels, none of that mattered to her.

"All of you. Here are my only instructions: terminate and destroy every last being and building on this property. We will build a new!" Daikoku shouted at the men that stood behind her ready for anything she told them to do.

The army erupted into loud roars and began to attack the first group of enemies they preyed upon. Each group of her soldiers descended upon an area of the stronghold grounds. Daikoku had her sights on the smaller building at the back of the property. She knew that is where Isis could be conducting the meetings with Dante and the other lieutenants.

She appeared directly in front of the door inside the small building using a power that she was restricted to use since she was the property of the Tor Crest. "Oh. It feels so good to be myself." She rolled her shoulders and blasted the door open with her power. She scanned the room and noticed Isis and General Krio sat with Dante with the passed-out Niko lying on a table in front of them.

"Well, I am so glad I don't have to search for all of you. You're all right here," she said as she seductively walked in the room dressed in her favorite short kimono. It was pink and white silk, lined in gold that included her all-black jumper underneath and her black heels. "Now, you can either surrender to me, or you can make this interesting and attack so I can destroy you ALL!"

The three were shocked, but Dante laughed, "This bitch really is like that. I am impressed." He stood up from his chair. "Do you really think you can defeat all three of us?"

"Three, not sure. Two. Definitely." She winked at Dante just as Krio unsheathed his battle axe and swung at the twin from behind, causing a gash on the back of Dante's back and vest.

Isis stood up to attack Daikoku as she did previously but to no avail. "What?" She shook her head. "Guards!" she called out to her personal guards as they came from the shadows to attack Daikoku.

Dante recovered from the sneak attack and stood with his back to the chair he had sat in. "Well. Ain't this about a bitch. You've been working for her this whole time. Zerrick probably didn't even know."

"Yea. Well, he was too young and dumb to understand anything. That's the problem with you power hungry motherfuckers. Never fully see the big picture," Krio sneered while he moved to attack Dante with his large left fist.

Isis said, "My family will not tolerate this disrespect and betrayal, Krio. You will pay for this." She ripped her dress up the side and ran towards Daikoku, landing the first physical blow of their fight. "I am so glad you are not as weak as I thought you were. Let me remind you: demons will always rule you!"

****

"Hi Lucy! What are you doing here?" Taki said to Lucy as she watched Adam lead her and a tall strange man into the apartment.

Lucy waved and looked around at the crowded place. She looked at a room filled with three angels, two gods, two Shinigami, and a former queen of Hell. "Well, I didn't know it would be a party. That's crazy, because I know everything." She put her head down. "Well, not everything. Because I did not see this one coming, ya'll."

M looked at the bulky, pale man. "Who are you? I sense that you are an original." She immediately felt the same purity of power that she sensed from Adam and Michi but more like the gods from before.

"Before we get into that, let me tell you something seriously important," Lucy interjected. "My shop was destroyed yesterday. But for some reason, NSA is investigating it as an unknown phenomenon since we can't prove where the water and gas pipes burst. Unfortunately, much of the brick is cracked too," she said shaking her head.

X jumped up. "What? You were attacked? How can that be?" He rushed to her but was stopped by the stranger as the hefty man stood in between X and Lucy. "Excuse you, homie."

"Do not come within her circumference," the unknown man said, shocking everyone with his booming voice.

X posted up and unsheathed his battle axe. "Lucy, what Shakespeare character have you accidently brought back to life?"

176

Mikael spoke out, "Lucy, please do not tell me what I think you are about to tell me." He shook his head as his suspicions began to grow.

"What, that the NSA found Deuce, M's nephew bleeding to death outside my building?" Lucy responded to the shocked crowd.

M asked, "He what? What was he doing there?"

"I don't know. I've never seen him in my store. I take it he can't come in," Lucy said and looked at M. "I wonder why you can."

"Because I am not a demon, demigod!" M replied through clenched teeth.

"Well, I don't know. Anyway, all I know is some men in black suits came in asking me questions about an individual who was outside and hurt. I went to see to make sure it wasn't Chain Face, but I found Deuce. I know it was him. I will never forget what he looked like when I caught him lurking around here before," Lucy revealed.

The large man still stood in between her and X. "Aye, my man. Can you move?" X said to the stranger.

"It's okay, Dad." Lucy patted him on the shoulder, letting him know that he could move.

With widened eyes, M asked, "When was this, and are you going to address this man you just called your father?" Looking directly at the strange man, she added, "Sir, you did not answer my questions."

"My Luciana asked me to let her explain everything. But you all are too occupied with your own thoughts that she can't complete her statements," he growled, pulling the hood off his head to reveal his long dirty blonde hair and caerulean eyes that glistened in the light.

Michi clapped for joy. "Okay Modelesque! Lucy! Spill!" she giggled, rushing over to the man and rubbing his arm.

Taki got up from the stool and grabbed Michi, dragging her back to the kitchen area away from the stranger. "Behave! We're trying to come up with a plan to rescue your man, girl!"

"You know I'm just playing," Michi said as she and Benzi giggled while Bisha shook her head.

Mikael raised his hand to his forehead, frustrated at the lack of seriousness from the ladies. "How?"

"Look. Let Lucy finish. We have other pressing matters," M spoke out and looked at Michi and Taki, causing them to calm down.

Lucy looked around at the group shyly. "Look, I still have a lot of dealings in Otherside and ran across him around my shop. He asked if I knew Taki, and I immediately knew it was the twin when Taki described him after the fight. I saw him before ya'lls big fight with them. At the time, I didn't know he would be involved in all of this."

M responded, "That's interesting. I wonder why he was back around your shop. He has to be involved with his brother."

Taki interrupted, "Guys, we're like two conversations behind. I've been trying to tell ya'll since Dante was involved with Niko's disappearance that Deuce might be the one involved with mine. I saw him today. He's the reason why I had an episode like that today!"

M added, "Right, too much has been going on that we forgot that Takisha here still hasn't told us what happened to her, nor has Michiko been able to tell us the full story on Daikoku."

Michi interrupted, "This is lots of storytelling, Sunny do you have popcorn?" She sat down on the floor with her legs crossed to watch as Adam ignored her question.

"Since I know my bestest friend probably won't hear 85% of this," Taki smiled at Michi, "let me just spit it out. Some random dude took me earlier from the field and was being a fucking weirdo, and then I woke up to some badass lady with red hair and a leather outfit out of this world. She—"

M walked closer to Taki, interrupting her. "Please describe this woman." She clenched her jaw. "Do you remember anything peculiar about her?"

Taki glanced upwards, deep in thought. "Mmm, come to think of it, she reminded me of Jade. Her skin color was lighter than you, like Jade, and her hair was huge!" Taki realized something but didn't express it.

X asked, "Seraphin?

"Xeno, mind yours," M snapped.

Taki glimpsed back and forth between the two. "Um. Who is that?"

M interjected before X could answer, "She is irrelevant."

Chain Face materialized instantly. "Yes, DF, she is."

Mikael questioned, "DF"?

"Get with the times, man, da fuck?" X said, laughing as Adam and Chike chuckled. "Hey Chain Face, long time, no see."

"Hey Xeno!" Chain Face waved, revealing he knew the angel by name. "I am only here for a second. She is detrimental to the path that has been set for the rebirths. Take heed to my words! Gotta go! Bye, Bestie!" He waved to Adam.

Adam stood in the background digesting the herds of information that he had been exposed to in the past two hours. "Bye, Chain Face!" Adam waved. "FYI, ya'll, in a little bit I will know who Chain Face is. He is getting easier for me to read." Adam held Taki tighter and continued, "Whoever he was talking about, he is extremely worried."

"That's because he has seen her in many of the conclusions of the universe. He gets nervous when he sees the same person in the different timelines causing havoc. Somehow, she is related to a lot of energetically connected outcomes that are causing major universal imbalances," Lucy explained.

Michi, antsy and bored, asked, "So, back to the sexy man?"

Lucy laughed. "Ya'll know how I told ya'll I don't know my parents? Well, come to find out, I had one of my parents with me the whole time. Literally." She smiled as she looked up at her father. "So, Dad, meet everyone. Everyone, meet my father, Mani, God of the Moon."

"Hi Mani!" Benzi gazed at the god. "So, yea. Seraphin sounds lame. Can we get to talking about Michi-ban's plans of rescuing Niko?" she said from the kitchen area. Michi playfully punched her as they giggled.

Mikael said, "Yea. We didn't get to that part yet."

Dillon interjected, "So, we know we have to rescue Niko, we have a new god in our midst, and the human authorities are showing their interest in Otherside matters."

X said, "The smart one!"

"Obviously, you're not. But we need to finalize our rescue plans along with gathering information about the new god. If I recall, Mani is not a new god, is he?" Dillon said, staring at the stranger curiously.

Mani replied, "I am THE Moon God."

Adam reached out his hand. "Hey! Cool. I'm Adam the Sun God. Don't confuse me with Ra," he added at the end.

"That failure of a Sun God? Why would I compare?" Mani replied.

Taki added, "Oh, your dad is an asshole!" She smiled at Lucy. "He will fit in perfectly with these jackasses."

Michi screamed suddenly. Taki rushed to her as Benzi and Bisha were already hovering over Michi checking on her. Michi's eyes and skin turned solid gold and she spoke in her trance-like voice, "It is time. Come, Taki. We about to fuck this shit up! Bye!" she said, grabbing Taki and disappearing.

LUCKY

Niko kept hearing screams, sounds of swords clashing and the sounds of battle. Gradually opening his eyes and not fully understanding what he was seeing, he sat up quickly and looked around at the chaos around him. He noticed the man he was fighting with earlier at his family's hideout. Niko attempted to move, but his body felt heavy and uncomfortable to breathe. He realized it had been a long time since he was able to siphon Michi's power and he was in Otherside.

Niko fell off the table while attempting to get up, his body still heavy as an EGU soldier came to attack him. Niko hunched over to cover himself as the soldier began to release a barrage of hits with a club like weapon. The soldier started to drag Niko by his feet. "Get the fuck off me!" He kicked forward, causing the EGU soldier to fly away from him.

Niko looked shocked as he felt the power starting to flow through him. He breathed slowly and felt the fiery sensation flow through his veins. He felt as if he had his first cup of coffee for the day. "Ya'll demon motherfuckers about to get fucked up!" Niko's body began to get bulkier. His hands grew with claws attached at the ends and he felt the teeth in his mouth grow larger. He ran to attack the EGU soldier that he had kicked away and turned his eyes on the large dark man with shoulder length curly hair. "You!" He leaped to the opponent.

Dante felt a malevolent energy approaching him. He stepped back to miss a gut punch from Niko and strode to the side watching the large half-demon land a blow on Krio.

The force of the blow caused the warrior general to fall back with widened eyes and a gaping mouth.

"Argh!" Niko growled as he twisted and used his right hand, throwing his second punch, striking Dante.

Dante spit a small amount of blood out on the rug. "I hope the stain comes out." He moved to attack Niko, but the half-demon was on him before he could recover.

Daikoku shouted towards the knocked out general, "Hey! I didn't know you were so weak!" She grabbed a chair and smacked Isis with it to distract her so Daikoku could help the general.

"Where are you going, bitch! I am not done with you yet!" Isis said, getting up and using her powers to make an ice wall between Daikoku and the general, leaving the general to Dante and the half-demon Niko with no backup.

Daikoku stopped at the ice wall and placed her palm on it, causing it to shatter. She huffed, "Isis, you are a mere child compared to me. I doubt very much you have any idea what's going on." Just then, one of Isis's personal guards stood separating the two women.

"Your Highness, we must retreat. We have received word that all of the Eastern strongholds have been invaded and most have already fallen." The personal guard hung his head low as he completed his sentence.

Daikoku laughed as she watched the rest of her army enter the meeting room. She smiled with pleasure at the look on Isis's face and Dante fighting with the half-demon. "Yes. You should retreat. Because if you don't, I promise you will return to Hell's fire."

"Shinigami, I keep telling you, don't forget your place, as the demons will forever rule you!" Isis angrily yelled, her eyes and hair turning white. "Do you really think you can go against a member of the Cressius? You fucking delusional bitch!" The intensity of her power started making the building shake. Her hands began to freeze up to her elbow. "Time to get serious. You will never see the day of ruling anything!" With that, she attacked Daikoku to start their fight again.

Dante continued to pummel on Niko, as the half-demon was no match for the seasoned fighter. "Looks like your little power boost is over." He grabbed the weakened Niko and threw him to the ground, standing on his head. "I can squish you like the bug you are. Half-demon. None of you will ever amount to a Royal Fallen!"

****

Deuce laid on what felt like a metal slab on his back. Unfortunately, he was unable to move as he opened his eyes. He stared at a ceiling that reminded him of all those places he used to witness other demons making deals with humans to heal them.

"What is your name?" a soft-spoken woman's voice interrupted his thoughts.

He turned his head towards where he heard the voice and noticed he couldn't move his body at all, growling at the restriction.

"I'm sorry. Unfortunately, it is protocol to make sure you are unable to attack anyone," the voice spoke out.

Deuce realized he was listening to a speaker as he paid attention to the distortion of the voice and tone. He closed his eyes, attempting to return to Otherside.

"My apologies. You can't do that either. This place is designed to block all Otherside powers. Including you demons. So, you can stop being so difficult and maybe we can see about getting you out of here."

His eyes widened with shock, but chose to not reply to the voice.

"Interesting. You're a rebellious one, aren't you? At least tell me your name." She sighed.

Deuce attempted to use his powers again, making the table shake.

"Ooohhh. You're a strong one? We may have to reinforce your area," she said. "The longer you take to answer my questions, the longer it will take for me to evaluate you."

Dante laid silent as he assessed his situation. He attempted to remember the bits and pieces of his transport to this place. He began to backtrack to what he heard Chain Face say: *"You will suffer."*

"You're still going to ignore me? Most of your kind likes my voice. Don't be shy," the strange woman whispered, disturbing him from his thoughts.

Dante continued to lay in the strange place as the woman kept attempting to get him to answer questions. He thought, *Now, why would these humans attack me? Unless they are working for another royal family.*

He made his decision to stay with the humans to see what they were up to. He knew that the humans were getting more curious about Otherside and had heard about their experiments and captures of Otherside creatures. The woman's voice rang through these thoughts.

"You can't tell me you are this boring? With that body and hair, I know you have a mouthful to say!" the woman spoke again.

Dante smirked at her comment.

"Oh, there he goes. I knew there was some personality in there." She chuckled.

Dante instantly tensed up from her comment then realizing he was being visually recorded. *Okay, stay focused,* he thought to himself as he went back to his expressionless face.

"Aw, damn. Just when I thought I had you," the woman teased.

She was interrupted by a knock on the door. "Be right back, handsome!" she whispered back, leaving Deuce in to his own thoughts again.

MICHI'S THERE

Michi and Taki had arrived at the Eastern EGU HQ in the midst of Daikoku's attack. Most of the entry gate and front area of the stronghold were destroyed. "Taki! I feel Niko here! I took you since I know Sunny can get to you fast! I hope you're filled with Sunny's powers right now." She put her finger on her head to think. "I forgot to ask before we left."

"Michi, babygirl, where the hell are we and—" Taki stopped to land a throat punch on an EGU soldier that was running up to Michi from behind. "Girl! This is not fun!"

Michi laughed as her body began to turn to solid gold. "We will make it fun! Come on. Let's go filet a Shinigami!"

Taki walked next to Michi as she sensed different energy signatures throughout the large area. "No, I didn't have time to. Someone snatched me for a cosmic war that I didn't know about." She stopped to look at Michi.

Michi returned the glare. "Sounds like a cheesy book line," she said and began to laugh hysterically. She and Taki stopped laughing and stood silent for a moment before n continuing to walk towards the area, she felt Niko.

"Are you sure you are ready to take her out?" Taki asked.

Michi sighed, "I don't know. But I do know, she will pay for what she did to my family. They're all gone, Taki." A tear began to stream down her gold skin.

"I know. I know. Come, let's kick this bitch's ass together!" Taki said as she grabbed Michi's arm to pull her.

Taki's hands began to glow with blue flames with a tint of golden hues. Michi clapped with joy since they didn't share that Taki could siphon Michi's powers too.

Taki jumped and attempted to wipe her hand of the flames but to no avail.

She yelped as Michi grabbed her flamed hand. "Taki, calm down. It's just the power that flows through you was ignited."

"But how? I haven't siphoned from Adam since I was kidnapped," Taki responded.

Michi shook her head. "Obviously, it's not his power. It is yours," she said as she felt Niko's spirit waver. "Come, Taki. We have to save him!" Michi grabbed Taki and began to head to Niko, just as Krio appeared in front of them.

"Who are you?" Michi called out to the large man. He was massive in size and height. He was taller than the angels and any demon she has taken down so far.

Taki stepped back. "This motherfucker is huge, Michi!" she said, assessing the EGU soldiers that had joined him.

"Don't worry, little one. I am the one that will bring you to Daikoku." Krio smiled then added, "On a platter." He lunged towards Michi using his arms, attempting to grab her in a bear hug.

While she ducked and moved to gain distance between them. It's okay. I'll take the big guy. You get rid of the EGU for me." Michi glanced over at Taki. "You got them?"

Taki's eyes enlarged. "Um. No. I am not letting you fight that big ass monster by yourself. I don't care who you are."

"Taki, I am the Shichifukujin. My friend, let me show you what I can do," Michi said as her eyes and skin gleamed gold.

****

Adam continued to try to search for Michi and Taki telepathically with no success. He asked M, "Can you feel them?"

"Unfortunately, no. Too much is going on right now. I'll be right back." She disappeared.

Dillon spoke out, "I am being contacted by our headquarters. I shall return. Send me a text if plans change." He proceeded to the front door to leave.

X and Bisha got up. "Well, looks like we are going to join the fight too. Bisha, can you find her?" he asked, then added, "What are we doing about the father daughter duo here?" He pointed to Mani and Lucy.

Mikael responded, "Someone has to stay with him and get him up to speed with the new world and possibly reason for his rebirth. We still don't know how he came to be." He moved from the couch and sat down at the counter, as there was more space with the departed beings.

"I am all caught up. Unfortunately, I was conscious in that prison," Mani's voice rang. "What we need to know is what happened to me and who did this?" His eyes turned a smokey white color with a blue hue.

Lucy reached up and touched his shoulder, "Dad, that is not important right now. We do have to get you up to speed. The other gods are gone. Adam and Michi were just reborn and now you are the third one in less than a year. This can't be a coincidence."

Mikael said, "I doubt very much so. So, Chike and I will stay here with Lucy and her father." He looked at Lucy. "Do you have arrangements for your housing?"

"I can't leave that place unprotected, Mikael. I have to stay there. I told you," Lucy said, determined to return to her home.

Mani questioned, "Do they know of you protecting the rift to Otherside?"

"Yes, Dad. I did tell them. If I didn't, you would have revealed it to them," Lucy replied.

Mani stood next to Lucy and glared at the others. "I would have had to kill them all if that was the case."

Adam stood eye to eye to Mani. "You know, you talk big shit for a dude that's not at full strength yet." His eyes evaluated Mani, dancing like flames.

"Baby G, chill. We on the same side, right?" X interrupted the showdown between the gods. He remembered how much the energy would clash in Earth Realm if they were to fight.

Adam huffed and walked away from Mani. "Yo, where the fuck is M? I am getting real antsy not being able to sense Kisha."

"Do not rush me, Sun God." M appeared in the penthouse. "I was gathering some info, and it seems that our Daikoku problem is a lot bigger than we originally thought."

Mikael raised a brow and folded his arms across his chest. "What do you mean?" He got up from his seat and watched as Bisha and Benzi finally looked interested.

"Daikoku had launched a full attack on the Eastern Region EGU and the ruling family, Cressius. She has also sent an army to annihilate the Vole Crest," M explained as she took a seat at the empty stool. "According to my informant, Daikoku is currently winning."

X sat back down next to M. "She is badass for real."

"She calculated this just right and had the right amount of demons in place to accomplish this." M looked down. "The fact that she is able to navigate two wars while attacking a base herself is pure genius."

Adam ran over to M. "When are we leaving? I don't even care if it's in Hell." He looked at her with sincerity while the flames in his eyes continued to blaze.

"We can't rush anywhere, Adam," Mikael answered Adam. "Let's listen to what M has to say."

M added, "Let's listen to someone that can assist." She snapped her fingers, revealing a shivering and tied up Putzin. "Ready to talk?" She said holding on to the ropes.

"Yes. They are at the Eastern Headquarters! I just left that area. It is crazy! Michi is turning the demons into gold statues while Taki is setting everything on fire." Putzin spoke clearly. "We have to stop them!"

Mikael was not convinced of Putzin's actions. "Where's Zerrick?" he forcibly asked Putzin.

"He's dead. Isis allowed Dante to kill him in front of Daikoku. She liked it," Putzin said.

X raised an eyebrow. "Oh shit. I keep liking her more and more, Mike!" He rubbed his hands. "How does she look?"

Benzi interjected, "She is not your type, Xeno. Even though she is gorgeous."

"It's not about looks, you know!" X replied back to Benzi.

Mikael said, "Can we get back serious, you two?" He looked at M and Putzin. "How do you know all of this information?" Mikael used his power of persuasion to get the truth out of the small demon.

"I was there." Putzin covered his mouth. "I hate when ya'll do this! I don't even see how this broad found me!"

Mikael cocked his head to the side. "Why were you there?"

"I was checking in with my master Isis." Putzin closed his mouth again.

X chuckled, "You're lucky Michi isn't here."

"For real, I told her ass he couldn't be trusted," Adam added to X's statement.

Putzin scowled at all the taller beings. "Not my fault Michi is crazy! I told you all I wanted to use her to defeat my master. Well, now you know who my master is." He folded his arms.

"Okay. Now since the little demon told us where they are, we need to get there. Where is this place? Why can't I feel Taki?" Adam said to everyone.

Bisha finally added her own thoughts, "Most likely Daikoku's doing. She is not stupid. Especially if she already saw that Michi is there."

"Come on, little demon. Show us how to get there!" Benzi grabbed the demon by the horn just how Michi did.

Putzin kicked and squirmed. "Put me down!" I can't take all of you. Max is three."

"I'm going." Adam immediately stepped up.

M moved next to Adam. "I am joining the Sun God."

"I am not staying here," Bisha added.

Benzi flayed her arms in the air. "Oh, come on! I wanted to go."

Mikael smiled. "Benzi, we can assist Mani here on what he needs to know and get him some clothes."

"Did you just say shopping?" Benzi whipped her head around and ran to Mikael and stared at the light brown colored man. "You're treating me too, right?" She placed her hands on her hips.

Mikael nodded his head. "Yes."

Adam interrupted, "Settled. Let's go, demon," he said, dangling Putzin in the air by horns.

"The disrespect is unnecessary. I am trying to help you. I can get in big trouble for bringing enemies there," Putzin said as he disappeared with Adam, Bisha and M, heading to the Eastern Headquarters.

Benzi walked over from the kitchen and plopped down with her arms sprawled out on the back of the couch. "So, how did you know he was your father?" she said to Lucy. Before Lucy could answer, Benzi randomly spoke to Mikael, "Mikey, you better be rich on this side. I only purchase the best."

SHINIGAMI'S FINAL PLANS

Daikoku wiped her mouth as she and Isis continued their brawl. Each woman landed multiple blows and hits and now were beginning to use their power to battle.

"I didn't expect you to be so strong for a young demon," Daikoku said.

Isis smirked. "There's a lot you don't know." She moved to her right and then jerked left, causing Daikoku to miss her punch.

Daikoku read the demon's next move and landed a high kick to the head. "Bet you felt that one!" she said standing over the passed-out Isis.

She turned to speak to one of her soldiers. "Gather up all the Fallen so we can burn them all! They will return to their fire as they proudly say!" she mocked the demon's praise of their hellfire.

As she spoke to her army, two of Isis's personal guards snatched Isis up and disappeared. Daikoku never turned back around. "Find them and return them to me. I will make sure she and her lackies are ended for good."

Another soldier approached Daikoku to speak. "General Krio is outside engaged with Michiko Tanaka." He bowed and left.

"Nice. Bridel, my plans are going so well. We are about to be where we want to be." Daikoku reached out for Bridel's hand.

Bridel grabbed and held onto Daikoku's hand. "I am proud of you, my love. But what of Dante? He did not lose to Krio."

"You are correct. But, both of them ran. Dante and Isis. So, they lost. I now have control of the whole Eastern Region!" Daikoku shouted proudly.

Bridel looked at Daikoku nervously. "So, what's next?"

"You already know. Time for me to become the Shichifukujin. Now that Michi is here, all of my plans are coming into fruition." She turned to face Bridel. "Go and confirm that each stronghold is prepared for the next phase of my plans. Time to blow this place," she said before walking out of the former meeting room.

****

Due to the decimation of the headquarters buildings, Daikoku now stood in debris that was the former grounds that housed the leadership of the Eastern EGU Faction. She searched around for the battle she felt not far away. "There you go, little birdie." She disappeared, allowing herself to reappear next to Krio.

"If you've come to scold me, I will scold myself later for taking so long with this munchkin," the general said as he struggled with fighting Michi.

Michi kept using her smaller size and swifter attacks to try to beat the large man down.

Daikoku stepped forward. "Michiko. I really don't want to hurt you. You are a mere human and do not understand the hierarchy and what it is needed to rule that kind of power. Just surrender and you can go back to your little life." She added some force at the end of her sentence, attempting to flex some of her power.

Taki finished ridding the battlefield of the EGU soldiers, leaving only the main warriors standing. Daikoku, Krio, Michi and herself. "Michi! That's her, isn't it? She gives me creepy Bisha vibes!"

"Yep! That's Koku. Don't compare her to Bisha! Bisha dresses much better! Prettier—" She instantly crossed her arms to soften the impact as she watched Daikoku swiftly move to attack.

Taki moved as the general attempted to fight her. "Hm hm, big guy." She leapt a few more feet away and used some of her blue flames from her right hand to light a rock and hurled it at the massive man. "Ooooo. Nice weapon." She picked up a handful of rocks and began throwing them at Krio.

"Stop it! You're burning holes in my clothes!" He attempted to dodge the fire like bullets that were piercing his skin. He glanced over to see Daikoku and Michi engaged in a fierce battle, his eyes hardly able to keep up with their movement.

Taki landed a fire rock on the general's light brown skin. "Pay attention!" She picked up a larger rock and chucked it with extra force.

"You are making me angry, little girl!" Krio began to stalk Taki as his nose sizzled from the rock. He reached for her head as she ducked and punched his foot, her hand aflame.

The general screamed in pain from the fire on his foot. He bended down to put the fire out. Taki stood up and used her foot to kick the general in the chin with her foot still covered with blue flames. This caused him to fly upwards and then land on his back, shaking the ground slightly.

"Oops. I actually held back a little bit. I don't know where or how I got this power boost from Michi!" Taki stood in her fighting stance. She gazed over at Michi and Daikoku's fight and noticed the two women were really trying to kill each other. Taki used the time the general was down and ran over to stand next to the panting Michi. "Mich! You okay?"

Michi answered, "I'm fine. Just heavy practice," she panted.

The general snatched Taki up by her hair.

"You stupid disrespectful motherfucker! You touched my hair?" She held onto his arms and used her legs to wrap herself around the massive right arm, kicking him in the face multiple times while twisting his arm and bringing it up to her body. The bone broke and the big man fell to the ground. Taki stood up just as Dante appeared with a knocked-out Niko across his back.

"I guess this is goodbye for now, Daikoku. Can't let you accomplish everything in one day!" he spoke directly to her then turned his red eyes to Michi's gold ones. "If you want your boyfriend back, defeat her!" He pointed to Daikoku and immediately disappeared with Niko.

Michi rushed to the now empty space. "ARGH!" she shouted, falling to her knees. The air around her began to get heavy and her fists pounded on the pavement. Michi panted as her breathing became ragged. The ground she pulverized began to turn gold. The building debris, the metals and pieces of glass that started to float in the air instantly turned to gold and fell to the ground.

Daikoku watched as Michi's power grew and began to decimate the area. She called out to the laid-out general, "We have to go now!" Daikoku couldn't believe the uncontrollable power that Michi was showing. The ground started to shake beneath her, and she jumped to higher ground as the gold spread.

Taki yelled from atop a gold piece of brick, unable to get to Michi. The air whipped around her face, causing uprooted trees, bricks, rocks and dead soldiers' weapons to float around while Taki's hair disrupted her view.

Michi rose from her knees and glared at Daikoku. "I will destroy you and everything you represent!" The power had Michi's hair whipping across her face, her eyes and skin solid gold. She walked slowly to the panicked Daikoku.

Daikoku was fixed on staring at Michi, almost as if her body was in a trance watching the goddess. She shook her head to snap out of the daze and began to gather her own power to resist Michi's pull. The pull that made them feel like one; the feel of being one with Michi felt so warm and needed.

One of Daikoku's soldiers tapped her shoulder. "Master, we have to meet with Bridel. This is too much for us!" Just then, he turned into ash from the intensity of Michi's power. Daikoku remembered her defeat from before and accepted a retreat was in order. She vanished, leaving the Eastern HQ as her celebration for taking over was put to a halt.

Taki watched as Daikoku disappeared, leaving her and Michi in the middle of the annihilated former EGU headquarters.

****

Mikael looked around the lobby, as he had an uneasy feeling in his gut. He noticed a few individuals he wasn't familiar with since he was a regular in Adam's building. "Hey Bisha and Lucy, take the bags upstairs. Mani and I will check on a couple things down here."

"There are armed humans in this area. Is there a problem?" Mani responded.

Benzi looked around. "Yea. They are pretty weird around here. I sense a lot of confused and malicious intentions." She looked at the brown-haired woman staring at Lucy.

"Come on. Let's get to Adam's apartment and then see what we can find out," Mikael said to the group as he moved towards the elevators.

Lucy's vision showed her the next events that would happen. "Well. Doesn't look like we will have a peaceful evening," she said, rolling her eyes and holding a few of the shopping bags.

The group continued to walk towards the elevator, and a stranger walked around the corner interrupting their stride. "Excuse me, I am looking for Adam Moore. Do you happen to know him?"

Mikael calmly responded, "Sorry, I'm new to the area. I don't know any of my neighbors yet." He smiled at the stranger and pressed the elevator button.

Benzi grabbed Mikael's arm. "I had such a great time shopping today! Let's take my sister and her father to the café down the street.

It will be awesome," she said, attempting to get away from the stranger.

"Dad, can you do something for me?" Lucy asked Mani innocently.

Mani looked at the stranger and grabbed them by their collar. "Who are you and what do you want with my daughter?"

The sweating and panting man, shivered, "I am from NSA. I am investigating a bizarre phenomenon here in this area that's been increasing."

"Why are you looking for Adam?" Mikael stepped closer to cover Mani holding the man. "Are there more of you?"

The man put his head down and closed his eyes.

"Are you alone?" Mikael demanded and added extra force to his sentence.

The man immediately replied, "No. we are currently searching for the entity, and Adam Moore's apartment for clues of otherworldly activities." The NSA agent whipped his head back and between the two men.

"He is not directly involved. The ones upstairs are the problem," Lucy said to the group. "My vision showed me we are about to battle some weird humans. Neither demon nor half-demons but not humans either,"

Mani spoke up, "Well, it seems as if these humans are aware of our existence in the universe. I say we go upstairs and give them the battle they deserve!" He dropped the human agent and raised his fist to the sky.

"Dad, I know you're part of Norse mythology and all, but fighting is not the answer for everything!" Lucy said, shaking her head.

Benzi bent over and observed the agent. "Just sit here and be quiet. Do not tell your friends about us!" she ordered just as the elevator door pinged and opened.

The group entered the elevator and Mikael's phone rang. "Hey Chike. Stay outside. We have NSA company. Come to the top floor the other way." He disconnected the call and sent a text to Adam and Dillon. "Might as well let the others know what's going on."

Benzi gazed at Mikael with lowered brows and her left hand resting on her hip. "There are going to be a lot of Otherside and Earth realm repercussions after this. There is no way all this will go unanswered."

"Yea. That will be another problem. Let's just concentrate on this one," Lucy said as the elevator doors opened to reveal a busy hallway leading to Adam's apartment. The strangers began to load the opposite elevator to exit the area, leaving the group to themselves. "Benzi, can you get in the apartment without us going through the front door?"

"I don't know. Let me check. I know how Queen Melchorde is with her barriers," she said, disappearing and returning less than thirty seconds later. "Yep! I can. Let's go!" Benzi grabbed Mikael's and Lucy's hands as Lucy grabbed her father's arm.

Benzi assisted the group in getting them inside Adam's place. The group witnessed others inside looking around the apartment. They attempted to be silent, but one of the strangers already sensed their arrival.

The agent called out, "Where is the individual Adam? We have some questions for him."

"Who? I have no idea what you are talking about," Benzi said, twirling a strand of her hair innocently.

Lucy giggled, "What are you men doing here? Who are you looking for? I'm just here for a good time." She walked over to Benzi and started to get flirty with her.

Mani had already assessed the humans in the apartment and realized they were not as weak as they led on. He called out to Lucy, "This is no game, child. They are serious." Just then, the NSA agent in the kitchen area ran to attack Mikael.

Mikael embraced the attack and landed a blow to the human's face, pushing him back. "Wait a minute. What is this?" He sensed a mix of demon and other beings from Otherside energy.

"You sense it too, Mikael?" Lucy yelled out. "These are some weird ass humans!" she backed up and blocked a punch from her right side as another agent in the apartment attempted to hit her but their fist was caught by her father.

Mani grabbed the soldier by the throat and began to strangle him. "Now, *this* I miss."

Benzi kicked the human out of Mani's grasp. "We do not kill humans regardless of how bad they are!" She looked at Mikael. "Take these things seriously. I think they are mixing human blood with creatures of Otherside blood."

"Yea. It looks like it. Dammit, we didn't need the humans to join this war," Mikael said, taking his stance to resume fighting. "Well, just another day with us, I guess."

CERTAIN HIDEOUTS

Dante paced the office as he finished explaining his dilemma. He used his Royal Fallen status to get assistance at the United Factions in NYC. He figured it would take longer for his mother to find out about his failure and he would have time to gather more men to go against Daikoku and Michi. Having the half-breed in his clutches was causing him to have to war with both. He knew Daikoku was going to attempt to finish him off along with trying to get Niko for herself to use against Michi.

A woman dressed in a blue pantsuit walked in. "Prince Dante, we have news to share about your brother. This was discovered just this morning."

"What? Where is he?" he asked curiously.

She gave Dante a large file full of pictures. "Here is what we gathered. Your brother is a prisoner of NSA at this time. We are unable to locate him, but we are actively working on it. We are awaiting the council's verdict on the human experiments with demons and Otherside creatures." She handed Dante another file. "This also brings The Gods into the fray. The humans are currently searching for the rebirthed Gods."

"Yea, I had a run in with both of them. They are definitely a problem," Dante responded to the news. "Okay. Did the council look at my proposal?"

The representative peered over her glassed with raised eyebrows, "Didn't I just tell you we have more pressing concerns? The humans are kidnapping demons and Otherside creatures and using them to enhance themselves. The council doesn't have time for your petty squabbles."

"You will have time! I told you to tell them that the whole Eastern EGU has fallen!" He slammed his hand on the conference table. "The enemy is probably on their way here now!"

The woman was unamused by Dante's antics. "I do not fear you, nor am I inclined to assist you further. I—" She stopped speaking as she began to receive orders in her ear piece. "But sir, we—" She paused to listen. "I understand. I will bring him to you." She glared at Dante. "Follow me." She turned around and began to lead Dante down a long hall to a massive set of doors. "Enter here and wait." She walked away.

Dante pushed the left door open to a huge study area that housed thousands of books. He directed himself to a set of chairs and sat down. He looked around to make sure he was alone. He pulled out his phone and sent a text to his twin, but noticed there was no delivery notification.

A council member that he was acquainted with seductively walked in. She spoke to the twin, "I am very surprised to see you here, Prince Dante. What is the grandson of Belial doing here looking for asylum?" She sat in the chair next to Dante. "Great choice of seat." They sat in front of the enormous floor-to-ceiling windows with their backs to the immense library.

"I explained my dilemma earlier to the council representative. I am seeking civilian asylum, as I became involved with a war going on right now in the Eastern Region," he responded.

The woman sat crossed legged in the chair. "We are aware of the issues going on over there. We have been in contact with the Cressius Crest."

"I doubt very much you are aware of the current events. At this time, the Cressius has lost their leadership of the Eastern EGU. The advising Shinigami Daikoku has taken over and is on her way to Earth Realm to attempt to become the Shichifukujin since one was reborn," Dante explained. He got up to gaze out the window. "Every one of the strongholds in the Eastern Region have been taken over by her."

The council member sat quietly for a minute. "When did this happen?" She got up and walked over to the desk, announcing over the intercom, "Bring the council rep to me please."

The large door that Dante walked through opened again. "Yes, Ms. Asirius." The council representative bowed.

"Prince Dante here has informed me of the loss of the Eastern EGU. Why were we not aware of the activities going on there?" Asirius asked with an eyebrow raised.

The rep looked slightly surprised at the news as her phone began to ring. She looked nervously, not wanting to disrupt the conversation.

Asirius said, "Please. Answer."

The rep grabbed her cell phone from out of her suit jacket and pressed the green button without speaking. She listened to the other line while details of the ongoing Eastern Region conflict were shared with her.

Dante and Asirius sat quietly waiting for the phone call to end. He knew it was probably confirmation of what he just explained.

The council's rep spoke to the demons, "It has been confirmed that Shinigami Daikoku has destroyed the EGU strongholds throughout the Eastern Region of Otherside. All strongholds have been demolished and soldiers annihilated." She spoke with her head down.

"What is the status of the Cressius?" Asirirus inquired.

"The former Eastern EGU leadership is currently unaccounted for. The attacks on the strongholds were completed simultaneously. So, we are unsure if they survived the attacks."

The council member stood up angrily and spoke with her voice raised, "What about the Vole Crest? Do we have any idea where this Shinigami is?"

"That is why I am here, Asirius. I have something that she may want. But there is a problem." He looked at Council Rep. "I have the boyfriend of the goddess she is looking to become."

Asirius looked at Dante, squinting her eyes while sitting back in her chair rubbing her fingertips together, "Who?"

"The reborn Shichifukujin. They were responsible for the random attacks on the bases on that side. Michiko Tanaka and I believe her boyfriend's name is Niko," Dante answered.

Asirius walked to stand closer to Dante. "Interesting. You're telling me you just so happened to come across all of this information and the young man?"

"I have no dealings with the Eastern EGU. Let's just say I was in the neighborhood and noticed this is what the Shinigami would want," he responded.

She placed her hands on her hips. "Begin the cleanup protocols and contact the leader of the United Factions and get him abreast to everything. Council Rep, you are dismissed." She paused, then added, "Thank you."

The council rep responded, "The Vole Crest has been annihilated." She left the study as directed and began her tasks.

Dante's eyes widened. "So, will you help me?"

"Of course, I will. I can't believe my sister allowed this to happen!" Asirius sneered. "She is lucky I wasn't there. I would have killed her myself for this shameless defeat!"

Dante placed his hand on her shoulder. "I know the feeling. My twin got kidnapped. How embarrassing. What am I going to tell my mother?"

"Nothing. I will make sure the UN resources are on top of finding your brother. We are going to destroy those humans for defying us," Asirius tightened her fist as she raised up from her chair.

****

Bridel watched as Daikoku slowly walked down the hall of their makeshift hideout. Bridel had successfully led the second phase of Daikoku's plans. All of the Eastern EGU bases had been destroyed. All soldiers loyal to the Cressius and Vole Crests were returned to the fire. "Daikoku, what are we to do now? The other families have most likely been informed of the defeat of both crests."

"Of course, they were. But with the minimal losses we have taken, we are ready for what they may try to attempt. At this time, they are probably running to the United Factions to get help." Daikoku stopped at a desk filled with documents, trinkets and random items. She pushed around some papers and found a letter with some information on it. "Isis doesn't think anyone knows that one of her sisters is a council member. So, it would be smart for them to go to the council for help." She started to think.

Bridel walked behind Daikoku and held her. "So, what about Michi?" She rested her head on the Shinigami's back.

"Since Dante decided to keep the boy for himself, the best thing is to get my hands on that boyfriend of hers and she will come to me," Daikoku said staring blankly at the page she held. "They don't know how much I've put into my plans. I will not let a mere demon brat and this new so-called goddess ruin my plans, Bridel." She turned around. "I have an idea. Contact the Hida Clan. I still have an insider there. I know he will get me what I want."

Bridel pulled out her phone and sent a text message. "Okay. Done. Let's send the army back to the castle and we can take a small entourage with us to Earth Realm to start the hunt for Dante and Michi."

"Great idea. I was thinking the same thing." She held Bridel's hand. "You will join them. I am going to take those bastards out at the same time. Don't worry. I might get lucky and take out half the United Factions." A smile spread on Daikoku's face.

Bridel looked at her nervously. "Why? I want to join you. We can stop them without a doubt together."

"I will need access to my full powers and won't be able to keep you on that side. Unfortunately, you know my powers are what allow you to go through the rift to the human world. I promise I will be back." She glared at Bridel. "You start the rebuilding phase of my plans while I finalize the rest."

Bridel nodded her head in agreement. 'Fine. I will be here waiting. I will contact General Krio to see that he knows the next phase."

"Have him meet me at our hideout in New York. He and I will be enough to finish Dante and Michi," Daikoku arrogantly stated. "No one will be able to oppose me anymore!"

Bridel's phone rang just as they were about to depart. She listened closely as she held her hand up asking Daikoku to wait. "That was Jason Hida. He confirmed that Dante has required able men to accompany him to the United Factions office and plead his case to the council. He has Niko using him as bait for you and Michi."

"Does this half-breed know where Niko is being held?" Daikoku asked.

"Yes," Bridel replied.

"Good. My plans just got even sweeter. Get Krio to me now! We leave for Earth Realm as soon as possible!" Daikoku stormed off leaving Bridel with her orders while Bridel watched as Daikoku walked away.

Adam, Bisha, M and Putzin arrived on the deserted battlefield looking at the surrounding demolished buildings, shreds of soldier uniform pieces, and areas on the ground were solid gold.

"It seems as if Michiko was indeed here," M said, assessing the gold ground under her feet.

Adam went to respond and suddenly heard a heart wrenching scream. "Michi!" he called out as he also felt Taki near the scream. He disappeared to find them.

"Where is she?" Putzin looked around for his master.

M called back to Putzin as she started walking towards the scream. "Demon! Do not run off!" she scolded.

The smaller demon sat with his arms crossed. "You don't have to talk to me like that. I'll just mind my business right here."

The group followed M towards the screams and approached a wailing Michi with Taki consoling her. The group witnessed the sad scene that Michi displayed with the crying, tears and shouting due to Niko's kidnapping. Taki continued rubbing crying Michi's back. "What are y'all doing here?" She looked up at Adam with tears in her eyes.

"Babygirl what happened?" he asked, looking around for more enemies. "Where's Daikoku?"

Michi bawled louder, "I am going to kill her!" She stood up. "I had her. I had her! That bitch ass mother—"

M interrupted her, "Watch your mouth! Takisha, tell us what happened calmly please?"

"We found them here about to leave. Dante had already escaped with Niko. Some big ass—I mean big ass—dude attacked us. Dante then returned to tell Michi she will get Niko back as long as she defeats Koku. Koku left when Dante left. So, we don't know where she is right now," Taki looked up at Adam while she continued rubbing Michi's back.

Bisha asked, "Did Michi and Koku engage in battle again?"

"Yes. I witnessed them fighting. It was amazing and scary to see," Taki replied. "I think Koku is up to something else."

Putzin finally joined the others. "Phase two of her plans is in motion."

"That's the annihilation of the Eastern EGU?" Adam asked.

Putzin put his head down. "She is going to kill me!"

"You better praise your hellfire that you survive *me*!" M glared at Putzin and then looked over at Adam. "We need to leave now! There's only one place my nephew can go without the repercussions of my family."

Michi's eyes flashed gold as she jumped up to face M. "Where is he? Tell me now!"

"No," M answered directly. "We need to reassess all the activities and make a plan. That's how Daikoku was able to stay a step ahead of us. She had all of this planned before we knew she was after Michiko."

Putzin responded, "Sounds like an excellent idea. Just maybe you'll get something accomplished this time." He rolled his eyes, "You know, between Isis and Daikoku, y'all about to get your asses kicked."

"You stupid little demon!" Michi kicked the small demon, sending him flying in the air and landing about fifty feet from the group.

Taki responded to her outburst, "Now, he is annoying, but did he deserve that kickball style kick, Michi?" She placed her hands on her friend's shoulder. "Don't worry! We are going to get Niko back! You were kicking Koku's ass! Did you see what I did to that giant demon dude?!"

"Yes! Girl! You looked like M but with a bigger butt." She covered her mouth to giggle. "Moved so fast like a snake! You kicked his ass!" Michi clapped with excitement.

Taki knew how to get her friend back in a positive mood but didn't appreciate the butt comment. "Girl! I should kick your ass now!" Taki said to Michi, shaking her fist towards her.

"Hey, glad we got Michi back calmed," M interjected. "Now, let's get to the dojo. Like I stated earlier, there is only one place my nephew can go. Once we create a plan, we will be able to extract Niko Black from Dante's grasp."

Michi walked to stand in front of the slightly shorter woman. "Lady Melchorde, do not leave me out of this. I am going to defeat Daikoku and I am going to get Niko back!" Her eyes flashed gold.

"I will not rob you of your duties, Goddess of Luck. But I will not allow you to continue to cause chaos in Otherside or Earth Realm," M responded.

Bisha interrupted the back and forth, "Michiko. Are you sure you are ready to take out one of your Shinigami?" Her head was bowed and her hands began to sweat.

"Are you still confused about how Michiko should handle Daikoku?" M folded her arms on her chest.

Michi calmly replied before Bisha could, "Um. I don't know about y'all, but I'm hungry and need a shower. Some clean clothes too."

"You are one of the most unfocused creatures I have ever witnessed," Adam said teasingly.

Michi stomped her feet towards him. "Be quiet, Sunny! I am hungry!" She smirked. "Like Taki said, no reason to worry. As long as I'm calm, M will tell me where Dante is. Most likely Koku will be there too. So, I will get what I want!" She smiled and skipped to stand next to Taki.

Bisha shook her head but kept her thoughts to herself. *How is this child wielding so much power? She can destroy all of us if she wanted to.*

"So, you don't feel the same way as Daikoku?' M asked.

Bisha ignored her at first and then answered, "No one deserves to die. But I will not ignore what I see."

"You better pick a side before it's too late," M said.

Michi replied to both of them, "I don't care what you think, Bishamonten. Daikoku is going to be destroyed. You can either agree or disagree. I don't care. She is going to pay for what she did." She rolled her neck and shoulders, "So, can we go now? I need a shower!" Michi glanced down at her clothes with a look of disgust.

Adam searched around. "We good? Everyone ready?"

"Yes!" Putzin yelled. "I want to get the hell out of here!"

Adam grabbed the demon by the horn. "M, do we need him to go with us?"

'Technically, no. But, do we want him to warn his master or possibly Daikoku?" M answered.

Putzin squirmed under Adam's hand. "Let me go! Damn bully! Humans with powers suck!" He continued to kick around.

"Yo! Chill. You can go. I wanted to make sure you didn't disappear. You should definitely keep in touch, little homie! Thanks for the ride," Adam said, letting the demon go. "Alright, Michi. You got this?"

Michi's eyes turned gold. "Let's go!" she shouted with excitement as she disappeared from the area, leaving the others behind.

"She is a hot mess," Taki said, shaking her head as the rest of the group followed Michi to M's dojo back in New York City.

****

Jason followed Dante quietly as he was ordered by his grandfather to assist the demon while the Hida Clan searched the city for Michi and the woman, Daikoku.

Dante glanced back at the half breed. "What is your name?" He continued walking down the hall of the building he sought refuge in with the coalition of the EGU factions that acted under the guise of the United Nations.

"Jason Hida." He continued to follow him, unsure of the destination.

Dante stopped walking. "The son of the last clan leader. Interesting. I have a job for you. I need you to watch the bait. You'll find it is someone you are familiar with." He finally turned around to face Jason. "Do not think you can help him. Nor do I need you to think you will save your clan. As of now, your clan is under the control of the Gilden Crest and you will now follow our ways."

"Yes, sir." Jason bowed with his eyes burning with anger. He always knew he would follow his father's footsteps and lead the clan. The fact that this was happening made his blood boil.

Dante smirked at the young demon. "I feel the murderous intent coming from you. You probably feel like, *who is the stranger taking my family?*" He turned his back again. "I promise you. I can help you hone those powers and maybe take what's yours in the future."

"Yes. Sir," Jason repeated through clenched teeth as the heated lava feeling that seethed through his veins began to scream with pain.

Dante continued their walk to an office door that he opened, leading Jason into a dimly lit room. "Half breed. Get up," Dante called out to a figure laid out on the floor of the empty office.

The sounds of chains rattled in the background. Dante continued, "Oh, don't worry. I'll let you loose in a minute. You know you can't beat me, and I doubt you want me to kill your cousin,"

"What the…?" Jason spoke out as he looked at the unrecognizable Niko. He stopped his body from rushing to his cousin as he watched the bleeding Niko struggle to move.

Dante witnessed the hesitancy from Jason and spoke in a slithering tone, "Do you wish to help your clan, Jason?"

"Yes," he responded.

Dante smirked. "Instant answer. If I told you he is the cause of all of this, and all of this has something to do with your father's sister, would you kill him for me?"

"No." Jason put his head up proudly. "I will not murder a member of the Hida Family."

The twin demon was impressed with the halfling's tenacity. "Then follow my instructions. Daikoku is going to play right into our hands with Michiko. Deal with her for us, and let my grandfather deal with Melchorde and the rest of the imbeciles."

"Who is Melchorde?" Jason asked curiously. He cocked his head to the side. "What about those Shinigami? They will come with Michi. Also, Michi's strong—she blew a hole in my house like it was nothing." He shifted side to side nervously.

Dante chuckled, "Those Shinigami are mere child's play compared to my family and the United Factions. This will end of all the human's interference and these so-called Gods that are returning."

"Yes. Sir." Jason stood quietly watching his injured cousin lay on the floor. He remembered the phone call he made prior to his family's arrival to assist Dante, the new head of their clan. He knew that help was on the way to assist him in getting the Hida Clan under his control.

THE DOJO

Daikoku sat quietly waiting for Krio in an apartment in Staten Island that overlooked the Goethals Bridge. "Is he here yet?" She and a handful of her soldiers were back in Earth Realm awaiting the general's arrival. "We must be prepared for the next set of plans," she spoke out to her current assistant. "Also, make sure the stronghold has extra protection." She stood and held her hand on her hip. "Bridel must survive all of this."

"Don't worry, Your highness. Your plans will be manifested." Krio walked into the sitting area of the large apartment. The big man was healed and cleaned up from the previous battle at the EGU stronghold. "Like my new threads?" He wiped his large hands on the fitted chocolate sweater, tan slacks and brown leather shoes that made the large man's feet look as long as his arms. The earth tone colors brought out the light brown sugar skin tone that held the strong muscles that surrounded his body.

Daikoku looked at the general. "You look like you're trying to apply for a slave position at the UN." Her piercing eyes stared at the bulky man. "I like. Anyway," she stood up and walked to a large window, "are you ready, Krio? This is the part where things will get messy but fun." Daikoku placed her hands on her hip. "Dante thinks the United Factions will help him. But, they won't if I tell them his real plans."

"His real plans? What do you mean?" The large man sat on the couch. "You need to get bigger furniture. I feel like I'm sitting in a child's seat." Krio was just as tall as a power forward in basketball, standing at about six feet eight inches, but was bulky like a body builder.

Daikoku smirked. "Yes. He and his brother is attempting to overthrow their grandfather."

"That is a very strong accusation, Daikoku. Those twins can't be that stupid. He is strong but not that damn strong. But he does have a lot of connections." Krio eyes glared at her, as he was familiar with the Gilden Crest's hierarchy.

Daikoku walked back over to her chair. "Believe me, I do not think that it is possible. But I do know those twins and their mother were connected to a lot of those major problems over the past few years here." She stared at the general. "I had a lot of information while

I worked for the Tor Crest. Those twins along with a degenerate soldier are the reason the United Factions are more involved with Otherside activities instead of Hell. That arrogant idiot Dante is probably attempting to unite Hell."

"Hahahahah!" the general let out a bellowed laugh. "No one is going to follow one family. He can't be that stupid. Too many families have been eliminated for their attempt at that. Also, he is in direct violation of a law created by his own family."

Daikoku rubbed her chin. "Exactly. That is why using the degenerate soldier, myself and whomever else he collected, while he tried hiding his and his brother's true intentions, my spies around Otherside confirmed that the twins were disciplined for their involvement with that soldier. We still don't know exactly what happened, but from what I learned it caused a strife with the humans, United Factions and the council."

"The Royal Council and the United Factions work together? That's surprising." Krio sat back and crossed his right foot over the other. "I like these shoes."

She stood up again. "They've always worked together. The EGU Factions are nothing more than the pawns of the most powerful royals. Most of the council members have some control of their EGU Faction. So, I am interested as to how they will respond to my attack. I have extra protection in place for the main stronghold. No one knows my connection to the Hida Clan. Our next set of plans is to ambush Dante at the United Factions building and have them give him to us. He has Michiko's boyfriend, so she will come to me."

"What makes you think they won't assist Dante?" Krio questioned with his left eyebrow raised.

Daikoku smiled. "Once we tell them that he was working with Isis to eliminate the Vole Crest, his deal will be null and void with the council. They will not be able to protect him."

"Use the council against him, but do you know how they will react to your annihilation of the Eastern EGU Factions?" the general asked.

She looked at Krio. "They will have no choice. Once they see that I already control the Eastern Region, the council will be obligated to recognize me as the leader."

"You give them too much credit. You are not a demon, Your Highness," Krio said. He stood up and adjusted the wrinkles in his clothing. "We will most likely have to prepare for a war with the United Factions and the Council. Are you up for it?"

He walked and stood next to the sitting Daikoku. "I am with you every step of the way. But do not think for one second that the Council will accept you with open arms. Just prepare for battle with all three."

"Krio, you underestimate me. I have a backup at the UN office. Not just the Hida Clan," Daikoku spoke up at the general. She rose and placed her petite hand on his arm. "Come, let's go say hello to our new partners," she said leading Krio out of the sitting area, heading to where Dante held Niko.

****

Michi had left the group to go shower and change clothes with Taki joining her in the locker room of M's dojo. M had already showered and changed while the group still waited for the other two to return.

Adam stood off to the side of the main training area of the dojo waiting for Taki. He yelled out towards M, "Yo M, where are we going next?"

"We are taking a trip up the street. The UN building is most likely where Dante is," M replied and then turned to the quiet Bisha. "Have you chosen a side?"

Adam was unaware of M's concerns. "M, what's up? Why you asking her that?"

Bisha interrupted before M could reply to the god, "Because she knows that I do not agree with Michi running freely with all of the power that she wields." She put her head back down. "Regardless of that, I care for the child but do agree that she is not ready for the responsibilities of the full Shichifukujin."

"Who are you to tell me what I am ready for? I was obviously born to wield this power," Michi interjected. She stepped in the middle of the room with a radiating energy that caused the air around her to sizzle; her eyes were solid gold along with her hair lashing around.

M was surprised that she didn't feel nor hear the goddess come into her presence. She realized that Michi was no longer on the level of control and that if Michi got out of control again, she would have to send her back to their God Realm. "Michiko, you must calm

209

yourself and stay focused. We have to go against the Royal Fallen Council and the United EGU Factions. Most likely, they will have sided with Dante and will want Michi and Niko to pay for the fall of the Eastern EGU."

"Um. Where are they located?" Taki asked walking in from behind Michi. She walked straight to Adam and placed her head on his shoulders as he stood silently.

Bisha sat cross legged, as she was unable to respond to Michi's outburst.

Adam placed his left arm around Taki to hold her. "Did you guys feel that power not too long ago? Someone else is here already. If I'm not mistaken, I also feel Mikael and Chike fighting right now.

"Mikael and Chike fighting?" Taki asked. "Should we be worried?"

Adam looked down. "I don't think so. From what I can tell, I think it's humans their fighting." He shrugged his shoulders as he attempted to sense the energy that he thought was coming from Mikael.

"You sure you don't want to shower and change clothes, handsome?" Taki glanced up at Adam and noticed the dirty shirt and jeans he had on.

Adam's eyes danced with flames as he playfully responded. "Nigga, I'm in the trenches. These clothes are fireproof so I won't end up naked at the end of the night." He looked down at the large dingy shirt and jeans. "I hope."

"What did your godfather tell you about that word, Adam?" M interrupted their private conversation. "God or not, I will personally remove that word from your lips if I hear you say it ever again!"

Adam's flamed eyes shined brighter. "What do you care for a word that doesn't mean anything to you! Ya'll don't care about what humans went through."

"You arrogant fool! How dare you use a word that disrespects your ancestors, your forefathers and very nature of your power as a term of endearment. For Hell's sake, and to the woman you love!" M stomped towards Adam.

Taki held Adam's arm to attempt to calm him but understood where M was coming from. "A, come on. It's okay. We always said we were going to stop using that word." She reached up to touch his face as she watched his eyes get brighter and brighter with a vacant stare.

"What is wrong with the Sun God?" Bisha got up and asked as she noticed the flux in his powers as well.

Taki reached up to grab his face and then glimpsed over at Michi and noticed that her eyes were gold but with a blank expression similar to Adam's. She instantly grabbed Adam's face and began to siphon some of his power and noticed the flames in his eyes began to subside. Taki ignored the burning sensation throughout her body as she raced over to Michi and grabbed her hand. "Hey! What do you see? How did you and Adam do that at the same time?"

Michi ignored Taki and began to skip around the room and tap everyone with her finger. "I am Luck and I will be your will to survive. She will die today, as she should not be here. Also, too, the humans are being very bad. Lucy's dad will reveal what they are up to. Soon the demon will know he is light. Now come, the connector of all, we have a job to do." Michi grabbed Taki and Adam and vanished, leaving Bisha and M at the dojo.

"The connector of all? Who is that?" Bisha asked.

M froze momentarily. "Adam is their leader. Come on. Let's follow them before this becomes another disaster here on Earth." Both women disappeared, following Michi's energy signature to the UN building.

Mani and Mikael finished removing the last of the knocked-out regular and altered humans out of Adam's apartment on to the roof of the building. They left Chike with Benzi and Lucy to clean up the apartment and to see if they could place more barriers to keep the humans away.

Mani stopped his task and watched the sky. "I haven't seen the night sky in over two thousand years. I do not know how a being can be so cruel." His eyes turned a grayish white color.

"Do you think it was one of the angel commanders? We were ordered to eliminate all gods and their counterparts. I never heard about an attack on you or your brother Sol," Mikael spoke out to the god.

Mani's eyes continued glow. "My brother Sol was captured and returned to the light long before my capture. His arrogance caught up with him." He stopped looking at the sky and shifted his gaze down at the angel. "Did you know Sol?"

"No. I was acquaintances with Ra the Sun God and now Adam," Mikael responded. "Sol, I heard was an interesting being. But, can I ask you something about your capture?"

Mani scrunched his eyebrows. "I will answer if I am able. I am unsure if it will resolve your question."

"Were you conscious the whole time in that ball?" Mikael watched the large man.

Mani looked himself up and down to see what the angel was staring at. "Oh. You're asking due to my size?" He smirked. "I was not always conscious, but there were times that I was aware of my surroundings and the conversations going on around me. At first it was hazy, but I can say the last five hundred years have been rather interesting to see. Especially after my baby girl, Luciana, got a hold of the crystal."

"That's another thing. How the heck did Lucy find you?" Mikael asked, as he was interested in how Lucy never knew her real parents but happened to have been holding one of them for over three hundred years. "Can it be a coincidence that she had this ball in her possession?"

Mani squinted his eyes at the angel. "Do not accuse Luciana of lying to you. She is one of many half-human children that I fathered.

Unfortunately, none of them survived but she and about two others." He stared back at the sky. "They did not survive the post war times as Lucy did, I learned later on." Mani put his head down sadly.

"I am sorry, Mani the Moon God. My name is Mikael and I am one of the lead commanders of the Western Region of the Angel Army. On behalf of the Ultimate High and the Angel Army of the West, I welcome your rebirth and hope we can assist you on starting over." Mikael held his hand out for Mani to shake it.

Mani ignored Mikael's hand and began to walk towards the roof access door. "I will not shake hands with the enemy. Your kind wanted me and my kind gone. I have seen you and that Xeno character in my daughter's shop on multiple occasions." His eyes began to shine a brighter all white color. "I do not care for that creature. He was not solely created from the light."

"I understand your concerns. I am unaware of what you know of our relationship with Luciana, but she will always be protected by us. You will never have to worry about the Days of Hunts happening again." Mikael looked at the god attempting to do a slight energy read on Mani.

Mani laughed as he grabbed the doorknob. "Angel, you will never read me. I am pure light. Your Ultimate High created us beings to be more powerful than his regular foot soldiers. What I will say, is you will help me find out who did this to me and Luciana's mother! I want to know what happened to her!" He left through the door with it slamming behind him.

Mikael stood quietly as he assessed what he learned. Sol was captured before Mani and that Mani was subconsciously alive in that crystal ball. "That is the work of a powerful psychic. There is no way he survived two thousand years in a ball." He shook his head and followed the god back to Adam's apartment.

****

The council rep pleaded her case to the council with approval that they would not interfere with the matters involving Daikoku and the Shichifukujin, in exchange for the evidence that Daikoku would supply them on the rebirth of the gods and the ones responsible for the attempt at conquering Otherside.

213

The rep placed a call and listened silently, as her role was complete. She took an elevator down to the lobby in one of the busiest buildings in the world that was now almost empty. She watched as the large tan colored man with a skin tone matching outfit and a pale petite woman wearing all red walked through the revolving doors with a handful of guards surrounding them both.

"Gabriela, they agreed to my stipulations?" Daikoku looked around the lobby and stared at the rep. "Get rid of all the humans. We do not need them causing us any more issues."

The rep, Gabriela, responded to the Shinigami, "I already had the building evacuated. Only beings left are demons or Otherside creatures." She bowed her head. "If you are defeated by the god, the agreement is null and void and the crest will have no choice but to eliminate all evidence." She backed away from Daikoku and Krio.

"Do not worry. Get the contracts ready, as I am ready to take my role as leader of the Eastern Region. Make sure all of my demands are met. The council has seen what I can do on my own. Imagine what I could do with them assisting me?" Daikoku smiled and slowly began to walk away. "Wait, where is Dante?"

Krio interrupted the conversation, "He is on the 27th floor of the General Assembly building. Are we sure we can fight in this building?"

Gabriela responded to Krio's remarks, "No. It is not in your best interest to fight Dante here. Get him to surrender."

"Easier said than done," the large general replied to the council rep.

Daikoku smirked and added, "Come Krio, we will pop in and surprise our friend Dante so he won't want to fight. I promise, Gabriela, any damages can come out of my budget." She held onto Krio's forearm and disappeared from the Lobby.

Gabriela walked away from the now empty space and alerted the guards to be on standby at the General Assembly Building and was instantly startled by the sound of a squeaky voice yelling out.

"Hello! Where is Niko! I can feel him here!" the voice kept calling out.

Gabriela turned around and noticed three beings walking in through the double doors of the building: a tall dark brown man dressed in a dirty shirt and ragged jeans with two women, tall black woman, and a shorter woman with Asian features. Both women had on black jumpsuits and sneakers with a golden flame logo on the front. "How can I help you?" Gabriela asked as the sensations she felt coming from them made her skin tingle with anxiety.

Michi skipped closer to the woman. "Hello, Ms. Demon. Where is my Niko?" Her solid gold eyes glared at the rep and her hands were behind her back.

"Excuse me, I believe you are in the wrong place. Please leave," Gabriela said to Michi as she watched the large man's eyes dance with flames.

Michi laughed and reached both her hands in the air as if she was choking something. "See, demon, I was trying to be nice. You got your little friends trying to creep up on us. I asked you where is Niko before I fuck this place up!" She squeezed her hands tight as two demons were revealed to be in her grasp. "Look Taki, I finally mastered that!" She smiled at Taki, whose eyes were wide.

"Well, I be damn. I saw them coming, Mich. Like as saw them lurking towards us," Taki added.

Adam suddenly used his right hand and shot a small fire blast at a group of guards that started walking towards them, turning them to dust instantaneously. "Look, lady. I know there are nothing but demons in this building," he said, speaking to the Gabriela. "Just tell us where Niko is. She is not going to leave, and then my girl won't leave. So, unless ya'll motherfucking demons want two rampaging gods here tearing shit up, I advise you to give us Niko."

"The council is not involved in this. It is the demon prince that has the hostage. We are not in the business of dealing in hostage negotiations at this time." Gabriela shook with fear, noting that she had in fact identified the two gods. She asked, "Can I go?" She was edgy, realizing she was in the presence of two gods and a being that did not have the aura of a human.

Michi touched Gabriela's shoulder before she could walk away. "There you go. You will survive this. Hope ya'll can pay the humans for the damage." She chuckled as she watched the rep scuttle away. "You ready?" she spoke out to Adam and Taki.

"I guess so, girlie." Taki placed one hand on Adam's forearm and her other one on Michi's hand. "This is amazing, guys."

Adam was concerned that they hadn't mentioned to anyone that Taki can siphon powers from him and Michi. "Baby girl, don't overdo it. You've been taking a lot of power from the both of us!" He grabbed her hand and led her towards the elevators.

"We're really going to take the elevator?" Michi scoffed.

Taki grabbed her friend's hand and pulled her. "Yes! Come on! This building is amazing!" The two girls chuckled as they walked towards the elevators with the Sun God leading them to rescue Niko from Dante.

IS THIS THE END?

Dante sat patiently waiting for the council member Asirius to return. He left Jason with Niko and some guards from the Hida Clan. As he waited for her, he realized he wasn't in the best position. "If Grandfather finds out about this, I am dead."

"Yes, you are, little prince." Daikoku swung open the large double doors that closed him in the massive office space. "Did you really think you rallying the council would save you from trying to play me?" Krio and a group of soldiers followed her into the room. "I told you. I had these plans laid out early on. There was no way you could win. You should have minded your business." She stood fiercely in her all-red pant suit with black and gold accessories.

Dante chuckled, "So, you did have an insider here. You think I don't know Jason Hida is your connection with the Hida Clan?" He stood up from the meeting table. "Daikoku, you are so easy to read. You're beautiful and smart. Evidently, you are just like the rest." He snapped his fingers as the wall panels fell, revealing his own soldiers. Dante leaned on the table in front of him. "Do you really think I would trust any of you! The council will kill you too, if the Shichifukujin don't get to you first." He winked at Daikoku as he shouted, "ATTACK!"

The dedicated soldiers that Dante always has at his helm, the Riot Hell Squad, descended upon Daikoku and Krio and the few soldiers they had with them. The surprise attack startled Daikoku and her men, but they braced for the attack as the rest of Dante's soldiers revealed themselves to the fray.

Dante paced the back of the battle watching as Daikoku and the general were giving the squad an intense fight. "My turn!" Dante raced towards Daikoku, landing a smack to her face and then her buttocks when her body twisted from his first blow. "You have no idea the spark you ignited, Ms. Goddess. Unfortunately, I already knew you were too greedy to share. That's why I came to the council, so I can pull your real card!"

"Do you think I don't know your real plan? You really think you can take over Hell?" Daikoku wiped her mouth from the hit. "You arrogant little brat. How dare you touch my face! I will kill you! Krio, get rid of the rest. The pretty little prince is mine!" She kicked her right leg towards Dante, missing and instantly using her left fist to land an uppercut on the demon's chin. "I will become the Shichifukujin. Now, where is the half-breed?" She moved closer to attack Dante again.

The twin dodged her attack as he left his back open and noticed Krio motioning toward him. "Shit!" Dante exclaimed, bracing for the blow that landed on his shoulder.

"I forgot how slick you were! That was supposed to break your back in two!" Krio shouted out as four Riot Squad Members jumped towards him to split him and Daikoku up. "Shit!' He hopped back to stand at a defense. "Dammit. I hate these guys!"

Dante laughed at the general's response. "You're definitely strong, but not strong enough." He dodged the incoming hit from Daikoku. "Sneaky little biteh!"

"Pay attention demon!" Daikoku missed the first punch but landed the second to Dante's right jaw. "You can end this. This has nothing to do with you! We can be allies!"

Dante kept dodging her blows. "I don't think so. I'm good." He instantly felt strange energy signatures approaching the disarrayed room. "Well, it looks like your time has run out, Daikoku. I will let you and the Goddess fight this one out. If you survive this, I'll see you again!" He moved to hit Daikoku just when a fire blast from a dark figure ignited the table that divided Daikoku and Krio. He felt the heat from the blast and yelled out as he wiped his clothing, "Riot Squad, let's go. We have some more hunting to do!" then disappearing from the now demolished office and leaving the Shinigami and the general with their new enemies.

****

M looked around the empty lobby. "This is a very busy human area. Why is it vacant?" she spoke to Bisha.

"I am confused as you. I sense nothing but demonic energy signatures in this area," Bisha replied.

M noticed a guard laid out on the ground still breathing. "Let's see if he can tell us anything?" She walked towards the guard. "What happened here?"

"Who are you?" the guard coughed out, dreadfully hurt.

M snatched the guard's collar and leaned into his face. "Tell me what happened here before I guarantee your return!" she said as her eyes turned red.

"They, they, attacked as the Shinigami arrived. I don't know who they were." The guard kept coughing.

M released the guard and stood up. "Looks like he's returning anyway." She looked at Bisha. "Do you sense your master?"

"She is not my master." Bisha turned to stare at the wall. "I sense Michiko's power growing as well as Daikoku's. I believe they are engaged in battle."

M sneered, "Interesting. I also sense Takisha in another location. You assist Takisha and I will assist Ms. Tanaka."

"You don't have to worry about me and my choice. Regardless, Michiko is who she is. I cannot change that. But she needs help to control this power she wields." Bisha looked back to glare at M.

M gazed back. "Your thoughts and will are no longer a factor. You are a previous Shinigami. It is Michiko Tanaka's will that allows you and Benzi to coincide with her. I suggest you think about your stance before you make her choose!" She began to walk away. "Now, as I stated, you go assist Takisha while I check-in on our gods and their battle."

"You know, for you to have sided against the darkness, you still act like the Queen of the Golden River Realm," Bisha said while attempting to locate Taki's energy signature, as it was not close to the fray that she felt coming from above her and M.

M chuckled and began to walk towards a being she sensed when they arrived, in hiding. "I am still the Queen that I was raised to be. Having subjects doesn't matter. Now, go. I sense Takisha will need your help."

"I'm going," Bisha said, leaving M.

M stood quietly assessing her environment. "I sense you here. Come out if you want a conversation." She looked at the exact spot she noticed a faint silhouette.

"You are very keen to your surroundings, former Queen," Gabriela spoke out, revealing her form. "I did not expect you to show up."

M said, "So, you are the new council rep connected to Daikoku. I wondered how she was able to move so freely." She squinted her eyes. "So, what does the council have to gain with siding with Daikoku?"

The council rep glared at M with squinted eyes and smirk. "I can call your family's EGU faction and have you captured immediately. Don't you remember you still have the bounty on you?"

M chuckled, "Little demon, you have no idea who you are dealing with. I advise you to tone down your arrogance." She placed her left hand on her hip. "Again, what does the council have to gain?" She added power to her voice that caused the air around them to start to crack.

"We will allow Daikoku's temporary siege of the Eastern Region of Otherside so we can control the demonic forces in that area. Along with figuring out who was responsible for catastrophe that caused the issues with the humans." She knew she was being forced to tell the truth.

M shrugged. "Thank you. I rather you would have told me willingly. Now, what calamity are you speaking of?" she asked curiously.

"The situation with the Gilden crest that involved Dante and his brother Deuce that is currently being held by the humans," Gabriela responded with malice. She hated the fact that upper ranked demons had the power to control her. It was one of the reasons she decided to assist Daikoku. Gabriela watched the demon hierarchy that toyed with the lower ranked crests and Otherside creatures. She believed in Daikoku's vision, as she promised Gabriela that the demons would no longer have control.

M's eyes widened and her heart raced. "Excuse me? What did you say about Deuce?"

"He is currently being held in an unknown location by the humans that are conducting experiments on Otherside creatures and demons." Gabriela shook her head. "Can you stop? This is giving me a headache. I will answer all of your questions without deceit."

M shifted to her right. "Good. I was hoping you would play nice. I am in no mood to return you to the fire."

"Why did you leave?" Gabriela asked. She was curious, as she always heard about the former Queen of the Golden River Realm. Being the council rep for over eight hundred years, lots of information about the high ranked offenders of Hell and Otherside was often discussed. The former queen's betrayal was the most discussed wrongdoing that the Royal Fallen Council and United EGU spoke of.

Gabriela also knew that the former queen was part of the highest ranked crest of Hell.

M glared at the rep and turned to walk away. "Child, learn your place. Once you choose a side, that is it. Be prepared for the consequences." Immediately, she disappeared from the area to engage with the gods and Dante.

SHE IS THE GODDESS

Michi followed Adam's initial fire blast with a touch of gold to the area in front of them, causing the soldiers that were fighting Krio to instantly turn gold. "Where is Niko!?" she shouted out to the room full of disorder.

"Michi baby, I don't feel Niko here. I think he is on this floor though! Be right back." Taki backed out of the doorway they stood in and turned to race down the hall towards what she detected.

Michi looked at Daikoku. "So, you did come! I was hoping I didn't have to look for you!" She immediately ran towards Daikoku and began a barrage of hits that could not be seen with the naked eye.

"Oh shit!" Adam excitedly exclaimed. He sprinted towards the massive Krio and landed a massive fiery hit that caused damage to the general's face. "Nice! You bitch ass—" He stopped his sentence, remembering his conversation with M earlier. "You pussy!" he added, continuing to land blows on the large man.

Krio stood with his arms crossed to block some of the hits that Adam threw at him. "Who are you?" he said as the hits began to burn the outside of his forearms.

"Don't worry about it, homie! You will be gone before you found out!" Adam responded to the man with his right hand lit aflame and landing another blow to Krio's face.

Michi continued her onslaught of punches towards Daikoku. Most of the hits were landing, as she was using her smaller physique to break through Daikoku's defense. "You will learn your place! I am the Shichifukujin!" She stopped the fast-paced punches and held her right hand that began to illuminate a gold light. "It is time," she said calmly.

"No, you don't!" Daikoku used her own power to keep the energy from Michi at bay. She held our both her hands as they began a white glow that caused sparkling electrical currents to flow between her and Michi. She struggled to hold herself against Michi. "You are not strong enough to wield all of our powers! You need me! They taught you all wrong! Our powers are needed in the different realms!"

Michi sucked her teeth. "You are wrong. I am strong enough. You are weak! Look what you sacrificed to accomplish your goals! Fukurokuji is so disappointed." She applied more force to her hand.

"I will not lose!" Daikoku yelled out as the glow from her hand exploded, pushing her and Michi apart. "You little witch! Who taught you this!" Daikoku swung to hit Michi and missed.

Michi dodged Daikoku's second attempt at hitting her. "You are no match for me, Koku." She called her the nickname Benzi had given her.

"Do not dare call me that!" Daikoku screeched just as another large boom came from the doorway.

Both women were distracted at the noise and turned to look at the cause of it. Adam had launched Krio across the room, resulting in the general creating a massive hole across the doorway.

"Oops. Sorry Mich," Adam said knowing he interrupted her fight. "I think he is done though." He panted from his immense fight with the general. "Shit." He bent over, still panting.

Michi turned her gold eyes back to Daikoku. "See, it's over. Might as well give up!" She launched herself at the Shinigami, attempting to start their fight again.

"I rather not! Krio! Let's go!" The Shinigami ran towards the passed-out general and bent down and touched his hand. They both departed, leaving Adam and Michi in the wrecked office area.

Michi shrieked, "What the fuck!" Her voiced carried, shattering all the windows on that floor. The building began to shake and the air began to sizzle.

"Michi. Mich. Come on. Don't go boom now! We almost got him. Don't lose your cool," Adam said as his fiery eyes danced. He sensed that Michi was at her wits' end with the whole Daikoku ordeal. He reached out to touch her but was blocked by her energy that surrounded her.

Michi's body turned solid gold and her jet-black hair whipped around like wind was all around her. "Sunny. I am going to kill her! No one better get in my way!" She slowly turned around to walk towards the doorway. She lifted her left hand and waved, the whole wall structure in front of her crumbling.

"Takisha, please come help with your crazy friend." Adam put his head down, shaking it while placing his right hand on his forehead. He witnessed Michi disappearing and attempted to follow her.

Just as he reached the doorway, M appeared. "Where were you? Michi is fucking shit up right now." he said.

"I can sense her, Adam. Did you rescue the half-breed yet?" M asked, unamused by the broken furniture and the large body shaped hole going across the doorway.

Adam looked around at the site. "Um, no. Didn't see him yet. I believe Kisha went to grab him. Michi is going to kill this Daikoku chick." He walked up to M. "She will be outta control as soon as she sees her," he added.

"I know. Unfortunately, the council and Daikoku underestimated how powerful Michiko is. Come, I believe they are only one floor above us." She turned around to leave as a soldier came crashing through the ceiling, landing on the floor.

Adam grabbed M to move her away from the debris. He snatched her hand and moved her to his left. He suddenly snatched his hand away remembering M's stance on people touching her. "Sorry. Didn't want you to get hit. I know how y'all are about your hair." He smiled with his white teeth showing.

"Thank you." She wiped herself of the debris from the soldier's fall. "It seems my assumption was correct. They are right above us," M said, looking through the hole in the ceiling.

Adam reached his hand out. "Come on, Lady Melchorde. Let's finish this. I'm tired."

"So am I, Sun God. So am I," M huffed as Adam placed her petite hand in his, allowing him to take them to the active fighting.

****

Jason watched as the battered Niko suddenly jolted up. "What's up, cousin?" he asked looking around for any sign of discord.

"No. You better mind yours, cousin. You really think your father will allow you to hurt me?" Niko coughed from the tight feeling in his chest and aching arms from his fight with Dante.

Jason's brows scrunched together. "That's your problem! Never feel like people can help you! You don't think you've had help all this time!" He walked up to the still chained Niko. "It's because of me, Grandfather didn't kill you! It was because of me that my father didn't leave you for dead when your mother disappeared!" His rage began to rise. "It's because of me Father took you to the elders. It's my doing that the Michi girl knew where to find you!"

Niko cocked head the side with furrowed brows, "What? We don't have time for this! Let me out of these chains! Something is coming." He reached his chained hands up to his cousin. "Help me now!" he yelled with spit foaming at the corners of his mouth.

Jason hesitated just as Daikoku and the still passed-out Krio appeared in the empty room. "Daikoku, what happened?" He reached down to touch the general.

"He is worthless! Didn't stand a chance against the other god," Daikoku responded looking towards Jason. She turned to stare at Niko's widened brown eyes. "Is this the boyfriend? We need to collect him and go now." She turned her back to Niko. "Bring the half-breed and let's go."

Jason was unamused with her demands. "What will happen with the Hida Clan once this is over?" he asked with his head down.

"Are you really asking me about this now?" Daikoku turned back around to face Jason. "I told you. We can only request an audience with the council to not acknowledge Dante's win against your father. Once they declare it was a hostile takeover by Dante, we will be able to appoint you as head. With me as your leader." She looked down at Niko. "Behave and you won't have to die." She strutted across the room to glance out the. "My men are gold statues right now. How many are here under the Hida name?"

Jason responded, "I am unsure now. Dante did not trust us and made most of us backup outside. There were only ten allowed to come in the building." He got quiet and asked, "Can you take us all back to Otherside and we can regroup there?"

"Not right now," she said just as a soldier was flung into the large empty office area.

Takisha had been fighting some of the soldiers with the Hida Clan in the hall and was making her way to the room with Niko. "Well, damn. How you get up here so fast, bitch!" she huffed as she noticed Daikoku and Krio were with Jason. She rushed towards Niko and snapped his chained hands loose, and he stood up to face Jason and Daikoku.

"What is she?" Daikoku glared at Taki with disgust as she observed Taki was not human. "So, who are you, girl?" Daikoku stood in front of Jason.

The exit to the room was open for Niko and Taki to leave. Taki turned to answer, "Don't worry about who—" Taki was interrupted by Michi's burst into the room through the left side of the wall behind Daikoku and Jason.

Drywall debris flew across the room, covering everyone. Michi grasped Daikoku's long ponytail and began landing a couple of hits on the Shinigami.

Taki looked around at the instant fighting that started and assisted Niko to get up so he could escape. Niko snatched his hand back. "I am not leaving her!" He stood up and sprinted towards Michi as she was still entangled with Daikoku in their fight.

He was stopped by Jason and a soldier that had entered the room while Michi was tussling with Daikoku. "Get out of my way!" he shouted, grabbing both their faces and slamming the beings to the ground then continuing to rush forward to Michi. The Hida clan soldier was down immediately while Jason hopped up and grabbed Niko's leg before he could rush off.

Niko tripped forward and landed on his hands. He turned to see Jason standing about to grab his leg. He spun around like he was in a breakdance battle and used his hand to land a blow to Jason's chest with a force that pushed his cousin through the floor, landing him in the room that the fight had started in.

Another Hida Clan member rushed towards Niko's back but was interrupted by Taki as she landed a high kick to the being's face. She made the half-demon, half-human fall backwards like a large tree.

"Timberrrrr!" she emphasized the sound at the end of the word. She chuckled and added, "Come on, Niko. Let's leave this bitch to Michi!"

Niko looked over at Michi fighting Daikoku as both women were throwing punches and kicks while dodging hits from each other. He looked in awe as he witnessed the petite women's movements and strange golden glow that was starting to form around them.

"Come on!" Taki grabbed Niko's arm since he was distracted with watching Daikoku and Michi's fight.

Just as Taki grabbed Niko's arm to run away, Bisha walked through the hole that Michi created and started a chant. The chant began to make the golden glow shine brighter with Michi's skin starting to return to its pale state. This caused Daikoku to slightly gain the upper hand in their fight.

"What the fuck?" Taki immediately noticed when M grabbed hold of Bisha's arm from behind her and squeezed it, making the Shinigami ball over in pain.

M held Bisha's arm as she slowly turned the Shinigami to face her. "I told you to pick a side. I didn't think you would pick the wrong one!" She side kicked Bisha to the other side of the room.

Bisha got up. "I am not choosing wrong. We've witnessed how many times that she is out of control and doesn't exert her powers appropriately."

"You think killing her and taking her power is the answer? How despicable." She sneered at Bisha. "Welp, I guess this is where you find who is stronger." She unsheathed her small twin swords from her boots. "I already know the answer." She crouched in a defensive stance.

Bisha glanced over at Michi and Daikoku's fight, watching as the women were almost evenly matched. Daikoku with more skill and power and Michi showing she was a natural fighter with unimaginable amounts of power. "That is not the answer. But maybe if we teach her properly and make her understand her role then she can be prepared to handle the responsibilities. At this time, it is not in the best interest of Earth or Otherside to have her wield this power alone."

"You are delusional if you think siding with Daikoku is going to change that your time is up, Shinigami! You nor Daikoku will ever be the Shichifukujin! So, learn your place!" M jumped at Bisha, closing the distance between them.

On the other side of the room, Adam had met up with Taki and Niko. He now stood in front of the entranceway, facing the hallway to watch out for other Hida Clan or EGU soldiers. He looked back at Taki talking to Niko. "Babygirl, you don't find it funny the EGU or council hasn't shown their face?" He was watching the fight with Bisha and M out of the corner of his eye.

Bisha unleashed an energy blast towards M that M dodged, sending the blast shooting towards Adam.

Adam ducked at the right time and the blast landed at the office entrance, blowing the hallway windows out and starting the building's walls to crack. "Oh shit. Guys, I think we are doing too much now!" Adam noticed the alarm bell ringing to signal the sound of approaching beings.

Michi grabbed hold of Daikoku's suit jacket with both hands, wrapped her left foot around Daikoku's right leg and used her hip to thrust Daikoku in the air, landing Daikoku on her back.

Michi immediately jumped on top of the Shinigami and delivered a thrust of punches that landed on Daikoku since Michi's power started to overwhelm her.

Daikoku started to shout as she allowed the punches to hit her, "You do not deserve to wield this power! We are the Shichifukujin, not some spoiled brat!" The tears began to roll down her face as Taki had grabbed Michi's arms with Michi still sitting on top of the battered Daikoku.

"I will not lose!" Daikoku closed her eyes as her body began to shine a slight copper color. "Do you think I didn't accumulate enough power to defeat you!" The air around them began to sizzle. Taki jumped back with Niko immediately standing next to the still crouched down Michi.

Niko extended his hand. "Come on, baby. This crazy chick about to be a problem."

"Niko!" Michi jumped off of the Shinigami and leapt into Niko's arms, wrapping her hands around his neck and legs around his waist. She jumped down and turned back to Daikoku. "You are my Shinigami. Know your place and role. Understand that you are not meant for this either! I did not ask to be born with the power of the Shichifukujin, but I am here and there is nothing you can do about it!" She stuck her tongue out at Daikoku and placed her head in the middle of Niko's chest.

Daikoku had stood up from her defeat. "Everyone keeps telling me learn my place. My place! My place is at the top of the food chain! None of you deserve it! The Eastern Region is mine, the council will be mine and the power of all the Shichifukujin will be mine!" Her hand lit up and the environment began to crackle with power that made it feel as if a gust of wind was whipping through the building.

Michi turned to face Daikoku, but paused and then looked up at Niko. "Here, take some. You need to heal. I am going to kick that twin demon's ass for putting his hand on you." She reached up and kissed his cheek. "Now you, Daikoku. You will pay for what you've done."

Adam interrupted the exchange, "Aye, time's up! There are like fifty dudes approaching. I can feel them coming." He turned around to face the fray, witnessing Daikoku's slight copper glow with her hair thrashing around her. He turned back. "Okay! I'm going to have to make demon barbeque." He walked out to the hall and began his fight with the arriving soldiers.

Taki rushed after him to assist with the soldiers. She yelled back, "Don't leave us or level the building girl!'

Michi chuckled, "Okay, so the party is just us." She looked over at the standoff between Bisha and M. "I'm sad. Because Bisha agrees with you. I always knew she wouldn't stay with me, but I never knew she would feel the way she feels."

"Little girl, I don't give a damn about Bisha or Benzi or the others. I respected Fuki. But I always knew I was supposed to lead them. So now, die like the rest of them!" She launched herself at Michi.

Michi pushed Niko to the side and blocked Daikoku's hit. "Ouch! That hurt, bitch!" her squeaky voice yelled out. "Niko, go help Taki and Adam; those are all demons they are fighting!" She sensed the demonic energy signatures of the soldiers that had come to attack them.

"No! I am not leaving you with this crazy woman!" Niko responded to the worried Michi. "Adam's a god, they are fine!"

Michi spoke to Niko softly, "I am fine! Let me do this!" She continued blocking Daikoku's hits but started to get irritated. "This is getting old." Michi stopped her defense and grabbed Daikoku's hand mid-swing. "I thought we really could do this diplomatically. Just an FYI, your freaky escapades got on my nerves over the years!" she said as she began the chant that would end it all.

Bisha instantly grabbed Daikoku out of Michi's grasp. "Michiko. I love you, but this is not the way!"

"Thank you, Bishamonten. Your assistance will not go unrewarded," Daikoku panted, standing next to Bisha.

Bisha sucked her teeth. "Do not thank me! I think we need to figure this out! Neither one of you are right!"

M slowly walked towards Michi. "Michiko, I am ready to end this!"

"Me too, Lady Melchorde," Michi responded, looking at the two women.

Just as the fight with the two Shinigami versus the Goddess of Luck and the former Queen of the Golden River Realm was about to begin, Krio had pushed Adam through another part of the wall.

Taki and Niko were fighting soldiers while more arrived. The now 27th floor looked like one large, wrecked area, as most of the wall panels and the windows were shattered.

Michi began to sweat more even with her skin being gold. The sounds of fighting and the sight of Bisha and Daikoku standing side by side against her started to make Michi's breath become more ragged and her body began to tremble. She covered her ears and let out a loud screech that began to shake the building. Her body began to glisten a brighter gold as her overwhelming power leaked from her body.

Daikoku and Bisha hopped back to get away from the fully powered Michi. Both women were unable to move, each one flaying their arms and attempting to move their body.

M stood back and watched as the Shinigami were unable to move from in front of Michi.

Michi began the chant with both her hands reached to the Shinigami. She closed her eyes and a bright gold light began to glow from within the formed circle of the Shinigami and the Goddess of Luck. All three women's eyes shined and Michi's skin gleamed the brightest gold with the energy in the air strengthening the gusts of winds. All loose items and the remaining passed-out soldiers in the office area began to whip around from the large winds.

Taki grabbed onto one of the columns as Niko copied Taki by holding onto one of the pillars that held up the building structure.

Adam held on to the pillar closest to him as he looked at the general Krio attempting to get back up. "Damn, this dude just won't stay down." He glanced over at the large golden colored energy globe that began to get larger. He yelled across the room to Taki, "I will get you out of here and we will return for Michi!"

M staggered to get up from being caught in the large energy blast. "Let's go! I think Michiko is performing the ritual for both of them at the same time!" She yelled out to Adam and Taki as M held onto a column as the winds were pulling her while the little bit of cloth from her remaining outfit whipped against the winds.

Krio was attempting to get up from his fight with Adam as the sphere touched his leg, igniting his whole body with a golden light and him instantly disappearing.

"I am not leaving her!" Niko called amongst the howling winds and the crackling energy. The large goldish circular energy ball started to absorb the loose objects that were floating around, creating a vacuum like pressure in the room.

Taki began to hold on tighter. "I don't know how long I can hang on!"

M had reached a column in between Niko and Taki and held on tight. She moved slowly to attempt to reach both of them. "Grab my hand! We have to go now! Niko! She will survive! But you won't!"

"Hmph," Niko huffed, not willing to leave Michi.

The golden sphere began to push towards the group as they held on to the pillars. The pressure started pulling the arriving soldiers into the circle, turning them instantly to dust.

"AHHH!" Taki screamed as the sphere got closer to her. It burned her skin as Adam appeared with his arms wrapped around her, his back taking the brunt of the aftermath of the sphere touching them.

Adam let out a bellowing yell as his back was burned. "Kisha baby, we have to go!" He disappeared with Taki.

Niko had started using the various pillars on the floor to get closer to the sphere. He did not want to leave Michi. He ignored the burning sensations that he felt from the sphere.

"What are you doing?" M called out. "You can't save her. Let her handle this!" She understood that Michi decided to return both of her Shinigami to the light, just as the angels decided before. M's heart fluttered with anger from the memory of before. She disappeared from the area as the golden sphere began to engulf the whole room.

Niko couldn't see within the sphere; the blinding light made it impossible. He could still hear Michi's voice in a language he did not recognize. Just as he was about to walk fully into the sphere, he heard a loud blast and was snapped out of his thoughts. Still unable to see or sense Michi, he rushed into the middle of the sphere and saw a dazed solid gold Michi with Daikoku and Bisha standing with their eyes blank of expression.

He began to shake Michi to get her out of the trance as she was repeating the same chant over and over. "Baby, come on. We have to go! You are going to make this place blow." He nervously continued to shake Michi to no avail. He paused and then closed his eyes and began to repeat the chant he heard from Michi. His body turned gold just as Michi's and he was surrounded by the golden light.

The area began to shake as the building's bricks started to crack around the windows. Within the shaking and the bright light, all

Niko could do was hold Michi's hands as the overwhelming light shined and continued the massive vacuum like pressure.

ARE YOU KIDDING ME?

Adam panted while attempting to hold on to the wall. He was able to get himself and Taki next to the UN building where Michi was still fighting Daikoku and Bisha.

Taki looked over Adam's back and noticed his wounds. "I'm sorry, handsome! I couldn't get away!"

He stood up straight to look down at her. "Babygirl, I was saving you and that's all that matters! I will be fine. By tomorrow these burns will be gone." Adam smiled and pulled Taki into a hug. "Now we have to make sure Michi survives this." He looked up and saw a massive explosion.

Adam and Taki moved to avoid being hit by the fallen building pieces. "Adam!" Taki yelled as she found M laid out in front of the building. "Is she okay?" She dropped down to her knees just as Adam arrived to assess M.

"Looks like she exhausted herself or something." He bent over to check her pulse.

Taki stood up. "Can you pick her up? I am going back inside to see if I can find Michi." She was about to walk away, but paused. "I hope she wasn't caught in that blast."

"Nope! I'm right here."

Michi's high-pitched voice startled Taki. Her skin was back to its pale color, but her eyes still solid gold. She clapped her hands. "I am so glad that is over! Whew, I am tired and hungry." She looked around. "Be right back." She vanished.

Adam and Taki whipped their heads back and forth, staring at the empty space and themselves, just as Michi returned.

"I forgot Niko up there," she said holding onto Niko's arm.

Niko waved at the couple. "Hi guys. Nice to be back."

"Y'all really going to act like we didn't just decimate the fucking UN building?" Taki said to Michi and Niko.

Michi laughed, "We didn't do anything. It was those stupid demons, and that's my story!"

"Girl! You been watching too much reality tv!" Taki responded. "Now tell us what happened."

Michi shrugged her shoulders. "Nothing. I returned them. But I still can talk to them if I want like I talk to the others." She looked up at Niko. "I'm hungry."

"I can imagine. Me too. You used a lot of energy there," Niko replied and leaned her to into his body while he rubbed her arms.

Adam looked at them. "Not the Michi version. Act like M was asking the questions." He was still holding the fainted M.

"I am asking the questions," M interrupted the conversation and slightly lifted her head.

Adam leaned down. "I hope you don't mind me carrying you."

"I am not bothered by this right now. Michiko, tell me what happened up there?" M said, laying her head on Adam's shoulder from exhaustion.

Taki reached out her hand to M. "I think we should go. Don't ya'll see the police and other authorities coming?"

"Yea, come on. Let's go check on Mikael and the other group. Any idea what happened to that big ass dude? I wanted to whoop his ass some more."

M sat up. "Watch your mouth, Sun God. Michiko, we will discuss in full detail what happened back there. I don't think this is over."

"Oh, it is. Don't worry. There will be no more rebellions or Shinigami attempting to take my power." Michi twisted her body like a little kid. "They both are at peace and will no longer cause any issues. But Koku did tell me something. She said that the humans are not playing nice. They are using Otherside creatures and demons for some gross experiments."

Adam shifted side to side. "Just like in those EGU bases in Otherside."

"Yes. Just like those. I didn't tell her I saw those though. She was being rather nice and I didn't want to start trouble. Also, Dante got away. But the council and the Gilden Crest will have to deal with the consequences," M replied to Adam.

Police cars and fire trucks sped in front of the building. Along with ambulances, SWAT and FBI vehicles. Officers began to rush into the building while others started creating a perimeter around the outside area, blocking the zone off to civilians.

"Come, let's go guys! We should go. We look like we know something," Taki said looking around at everyone's disheveled and ripped clothing.

Adam held onto Taki while Michi and Niko disappeared before he did. "Does she even know where we—" He was interrupted by Michi's return.

"Where are we going again?" Michi called out.

Everyone laughed.

Adam spoke out, "We are going to Taki and my house so we can check on Lucy and Mikael. They were attacked too."

"When did this happen?" M asked.

Taki spoke out, "We have to go, guys. Officer nine o'clock!" She pointed towards the approaching officer.

"We don't know anything, officer. Leave us be," Adam said, adding some power in his voice so the officer wouldn't target them.

The officer scrunched his face. "Excuse me? I was telling you all to move. Now you're going to make me want to question you."

Taki walked to the front of the group. "I'm sorry, officer. We all just had a heck of an exercise. Can we just call it a day? We were crossing the street." She smiled at the officer.

"We have to clear the area, so get out of here!" The officer turned around and walked away.

Michi clapped with joy. "Good, I want to eat now!"

They all disappeared, leaving the council and United EGU building with the demons and humans to clean up the mess.

EPILOGUE

The officer walked up to Mikael. "Do you know those men on the roof?"

Mikael stood in his chocolate brown suit with his eyes darting around the room, "No, I do not. I came down here like the rest of the residents as requested from management," Mikael replied to the officer. He leaned on the lobby wall. "Why are we all down here?" He was unsure as to why the full residential building was being evacuated.

Benzi shook her head. "Something is really wrong. I no longer feel Bisha, and Michi's power is faint.

"We can't leave yet. We are being watched by the humans," Mikael said.

Chike added, "Mikael, they are all over the building. They discovered the other humans, so they have to be involved. How do we warn the rest of the group?" They were unable to reach them for the past few hours.

"I think our best bet is to see if they leave soon, find Adam and Michi, and then regroup at the castle. So much has happened." Mikael looked around for a clue for the other group.

Benzi placed her right hand on her hip, poking her left leg forward to show off her open toed wedge shoes, "Mikael. I think they are here to capture Adam and did not expect us." She felt someone staring and noticed a brown-haired woman that was looking in their direction. "Hey Lucy, your pretty dad is going to get us in trouble. It's like the women just won't stop."

"No, they don't. This is going to get annoying," she said, looking over in the same direction that Benzi was, immediately recognizing the woman but turning her head so the woman wouldn't notice her.

Benzi clapped her hands. "This is lovely! Michi-ban is back!" She raised her hand in celebration just as the group from the UN building returned.

Michi and Benzi ran to each other and embracing in hug as Taki walked over to Lucy to check on her.

Adam strolled over to Mikael. "Unc, what's up? Why can't we go upstairs? We came in this way when Michi pointed out you were down here."

"Unfortunately, your apartment was attacked and then the human authorities came to evacuate your building." Mikael folded his arms while talking to Adam.

Adam reached out to shake Mani's hand. "Hey Mani. I hope they were good to you. We should talk sometime." He looked at Mikael. "Where is Dillon? Everyone should know this information."

"Yes, Sun God Adam. We shall." He looked away past Adam and noticed the brown eyes that he saw before. His eyes turned white while the air around him began to sizzle and crackle. "I will have my revenge."

Adam turned around and noticed a red aura mixed in the crowd. "Aye! Come here!" He walked towards the being.

"You see him too, Sun God?" Mani asked.

Adam continued his stride towards the crowd. "I do. Come here!"

The being that caught Adam's and Mani's eye turned around and swiftly began to walk away from the area. They turned around and noticed Mani and Adam hot on their heels.

The being stopped and turned around to stare at the large men that was walking towards them. They pulled the drawstrings tighter on their hoodie blocking any vision of their face. The red eyes met Adam's and Mani's followed by a smile that showed sharp white teeth. The being disappeared, leaving the two gods confused.

THE END